S
TO DIE

A totally gripping serial killer thriller with a twist

REBECCA BRADLEY

DI Claudia Nunn Book 2

JOFFE BOOKS

Joffe Books, London
www.joffebooks.com

First published in Great Britain in 2021

This book is a work of fiction. Names, characters, businesses, organisations, places and events are either the product of the author's imagination or are used fictitiously. Any resemblance to actual persons, living or dead, events or locales is entirely coincidental. The spelling used is British English except where fidelity to the author's rendering of accent or dialect supersedes this. The right of Rebecca Bradley to be identified as author of this work has been asserted in accordance with the Copyright, Designs and Patents Act 1988.

Cover art by Nick Castle

ISBN: 978-1-78931-735-0

PROLOGUE

Claudia's eyes were heavy. Her head fuzzy. Her body leaden.

She had no concept of where she was or what was happening. Whatever it was, it wasn't good. She wasn't at home or at work. This wasn't her bed. Something rigid was sticking into her neck, which was at a weird angle.

She clawed through her mind for her last memories. The killer they were investigating had targeted her. Her father had come home with her for protection. She'd made dinner.

Pain sliced through her forehead. She winced. Whatever her location was she was moving. Rolling and bumping. But it was dark. She still couldn't open her eyes. They were heavy, weighted down in the fog of unconsciousness. Her shoulders were killing her.

She remembered the police car. Something was wrong with the cops inside. They were supposed to be protecting her, but they were too still.

Fear gripped her stomach at the memory.

What happened?

Where was she?

Something about slippers?

Things had gone fuzzy then, and all she remembered was fighting the darkness that was grabbing her brain, pulling her down into the inky black. Before it took her, she remembered being pushed into the back of a car.

Shit.

Her eyes flew open.

The darkness barely changed. She blinked to make sure she'd opened her eyes. She was awake.

She was no longer on the back seat of a car as she'd recalled, she was in the boot. Her face pushed towards the carpet and she could smell . . . oil and something else. Something dark and metallic, like it was rusting. But it was a crude scent.

This was how he'd transferred the bodies.

Claudia tried to move, to find a more comfortable position, but she couldn't. Her wrists were tied. She twisted her neck. Tried to ease the discomfort from the position someone had dumped her in. But there was little room for manoeuvre.

She flexed her wrists. Tried to see how much give was in the ties, but they were tight.

Behind her was a huge blanket. Rough against her bare arms. She shuddered as she thought about why he'd want a blanket in the boot. To transfer a body?

Fear was eating her up. Slowly, second by second, it crawled onto her skin. Owning her.

She shook her head as much as she could. She wouldn't allow this to happen. No matter how things looked now, she would not be his next victim.

The team would have been alerted. The whole force would be looking for her, in fact. They'd not rest until they found her. Until then, Claudia had to rely on her own wits to keep herself safe. To prevent this man from fulfilling the act he had her in here for. That was her one job. To stay alive until the cavalry came.

CHAPTER 1

Seven weeks earlier

Well, that was what he called a bad day.

He let himself into his apartment, brown cardboard box — the only sign he'd even been in the relationship — clasped in his hands. Struggling to juggle the box, he bent to retrieve the post from the floor and then slammed the door behind him.

After two years together Dani had decided they were no longer working as a couple.

This was news to him.

As far as he was concerned they were doing brilliantly. They both had their own homes but had progressed to having a toothbrush and a few clothes stored at the other's.

Today Dani had packed those clothes and that toothbrush into a box and handed it to him, telling him that she wasn't ready to move onto the next stage and that to her their relationship wasn't working.

She told him her biological clock was ticking and the louder it got the more she'd had to assess her life and her life decisions. This was not about him but about her, and her biology. She hoped he understood.

He'd apologised to her. He'd actually apologised.

She'd given a faint smile, clearly grateful he was making this so easy.

He was sorry she had to do this. Said he understood why it was happening.

Now he placed the box containing his few belongings and the post on the arm of his sofa and collapsed beside it.

Dani had been his world. What would he do with himself now? He supposed he had more time to focus on his real dream. He'd made some inroads recently but now he could really give of himself.

His art, real creative work, was what drove him. Creating art for the masses in the form of an exhibition to attend and view. His name in lights. Known to critics. Reviewed. Critiqued. His soul soared at the thought of what he could create with the time stretching out in front of him. He could pour his emotions at the loss of Dani into the sculptures he would design.

He looked at the box beside him and the small pile of letters beside the box. One was his past. The other could hold his future.

He'd applied to a few museums and some art galleries a couple of weeks ago, requesting to hold an exhibition in their premises. There had been some rejections, but that was to be expected within the creative arts field. You didn't get anywhere without rejections under your belt. If you weren't rejected you couldn't call yourself a real artist. But he was expecting to hear from the rest and at least one would accept him and that would be his starting gun. You only needed one to get going.

Excitement fluttered in his stomach like a butterfly cornered in a window as he stared at the mail.

He picked them up.

Five in total.

The first was a gas bill. The second an offer of a credit card.

The third one was the important one, in a plain white envelope without a window. He tore it open and read down the single typed sheet, a cold knot curling in the pit of his stomach.

How could they?

His fist clenched. The paper crunching in his fingers.

How could they?

He tried to breathe. There were two more envelopes in his other hand. This meant there was still a chance he could hold an exhibition and show the world, the art critics, his work.

The first of the two envelopes went straight on the floor with the scrunched-up rejection. It was a brown envelope with a clear window. Not what he was interested in. The final one was the all-important one.

He tore it open.

His world ended.

The paper fluttered to the floor with the rest. Scattered around him like large pieces of confetti.

Time slowed. His mind struggled to grasp what had happened. How could they all reject him like this? He was good. Dani had told him how good his work was.

Had she lied to him?

Was that all she was, a liar? His fury at her built up like the rejections on the floor at his feet.

She'd rejected him and he'd apologised for it. Him. He'd apologised instead of her. He certainly wouldn't apologise for these rejections around him. He would do what Dani had said and assess his own life and his decisions and that meant his choices in pleading for space to show his art.

He would turn this around on them and show them he didn't need them. The world would be his stage. There were plenty of spaces that could host an exhibit. Bring it to life and have people awed.

What he needed was an installation that would have everyone talking. Something that no one had ever done before. Something real.

That was it. He needed for it to be real.

That would draw their attention.

An amalgamation of constructivism and assemblage sculpture with live and performance art. But it would have to have a standout twist for people to take notice of his creation because people rarely took notice of art. Too busy living their lives. Busy while at the same time doing nothing of note.

He had so much to say. And he had the creativity with which to say it.

With a little extra thought he could come up with the perfect installation idea and the twist that would make the masses take notice.

He looked down at the envelope still in his hand and at the logo printed on it. The inspired design that represented the organisation. It was beautiful and yet simple.

That was what he could do.

Create invitations to the installations. Make them part of the exhibit somehow.

He'd need to think this through. Brainstorm ideas for the installation and in turn how he'd create invitations that linked to them creatively and who he would send them to.

It would need to have critics talking.

No one would have done what he was imagining. Pieces set in different locations. He would set the art world on fire. You couldn't reject him this way, he was somebody worth talking about. And soon everyone would be talking about him.

CHAPTER 2

The pile of envelopes landed on DI Claudia Nunn's desk with a thunk. Claudia thanked the front counter staff member who had traipsed through the building to bring the mail and selected the top envelope.

Claudia was bored.

It wasn't something you said within the police. The service was overstretched at all times. And yet here she was, sitting in her office, waiting for a job to fall into her lap.

One month ago, after a tough case, Claudia's supervisors had created a new task force and asked her to lead it. Complex Crimes. A unit designed to pick up investigations that were not so run-of-the-mill, that were more difficult in nature. She had chosen the staff she wanted on her team, other than the detective sergeant. He had, like her, been allocated by the top brass, Detective Chief Inspector Maddison Sharpe and Detective Superintendent Connelly. The DS in question was Dominic Harrison. A good cop on every level, but Claudia's problem with the choice was Dominic being her father. It was a position neither of them wanted to be in. Her supervising her father and him taking direction from his only child.

Particularly in the aftermath of his wife's death.

Ruth Harrison, Claudia's step-mother and one of her closest friends, had died at the hands of the Sheffield Strangler, Samuel Tyler, the serial killer whose case Claudia had closed and which had landed her this role.

She thought of Ruth and missed her as deeply in this moment as at the time she'd first heard of her loss.

Her father was throwing himself into his work, but that was where they had a problem. Since they'd locked up Tyler for the murder of Ruth and the other women, no such complex jobs had come through their door. Tyler was currently on remand awaiting trial and they were sitting twiddling their thumbs. They supported other teams on homicides where they could, as they waited for something they could get their teeth into and use their so-called expertise on.

Claudia looked down at the sheets of paper in her hand that she'd pulled from the envelope. The minutes of a multi-agency meeting run by Social Care for one of the children affected by the murder of his mother. The ripples of a case that continued to flow. All the women who had been murdered had children, children whose lives that would never be the same again.

Claudia skimmed the document and put it in the internal mailing system for the officer pulling the Tyler case together for court. As Ruth was family the task had been given to another officer. Yes, she'd stepped in and helped when they'd needed it, but it was temporary and for a specific area. Now another SIO was wrapping it up.

She picked up the second envelope. It was a little damp. Tiny splodges where rain had hit it patterned the paper. The day had been dry when Claudia arrived at work that June morning, but it looked as though there had been a shower in the meantime. Turning to look out the window behind her, Claudia saw an overcast day, but no rain. She hoped it held off as she didn't carry an umbrella around with her in the summer months. Though she probably should, being in Sheffield.

The sheet of paper within the envelope slid out easily. It was A4 in size, good quality thickness and folded in half, so Claudia had no idea what it was or who it was from yet.

She unfolded the sheet and stared down at a drawing. Mesmerised. Claudia had never seen such an intricate drawing before. Not that she was an art critic or anything. But the detail in this image was as beautiful as it was horrific.

Horrific because the image depicted what looked like a crime scene.

Claudia idly wondered who would send her this drawing. It belonged in some macabre display, it was that good.

In the middle of what looked to be a rundown industrial building was a bed. On the bed lay a man, on his front. Arms stretched out above him, tied with rope to the bars of the bedhead. He was naked. A sheet tangled around his feet. And in the middle of his back, dug in deep, was an elaborate-looking blade.

The man's neck was twisted sideways so a slice of his face was visible. As with the rest of the picture, the detail was painstaking. A look of sheer horror — or was that agony — marked his features.

Taut arm muscles pulled at the binds that tied them to the bed.

There was a knock, and Claudia's second DS, Russell Kane, poked his head around the door. Claudia dragged her eyes away from the paper in her hands and looked up.

'DI Simpson called and asked if you had anyone available to help out for a few days on a murder she's running. A nightclub fight gone wrong.'

Claudia tried to pull her thoughts from the fear niggling at the back of her head as she'd immersed herself in the drawing. She shook herself and returned to the reality of her job. 'Of course. Select a couple and tell them they'll return as soon as we need them.'

Russ rolled his eyes. Like Claudia, he wondered at the sense of the new task force but kept his thoughts to himself, and she was grateful to him for that. It had felt like a knee-jerk reaction to the murder of a serving police officer to her. But she was not one to fight the top brass. Especially not Sharpe or Connelly. They ruled Major Crimes with an iron fist and you stepped out of line at your own risk. Not that she and Russ disagreed with the Complex Crimes Task Force entirely. Not if they were going to be busy. But the last couple of weeks had shown them they really were only going to deal with difficult — be that investigatively tricky or publicly sensitive — cases. And neither of them were ones to sit around and wait. They wanted to work.

Russ stepped into the office further, his broad shoulders from his days of playing rugby filling the doorframe. 'What do you have there?'

Claudia flipped the paper around at him so he could get a glimpse of the strange arrival. He narrowed his eyes, attempting to grasp what he was seeing.

'It looks to be a drawing of a crime scene. Quite beautiful, if you take out the gruesome murder side of it,' she said. 'With the blade, it looks like it could be a piece of fan art or something, you know . . . something from a book or a TV show, or something historical.'

'And they sent it to you? You have a fan?'

Claudia peered inside the envelope it had come in. 'I've no idea who sent it. Strange as far as gifts go.' She folded the drawing back in half, but not before noticing the big round clock in the top right-hand corner. It was shaded so as to appear insignificant. But it was there, nonetheless. The hands of the clock were pointing to 9 a.m., and on the outside in a box was written the word 'Friday'.

As she pushed the paper back into the envelope a tiny shiver ran down Claudia's spine at the level of effort that had gone into this artist's work. Opening her top drawer, she dropped the envelope into it and closed it again, adding it to the mess contained within, knowing she would leave it to fester in there for months until she got around to clearing the drawer. But right now it seemed too harsh to bin it.

'You're not worried?' Russ asked her.

Claudia had already moved on to the next envelope. 'About?'

'That someone has taken the time to draw something for you?'

She waved a hand dismissively. 'It's a drawing. How much harm can it cause me?'

CHAPTER 3

The art installation was nearly ready. He'd loved the location the moment he set eyes upon it. The fact that there was already a steel bedstead in situ was a stroke of luck. He'd found it when he'd been scouting for locations and decided it was perfect for his needs. The place was derelict. He hadn't seen anyone in weeks.

It really was ideal.

Light through the windows set the perfect scene. He'd been at different times of day to check. Light levels should always be maintained between 50 and 100 lux. Not that the materials he would be using would degrade at speed, but light was always a factor you had to consider. And as long as the audience saw the installation at the time he'd sent the invitation for, then there wouldn't be a problem.

There were still some parts of the exhibit he had to source, but he was comfortable he could complete it in time.

He was so excited his whole body pulsated. He'd never felt like this.

This installation would have everyone in the art world talking. They would regret turning down his requests for gallery space.

He would show them.

CHAPTER 4

Russ had left her about an hour ago. Claudia had no idea who he'd sent to the nightclub homicide. She closed the lid of her laptop and opened the door. Her office was within the confines of the incident room. The blinds had been down so she couldn't see out. She needed to fix that. She'd obviously pulled them down during a meeting or phone call. Glass walls were all well and good, but they didn't offer a hell of a lot of privacy to the occupant.

Russ was standing over DC Rhys Evans. Quiet laughter was bubbling up between them. Across the other side of the room, DS Dominic Harrison was at his desk. She made a move towards him. There was a fine line between being his supervisor and his daughter. Particularly as they were both still grieving the loss of Ruth.

Empty desks indicated DCs Graham Dunne and Lisa James were missing, so Claudia figured they'd been sent to the murder investigation.

'Hey,' she said as she grabbed a chair and wheeled it over to Dominic, sinking into it as she pulled up next to him.

Dominic looked up. 'Hey, yourself.' He smiled at her. 'What's new?'

She shrugged. 'Not much. Looks like Graham and Lisa have gone off to support Simpson on a job.'

'And you're spinning your wheels.' He was observant.

Dominic could have taken unlimited time off to grieve Ruth, bearing in mind the circumstances of her death, but he'd returned quickly. Too quickly if Claudia thought about it for very long.

'What're you working on?' she asked, instead of mulling on what lay between them.

'CPS want some more paperwork for a case I put together a few months ago.'

It didn't matter to her team that there was no new work coming in. They all had a pile of casework to be getting on with. Police work was ten minutes of excitement and then six months of paperwork. The public only ever saw the exaggerated side in books and in television dramas. If real life was depicted they'd soon get bored.

Claudia realised Dominic was staring at her.

'You're working on the Tyler case, aren't you?' He knew her so well. He was her dad, he could read her even when she wasn't talking. Not a trait she wanted from a member of her team. Even if she wasn't officially putting the file together, he knew she would wheedle her way in somewhere. She rolled her eyes at him.

'Don't do that,' he chided. Like a father.

'And don't do that,' she commanded. Like his supervisor.

Dominic laughed. Breaking the tension around the mention of Tyler.

'I'm not working it, no. Keeping myself apprised as it's going along.'

Dominic nodded. 'You're coming for lunch on Sunday?'

She looked at her watch. No idea why. It would not tell her anything. 'Of course.' She'd been for Sunday lunch with him on as many Sundays as their shift pattern allowed. They were both due rest days this coming weekend. If a job didn't come in.

Claudia hoped for a case. Not that she wanted anyone's life to be so disrupted that her team needed to be involved, but she would at least like to be busy. It was one of those things.

Krish stood and announced to the room he was making a brew. A small cheer from those in the incident room met the announcement.

Claudia had selected DCs Krish Dhawan and Rhys Evans from Dominic's old team. Dominic had tried to get the whole team transferred over — there were only four DCs under him — but there wasn't the capacity yet. Sharpe had said it might be possible once Complex Crimes found its feet.

It had been a simple decision to leave Hayley Loftus behind, as Dominic had admitted to an affair with her before Ruth had been murdered. Claudia didn't think she could face working with the pair of them together. Dominic was adamant that it had been over before Ruth's murder and that they had barely even spoken since her death.

Paul Teague was a little more difficult. He was a great cop and Claudia was disappointed not to have him on the team. She'd also had to drop Harry Harbor from her own team. He'd been gutted, but if Sharpe was as good as her word, which Claudia knew her to be, then one day they both might work with them again.

Claudia rose from her chair. Her father watched her.

'Be careful how deep you sink into the Tyler case,' he said.

He was looking out for her.

'It's just some paperwork I have to do for my part in the investigation.' She pushed the chair under the desk. 'It's nearly over.'

He was still watching her. 'And you're doing okay?'

She smiled before she walked away. There was no way she was going to tell him how confused she was by the whole case. How it had gotten under her skin. He was grieving for the loss of his wife. Yes, Ruth had been Claudia's friend, but Dominic had lost the love of his life. Claudia would figure out the truth of the case as it finally came to a close.

CHAPTER 5

At her desk on Friday morning Claudia swivelled her chair around, turning her back on her office to stare out of the window. The caller was still talking at her through the phone in her hand. A hand that was going numb with tension at how hard she was gripping the handset.

The sun was out and the residents of Sheffield were mulling about their business, short sleeves exposing skin that spent most of the year wrapped up. The women — and some men — wore sandals, and faces were upturned towards the bright globe in the blue sky, sunglasses protecting them from the glare. If you were so minded you could practically feel the summer joy through the glass.

But Claudia was not so minded this morning.

This caller was Samuel Tyler's solicitor, and she wanted to relay a message from the killer. The man who had murdered an undercover cop, Claudia's step-mother and closest friend.

'What makes you think I'd even contemplate this?' asked Claudia. The tips of her knuckles whitening, bile rising in her throat.

'I'm not here to reason one way or another,' the solicitor said quite calmly. 'My role here is to convey what my client has said to me and nothing else. What you decide is entirely up to you.'

Of course it was.

'What does he want?' Her office was warming, the glass acting like a greenhouse in the small space she'd been allocated. The title Complex Crimes might be grand, but the office they'd provided her didn't match the name. She missed her spacious old office, though the building was getting on. Opened by Her Majesty Queen Elizabeth II in 1975, it was creaky and drafts were inevitable. But she'd rather the airy space of her old haunt than the pocket-sized box that she was placed in now. Maybe they would upgrade her in the future, as they'd promised to do with the staff, if the team proved their value. She could only hope.

There was a sound as though the solicitor was flicking through papers. 'Mr Tyler hasn't passed on why he wants to meet, other than to say it'll be worth your time and you'll be glad you went.'

There was a long stretch of silence as Claudia contemplated what this could mean and what her own response would be. 'Can I think about it?'

'Certainly. I'll leave you my number. Call me and I'll set up the meeting whenever you're ready.'

The solicitor thanked Claudia for her time and hung up the call.

Claudia continued to gaze out of the window. Her mind was racing, trying to grasp for meaning in the request, and as a potential answer was within reach, her thoughts froze. Though she couldn't imagine what possible reason Tyler could have for wanting to see her, she was nonetheless intrigued. And at once, horrified.

This was the man who had murdered multiple women and a well-respected undercover police officer, wife, stepmother and friend.

She wondered how he was faring in prison. In normal circumstances it would be difficult for him because he'd killed women. But he had the kudos of killing a police officer. Did that trump the women in the eyes of Tyler's fellow inmates?

Whether she wanted to see him was one thing. The other was, could she? Did she have it in her to face him again?

Claudia gritted her teeth. If she did, then she would show no fear.

She would discuss this with her father. He deserved to know about the phone call. It would upset him. Anger him even. But as Ruth's husband, he should know that Tyler had reached out.

Claudia narrowed her eyes as she thought about her dad being Ruth's husband. Was Tyler reaching out to her as the officer who had arrested him or as Ruth's step-daughter? And why hadn't she thought to ask? Shock at the request had sent all sense flying from her head. She should follow up with the solicitor before she decided.

With her mind made up on that point, she twisted her chair so it was back in place at her desk, the sunshine behind her.

Today was their last shift before a long weekend off. And she was ready for it. She would make the most of the sun and maybe take off to the coast for the day tomorrow. Blow some cobwebs from her mind with the sea breeze. Eat her body weight in junk food and return home to a bottle of wine and a good book.

It was as the smell of the sea air tickled her brain cells in anticipation, along with the salt and vinegar of the chip bag, that her desk phone rang again and everything changed. Her long weekend was forgotten as the caller mentioned a dead man in an industrial building, wrists strapped to a bed with rope and staked to the mattress with a long blade through his back.

CHAPTER 6

Claudia walked up the stairs to Sharpe's office, each step heavier than the last, the sheet of paper in her hand heavier even than her feet.

Maxine, Sharpe's PA, looked up at her in surprise. 'She's not expecting you.'

'It's important.'

The look on Claudia's face must have confirmed this, and after a few mumbled words into her phone, Maxine ushered Claudia through.

Sharpe was immaculate, as always. Highly polished nails tapped on the edge of her desk in barely held patience. 'I'm due on a call to the assistant director of children's services in ten minutes. What's so important, Claudia, that I had to risk being late?' There was none of the recent warmth that Sharpe had shown Claudia since Ruth's death. Today was a stressful day for Sharpe, or so it seemed, and Claudia was about to make it ten times more so.

Claudia waved the paper she was holding in the air between them.

'Is that supposed to mean something to me? Didn't I hear you have a case? Does it warrant your attention as Complex Crimes? And why are you even in the building?'

Sharpe asked multiple questions and expected an answer for each.

Claudia was still standing, and Sharpe, she knew, had no intention of asking her to sit. She had the all-important call shortly. Social Care would feel snubbed if Sharpe was late, and Sharpe, in turn, would bring all her anger down on Claudia.

But this was worth crashing that meeting.

Sharpe stared at her, waiting for Claudia to respond.

Claudia took in a deep breath. She waved the sheet of paper at Sharpe again. 'This is a printout of a photograph I took of a drawing—'

A loud sigh stopped Claudia in her tracks. She was losing Sharpe.

'The drawing,' she continued, 'is in an exhibit bag, ready to go to forensic submissions, because from what I've been told, it sounds as though the image is an exact replica of the crime scene I should be on my way to.'

The lines between Sharpe's eyes deepened. 'You've had a sketch artist at the scene already?'

Claudia threw the paper on Sharpe's desk. It fluttered down slowly, landing gently in front of her. Face down. 'No, it's not a sketch artist's interpretation of the scene. This is a drawing I received earlier this week.' She waited for her words to sink in.

Sharpe picked up the sheet of paper and turned it over, staring down at the perfectly drawn image of a man tied to a bed in an industrial building with a blade through his back. 'This is the report that's come in?' She was querying rather than making a statement, wanting facts as she tried to get her head around what Claudia was saying.

'As far as I can tell.'

'How . . .' Sharpe had no other words. Her eyes widened as she flicked between the image and Claudia for answers.

'It looks like we were prewarned,' said Claudia.

'In a drawing?' Sharpe nodded towards the chair in front of her desk, calls with the assistant director of children's services long forgotten.

Claudia dutifully sank into the chair and waited for Sharpe to speak again. When she did, it was to tell her that the team had their first complex crime. 'Oh, and Claudia . . .'

Claudia waited.

'This drawing thing, it's not to get out to the press. Not until we know what on earth this idiot is trying to say to us.'

Claudia couldn't agree more. They'd be inundated with drawings if this got out. There were some real nutjobs out there. Not that that was the official term for them, but putting it bluntly, they really were. And they made Claudia's job so much more difficult.

Sharpe looked down at the drawing again. 'It's rather intricate, isn't it?'

Claudia agreed. 'Whoever did this knows how to work a pencil, that's for sure.'

'You think this is our murderer? Or does our killer have an accomplice?'

'That's a big question and one I'm in no position to answer.' Claudia rose from her chair. 'I thought I'd better make you aware before I headed out.'

Sharpe's phone rang. She picked it up. 'Tell him something has come up and reschedule, please. Thanks, Maxine.' The handset was quickly returned to its cradle.

'Keep me updated on this, Claudia. I want to be apprised every step of the way. This—' she waved the drawing in the air between them — 'would certainly place the investigation firmly within your remit.'

It took Claudia everything she had not to roll her eyes. She did not need supervising when it came to murder investigations. That was one of the main reasons they had given her this task force. But she kept her mouth shut, knowing Sharpe was likely interested rather than needing to tell Claudia what to do.

'Before I go,' Claudia said, halfway to the door. 'I received a call from Tyler's solicitor.'

Sharpe raised an eyebrow.

'He wants to meet me.'

'How do you feel about that?' Sharpe had been nothing but supportive throughout the investigation, first into Ruth going missing and then into her murder.

Initially they'd had to arrest Dominic for her murder and had drafted Claudia in to interview him. The top brass thought it would unnerve him and make him talk if his daughter was running the case. But it had become clear when they found her body that he hadn't been responsible.

Interviewing her father had been one of the most difficult things Claudia had ever done. Sharpe had pushed her onwards with it, but she'd also supported her. Nothing had been too much trouble. Whatever Claudia had needed Sharpe had got or done for her. Now she wanted some honesty. Yet Claudia didn't know her own feelings. She couldn't be honest with herself, so how could she be honest with Sharpe?

'Uncertain.'

Sharpe inclined her head. 'Don't let him destroy you, Claudia. You did an amazing job bringing him in. Remember you only have to face him across a court room now. You've done your part. You need not meet him again.'

Claudia pulled on Sharpe's closed door. 'I'd better get on with this new case. It'll keep me occupied and out of trouble.' She smiled. Someone might be dead, but she was actually looking forward to getting her teeth into a decent job.

CHAPTER 7

It was eerie. The building as Claudia entered it — all kitted out in her white Tyvek suit, mask, gloves and booties — was identical to the printed-out drawing she was carrying in her pocket. Even down to which windows were broken and which floorboards were smashed.

She'd pulled her officers from Simpson's case, but they'd not yet made it back.

For now, she only had a partial team.

Russ was at her side. She'd filled him in on the drawing as they travelled to the scene, not knowing what to expect. She'd shown him the printout so he had something to compare it to when they got there. He was equally as stunned as she was.

It was incredible.

A metal bedstead was placed in the middle of the large open space. On it was a bare dirty mattress and on that was the murder victim. Exactly as the drawing depicted. Naked, laid on his front, with his arms pulled up above his head, tied to the bed by rope. His neck was twisted to the side, a look of utter horror on his face.

Claudia and Russ took a couple of steps closer on the metal plates the CSIs had laid down.

In the centre of the victim's back, deep in his flesh, was a long blade with an intricate handle, culminating at the top with a ball of the same intricate design. All of it in a silver or steel composition.

Blood slipped down the sides of the victim onto the bed to pool beneath him, and wrapped around his feet was a single sheet. Both dirty and bloody.

Claudia looked at the man's face. She didn't recognise him. Other than from the drawing.

He was the exact man from the image.

'It's him,' she said in hushed tones to Russ, as though the killer were here in the walls.

He turned to her. 'What, the man in the drawing? You're sure?'

She nodded. 'Absolutely. He has a dimple in his chin. Look.' Claudia pointed to the dead man's chin and opened up a copy of the drawing she had on her, showing the same indentation.

'Jesus,' sighed Russ. 'He even had his victim selected, as well as his location and MO. This is warped.'

'He's so young. How did he get such a young man here, in the middle of nowhere, stripped off this way without any other visible injury?'

'Let's hope Nadira can provide some answers.'

Claudia shook her head and looked down at the floor.

'What is it?' Russ had worked with her long enough to know when something was wrong.

'I had a heads-up. I could have prevented this. I *should have* prevented this.'

Russ stared at the dagger plunged into the man and back to Claudia. 'There's no way you could have prevented this. How were you to even know it was nothing more than a weird gift from crime fan?'

'I ignored it and threw it in my drawer, Russ. This poor guy is staked to this bed because I couldn't pick up on the clues straight in front of my face. What the hell does that say about my detective skills?'

'What it says about your detective skills is that you're not a psychic.'

Claudia shrugged.

There was the sound of voices behind them as someone else entered the crime scene. Claudia and Russ turned to see Home Office-registered forensic pathologist Nadira Azim striding towards them. Though she was a petite woman, she swung a huge black bag in her hand as though it weighed little more than a feather.

'Claudia, Russ, what do you have for me today?'

They both stepped to the side so Nadira could see.

'Oh. That's different. Poor chap. Can't have been very pleasant.'

'Obviously, what we want to know is if the blade killed him or something else,' said Claudia, thinking about how the young man had got here.

'And as always, I won't be able to tell you until I get him on my table.' She tilted her head to get a better view of the blade and its positioning. 'Though I will inform you if there are any other signs of injury, if that helps.'

Claudia thanked her and stepped back slightly so Nadira could get to work.

As she did so she saw something underneath the bed. She bent over for a closer inspection, careful not to touch anything.

Russ saw her and followed suit to check out what had caught her attention.

Under the bed in a neatly folded pile were what would probably turn out to be the man's clothes. Claudia couldn't check them. They needed to be recovered by a CSI and processed properly.

'Kind of him to leave his clothes for us,' said Russ.

'Not that he's going to need them again,' Nadira murmured.

She continued to work, taking swabs and clippings, and bagged the man's hands before agreeing he was ready to transport to her morgue.

Claudia, along with Russ, walked outside in the bright sunshine, at odds with the grim scene inside the building.

They were at an old disused industrial site on the outskirts of the city, one of the few that had not yet been caught up in the regeneration of Sheffield. Once the steel city, it now had only one remaining steel works, the Forgemasters, which had a global reputation and was responsible for defence and marine contracts, civil nuclear contracts and many others, including all-important renewables.

Looking around her, Claudia wondered if their location would give them any clues as to the home of the killer. Was his kill close to home? Or had he gone wide of the mark to put them off?

Parked in front of the derelict building was an old, dark blue Audi A3. It was in good condition and appeared to be well cared for. Humming around it were several CSIs. They were clearing the ground around it first in order that the car could then be lifted to a garage to be forensically examined. But before a truck came in to lift the A3, investigators had to search for evidence that may have been accidentally dropped around the vehicle.

'The victim's?' said Russ.

'I'd guess so. I don't see our killer still being here and leaving his only way out in full view of the cops.' She grinned at him and he laughed.

Around them there were multiple buildings in the same disrepair as the one they had exited.

How, then, had the witnesses found the victim? Claudia unzipped her Tyvek suit, tied the arms together around her waist to keep it secure and pulled the printed image from her pocket. In the top right-hand corner was the clock drawn at 9 a.m., and written in a box at the side of it was the day: *Friday*.

Today was Friday.

How had they found the victim in this specific building out here, and on this specific date, and around the time on the clock?

She looked to Russ and pointed out the clock on the paper.

'The young lads who found our guy are over there with a uniformed officer,' he said, pointing to a marked car in the distance, away from the main scene. 'Let's talk to them and see what they have to say.'

CHAPTER 8

Claudia and Russ approached the boys. Dominic was with them. They couldn't be more than fifteen years of age. Their faces had a damp sheen. Eyes dark. Fear emanating from them with every shaking breath.

'I've contacted their parents,' Dominic said. 'They're on their way.' His notebook was out, and Claudia could see he'd already taken an account from the boys.

She looked at them kindly. The smallest of the two had arms like narrow sticks. She imagined if he got into any sort of fight, they'd break at the slightest touch. She'd never seen a kid so skinny. His mate, on the other hand, was wide. Cheeks like a hamster and fists like little meat tenderisers. There was something about them, an air of loneliness maybe, that made Claudia feel like they were both outsiders, and perhaps that was why they'd buddied up.

'What were you doing here this morning?' she asked, recognising they needed to be interviewed independently but needing the answer to her question sooner rather than later.

The two boys looked at each other. This was the reason you split witnesses up. So they didn't confer. You wanted their individual accounts. Not a joined-up, compared, single account. Separately they could remember something the other didn't and you could paint a bigger picture. Witnesses were invariably unreliable, but you could glean just enough information to start you on a line of enquiry that would prove helpful.

'Hey,' she chided quietly, so as not to scare them. 'Don't check with each other. Just tell me. Don't worry that you shouldn't be here. You're not in trouble for that. You hear?'

The boys nodded in unison.

Dominic smiled.

'Okay,' she tried again. 'So tell me, why aren't you in school?'

The skinny-armed boy jutted his chin out. 'It's an inset day.'

'So, what were you doing here?'

He stepped forward. Braver than his stature gave him credit for. 'We were messing about on a UE website and eventually asked if anyone knew of any places in Sheffield.'

Claudia frowned. Russ and Dominic shook their heads.

'What's UE?' she asked, totally showing her age, and she wasn't even thirty until next year. It felt ridiculous.

She'd joined the force at a young age and immediately applied for the fast-track promotion scheme. That was how she was running her own unit at such a young age and probably why it was so difficult for her father to take his instruction from her.

The boy looked surprised. 'Oh, erm, urban exploring. Where you explore abandoned, derelict buildings and tunnels and stuff.' He waited for her to say it was okay to carry on.

Claudia had heard of urban exploring, but not UE. It was official. She was no longer down with the kids. Had she ever been? It wasn't likely. She preferred to study, have her nose in a book. You wouldn't catch her doing UE. Mostly because it was dangerous and often illegal. She realised the phrase 'down with the kids' showed how out of touch with the youth of today she was. She groaned to herself silently.

'What does the website have to do with being here?'

The lad with the cheeks took over. 'We got a DM telling us about a great place, and if we came at a specified time, we'd have a professional photographer do the photos for us. You see, it's all about the images.'

'So you were told to be here today? In that building specifically?' She pointed back to the building they'd exited. An army of white ants, the CSIs in Tyvek suits, were crawling all over it.

Again they nodded enthusiastically. They were clearly trying hard not to look at each other.

'Do you have a name?' asked Russ. 'For the photographer who DM'd you?'

DM, direct message. Claudia was aware enough to not need this explaining. A way of conversing on a website directly without everyone else seeing what you had to say.

Their previous enthusiasm ebbed away. Something akin to fear started a slow crawl across their faces, unsure if the promise of not being in trouble only stood if they gave the cops actionable information.

There was a pang in Claudia's stomach, an uncomfortable urge to protect them. It was unlike her. She was all about the job. Surging forward to identify and locate offenders, killers, child abductors. But here she was, standing in the sunshine, wanting to mother two bewildered boys.

'Erm . . .' The chubby-cheeked boy couldn't help but look at stick arms before eyeing up Claudia and yanking his gaze away. 'He didn't have a name. It was a random handle.'

'And do you remember what it was?' pushed Russ.

The boy flushed. Considered the question. 'Yeah. He was PixPositive. One word, two capital Ps.'

Russ wrote in his notebook, then turned it around to the boy. 'Like this?'

The boy stuck one of his thick fingers on the page in his excitement. 'That's it.'

They had something to work with. 'And the name of the site you were on?'

'Enter at Your Own Risk.'

At least they acknowledged the dangers of urban exploring straight up before anyone even posted or read anything. The title of the site said a lot. They'd have to do some research. Now, though, they needed to get the boys to the station, split them up and take their statements. Their parents were on their way and expecting to be updated. They'd be horrified by what their boys had come across.

'Before we go and take your statements, I need one last thing from you.' Claudia was both hopeful and doubtful about where this next question was going to lead. 'Did PixPositive meet you here?'

CHAPTER 9

Claudia wondered what effect this would have on the boys. At this age, seeing death was not the norm — though some families might allow them to see loved ones who had passed away, murder was a different matter altogether. It was brutal and violent. And this scene had no equal.

Dominic ushered the boys into the marked police car, spoke quietly to the uniformed officer, then walked back to Claudia. 'I'll go with them. A friendly face. Well, someone they've come across from the start.' He studied his daughter. 'If that's okay with you?'

It was fine as far as the job was concerned, but she wanted to talk to him. Work was not the ideal place to do it, though. 'I need to grab you at some point if I can,' she said.

'I know, Sunday lunch is off.' He scrunched up his face in disappointment. 'There'll be other weekends. It can't be helped. If I didn't work on the same unit as you I'd think you were trying to put me off.' He laughed at his own joke.

Claudia tried to smile along with him, but it felt forced, like her skin would crack at the effort.

Concern skimmed across his face. 'What is it, Claudia? And please don't say nothing. I know you well enough to see when there's something wrong.' He looked back at the boys in the marked car. 'And we've been through more than any other father and daughter for me to understand when you have a problem praying on your mind.'

Claudia hated that he worked so close to her at times like this. She wanted to work her own way through the issue, before she had to confront her father with it. As it was, she needed to tell him about the meeting with Tyler before he heard it from anyone else. She felt guilty for sharing the information with Sharpe before Dominic. Not that she expected Sharpe to disclose what she knew, but that wasn't the point. She hadn't come straight to her father. Why was that?

What was the reason she was putting off such an important conversation?

'Claudia?' He nudged her. She'd wandered off in a world of her own.

'I'm sorry. I'll catch up with you later,' she said and moved off towards Russ, who was already halfway back to the primary crime scene, pulling up the Tyvek suit again ready to re-enter.

'So it was a ruse to get the boys here at the right time,' Claudia said as she strode up behind him. The sun was so bright it was burning through the Tyvek suit, her arms prickling with heat. Sweat was dribbling down her back and gathering along the elastic of her knickers as it went around her hips and stomach. She hated being cold, but there was nothing as disgusting as being too hot. She wriggled in an attempt to ease the discomfort of perspiration. It did little.

Russ started, his large frame jumping slightly in his skin. 'To match the time and day on the clock in the drawing?'

Claudia pulled it out of her pocket again before she zipped up the white papery suit.

Russ and Sharpe were the only people who knew about the drawing so far. This was another question. Why hadn't she told Dominic about the drawing? Probably because the boys were there in front of them. But before that? Before they set off. She should have informed the team before they headed out.

Her stomach twisted in on itself. She was raw with anger and guilt at how badly she'd let this victim down. It was these emotions that drove her actions, prevented her owning up to her mistake. She would, of course, have to explain everything back at the incident room. For now they needed to process the scene. So she would hold on to her self-loathing for a little longer.

'He needed a way to get us here at the hour he predicted. There's no way we'd have known about him in time without the killer preparing it for us in this manner,' she said. 'It's macabre, but I do think he set the boys up to find the victim, to match up to his drawing.'

'The big question is,' Russ said, 'was he here, watching somewhere? Soaking up the boy's reaction?'

'They didn't see him,' Claudia replied. 'But there's nothing to say he wasn't here, revelling in his work. Let's have another look around, shall we?'

Claudia and Russ signed back into the scene and entered the building. They stared around the space with fresh eyes following Russ's last query. Had the killer been here watching the discovery of his live drawing? The space was cavernous. It was as tall as it was wide with an open second floor you could see from the ground. Steel stairs led up from the rear of the building. It hadn't been emptied out. Remnants of what used to fill the site before it was left to rot still remained. Huge boxes and canisters on wheels that anyone could hide behind. Vast tables and bits of machinery. Claudia was sure they would find that the bedstead the victim had been found on had come from inside the building somewhere and been dragged to its central location for its performance piece.

'You think that might be what he needed?' Claudia asked. 'An audience. The boys. Poor lads. It's grim to consider they could have been part of his entertainment.'

'But why send the drawing to you?' asked Russ.

Claudia furrowed her brow. It was a question she didn't have an answer to.

CHAPTER 10

Back at the station, Claudia gathered the team together for their first briefing of the case. Graham and Lisa had returned from supporting Simpson, and she had a full complement of staff.

She paced around the incident room with the photocopy of the drawing folded in her hands. Time to let the unit in on what was really happening.

When she finished talking and had passed the sheet of paper out into the office for everyone to look at, there were faces staring back at her with incomprehension in their eyes.

'You're saying whoever killed this guy knew he was going to kill him and how, and drew a picture of it and sent it to you days before it happened?' said Lisa, shock edging her voice. 'Why the hell would he do that? The drawing, I mean.'

It seemed this was going to be a common question in this case, and one Claudia had no answers to.

'This is why we're the Complex Crimes Task Force,' Claudia said instead, hoping to lift them from their confusion and encourage them to be excited by the new job. 'To look at unusual cases like this. You all signed up to be here. This will be interesting, something to get our teeth into.' She looked around her and she turned and paced some more, activity making her brain cells function. If she had a problem she liked to go for a run, but that wasn't possible here, so she paced the incident room instead.

'Tell me about the victim.' She'd told them what was strange about the case. Now she needed to get on with the job.

'We have an ID because his car was at the scene,' said Krish. 'The victim was Oliver Kennedy. He was twenty-seven and single. Lived alone. His parents are separated.'

Claudia thought back to the crime scene. Oliver Kennedy had been youthful, even in death. There was something so young and naive about him. How had he ended up on that killer's bed? 'What did Oliver do for a living?'

Krish checked his notes. 'HMRC has him down as working in a coffee shop and also as a model.'

Claudia thought again of the baby face she had looked down on. The hopes and dreams the man must have had. It made her sad. 'So why was Kennedy in that industrial building today?'

There was a deadly silence.

Claudia let it play out. She wanted her team to think, to allow scenarios to play out. This was their first case as the Complex Crimes Task Force, as a team together. They couldn't fall at the first hurdle. There was a lot riding on this. Not just for Kennedy and his family, but for Claudia, her reputation and her future.

She rounded a desk and paced on. 'The car being at the site tells us it was likely that Oliver drove there of his own accord. He wasn't dragged there kicking and screaming. Obviously there's a possibility the killer has been inside his vehicle, which is one of the reasons we've recovered it. That information will take a few days to come back from forensics, though. What we have to ask ourselves is why he would meet someone in such an isolated spot? Did he know the killer?'

'Something to do with his modelling work?' asked Rhys.

'Good question,' she said. 'Find out if he works for a specific agency and then check if they sent him there. In the meantime we have to wait for forensics and the post-mortem, which I'm attending with Dom later today.' She only called him Dad out of hours or when they were alone.

Dominic lifted his chin in acknowledgement.

'We need a media plan to arrange a press release.' She looked to Lisa. 'Can you liaise with the media department and pull something together with them, please, and let me check it before it goes out? Do not, under any circumstances, mention the drawing we received before the murder occurred. This has been requested by Sharpe. Not only do we want to prevent an influx of drawings from the nutters out there, but we want to hold the pertinent information back for when we make an arrest. Something only the killer will know.'

Lisa agreed.

'The first thing I have to do is to inform Oliver's next of kin. Russ, if you can appoint a FLO to follow me on there, that would be great.'

* * *

The semi-detached house in Greenhill was well tended. The grass was neatly mown and the bushes across the front of the premises were well groomed. Horizontal blinds lined the bay windows, keeping the home private.

The woman who answered the door was youthful like her son. For some reason, this made Claudia more anxious than usual. Parents should never have to lose a child. Especially in such a cruel way. But this pair were like a Peter Pan couple. This mother was where Oliver had got his good genes from.

Claudia and Russ showed Louise Kennedy their warrant cards and with worry etched on her smooth face she allowed them entry, moving straight into the kitchen. Louise Kennedy grabbed the kettle as she spoke, asking if they wanted drinks and not waiting for a reply. Electricity coursed through the air. A frisson of fear emanated from Louise, who probably sensed it was bad news and was cutting off any opportunity for them to speak and destroy her life.

Water gushed into the kettle, the sound loud and brash in the fragile world the three found themselves in.

With a click the kettle was on and Louise moved to the cupboards to gather mugs and then the fridge for milk.

Claudia took a step towards her and placed a hand on her arm. 'Louise, if we can have a minute of your time?' The act of making drinks was soothing her. But Claudia had to stop this and do what they had come here for. No matter how painful.

Louise Kennedy jumped as if Claudia had electrocuted her.

'I'm sorry,' Claudia said.

'No.' Louise backed away. Her hips hitting the edge of the counter top.

'We need to speak to you about Oliver. Can we sit somewhere?' Claudia looked at the kitchen door, hoping Louise would lead them to the living room.

Louise, wide-eyed and mouth slightly agape, stared at her, then she spun and started on the tea-making ritual again. The kettle was now boiled. She started to pour the water, making drinks for everyone, keeping her hands and her mind busy.

Claudia tried anew. 'Louise, there's been an incident this morning involving Oliver. We need you to listen to us.'

The tension was palpable. Louise was vibrating. It was obvious to Claudia that she was keeping the truth at bay, but how much longer could she put them off? She grabbed the tea caddy as Claudia spoke behind her again. The canister dropped from her hand, hit the edge of the counter and slammed onto the floor.

Louise let out a small yelp as the jar smashed to pieces on the tiled ground. Tea bags scattered to the corners of the room with flecks of white ceramic that had broken away. Her eyes welled and her hands went to her chest.

Russ went for the floor and Claudia to Louise. They were a practised team. Claudia wondered how they would have operated had she brought Dominic with her. She had never worked with him before, and it was a strange situation. They both had to get their footing. Learn how the other performed.

Louise crumbled, her knees buckling. 'Oliver?'

Claudia ushered her out of the kitchen, hoping to find the living room. It wasn't hard, it wasn't a large house. She sat Louise down and crouched in front of her.

'We found Oliver dead this morning, Louise. I'm so sorry. He was murdered.' It was always best to deliver the facts as succinctly as possible, so there was no confusion as to what was being said.

There was a heavy silence as the two women watched each other.

Then Louise started to break. Her voice came in a fractured hum that gradually grew into an ear-splitting howl. She clawed at her clothes, her chest and her face, her distress raw and fragile.

Claudia reached out and touched her. Shock shuddered through Louise.

'What happened to my boy?'

Russ entered quietly behind Claudia.

'We don't know. We're investigating it now. He was found on an industrial estate on the outskirts of Sheffield. Do you know of any reasons he would be there?'

Tears were slicing down her cheeks. Louise shook her head. 'Why would someone kill Oliver?'

To Louise, Oliver would always be a small boy set in amber forever. Never to grow old. Claudia could do nothing to ease the woman's pain other than investigate the murder and bring some justice to the case. Of course they would provide her with more details on the actual murder in time, and they would come out at any trial in the future. But right now it was enough that she knew her boy was dead and had been murdered.

Claudia pulled a small card from her pocket. 'We hope to find out. These are my contact details. Call me if you have any questions. I'm sending a family liaison officer to your home to talk to you about Oliver and to keep you apprised of the investigation.'

Louise took the small offering, though Claudia was aware she wouldn't be able to read it through the tears.

'Did he have any new friends recently, that he'd talked about?' she asked. It was difficult when your child had flown the nest, you didn't always know their life.

Louise was still shaking her head from the last question. A continual motion of denial. The hope that this was not her world. That Oliver was somehow fine out there somewhere. Desperation emanated from her.

'No one new in his life?'

Louise bent double. 'Nooo,' she howled. And Claudia couldn't tell if it was in response to her question or at the fact Louise didn't want this to be happening.

She turned to Russ, who just looked saddened. In his hands was a steaming mug. He'd made a tea for Louise. The action of sipping on a warm drink was soothing. Not the brew itself, but having something to hold, something warm, and something to do with your hands and your thoughts as you ran through the motions of drinking.

Claudia nodded him forward and Russ stepped towards Louise, holding out the mug.

'Do you have anyone we can call who would come round and sit with you, Louise?' she asked, not wanting to leave the woman alone when they left.

Louise rubbed at her face with her fists, tears smeared over glowing cheeks, eyes highlighted red and angry. 'My mum. I can call my mum.' She sniffed and wiped again, but it didn't stop the torrent of tears that were falling.

'Let us have her number and we'll arrange that for you.'

Louise took the drink from Russ. Her tears slipped silently down her face, her angry sobs more subdued. 'Her number's in my phone, in the kitchen. It's not locked. Listed under Mum.' It was the most she had spoken since Claudia had informed her of her son's death.

Russ headed to the other room.

'We'll get your mum here for you, Louise. We need to ask you a couple of questions though, if you're up to it?' This was never easy. As police they had a job to do, and yet this woman wanted to grieve quietly and privately for the loss of her only child. It was such a difficult balance to be had. Claudia felt the intrusion acutely but nevertheless ploughed on as she had to.

Louise stared at her with incomprehension etched across her face. The thought of answering Claudia's questions was an impossible task.

Claudia took the look to mean that it was okay to go ahead as she needed to. It may have meant the opposite, but the questions had to be asked regardless. 'How was Oliver this past couple of weeks?'

Louise stared up at the wall, where family photographs looked down at them. Oliver in happy times. A smile across his face. Louise grinning like they had all the time in the world. Unknown to her he would be stripped away from her so savagely. 'He was . . . Oliver.' Her voice barely a whisper.

'Did he mention any problems he was having?'

Louise tried to focus, tried to wipe away the tears, but they continued to fall. 'If Oliver had problems he wouldn't have talked to me about them. He'd have tried to protect me in his wonderfully kind way and kept them hidden. No, he didn't mention any problems.'

'What about new friends?'

This time she shook her head. Her words were failing her.

'Everything was okay with work?'

'The coffee shop ticked over. But his modelling, you'd have to speak to his agent.'

'His agent?'

'Yes. She's a lovely woman by all accounts. Audrina Post. I have her card somewhere if you need it?'

Claudia wasn't sure Louise was capable of searching out what they needed, but she needed those contact details.

Louise rose from her seat and stumbled. Claudia jumped up, reached for her elbow and steadied her. The woman turned her broken eyes on her. Claudia's heart ached a little. This was the most emotional part of the job and it never got any easier.

'Let me help.' She sat Louise back down. 'Tell me where it is and I'll get it.'

Louise directed Claudia to a kitchen drawer, where she found a small rectangular card with the details for Audrina Post, an agent based in London.

She thanked Louise and made her a fresh drink. 'When did you last see Oliver?'

Louise dabbed a crumpled tissue at her face. 'A couple of days ago. He called in after work. I made him some dinner, we chatted. He said he'd drop by at the weekend.' She broke down further. Oliver would never visit again. There would be no more dinners with him.

'Can I see him?' Her voice was weak — Claudia understood — at the thought of seeing her boy in such circumstances.

'Of course.' Claudia's own heart ached but she kept her control. 'We need you to do the official identification. We'll make arrangements for it to take place today.'

Louise bent double with the pain of what she had asked and was being asked to see.

For Claudia it was this pain that cut through her professionalism the most. She took a couple of quiet calming breaths before she spoke again.

'Was he at work yesterday?'

Louise held her head in her hands. She blinked as though trying to clear the fog in her head, trying to focus on the discussion. Her voice was thick with emotion. 'Yes . . . yes he should have been.'

Claudia needed to know who the last person to have seen him was and at what time. They'd need to attend the coffee shop.

Russ quietly informed Louise that her mother would be here shortly. They'd wait until she arrived before they left. They wouldn't leave her alone with grief as deep and painful as hers.

Claudia tried to reassure her. 'We'll keep you updated on the investigation into Oliver's murder. The family liaison officer will help pass information between you and the investigating team, so please don't worry that you'll be out of the loop.'

Louise looked up in horror as a thought crossed her mind. 'What about Oliver's dad? His dad. Oh my God.'

'Another officer has gone out to inform Oliver's dad.'

Louise settled again. Settled as much as a mother could whose life had just been altered in a way no parent should ever have to experience.

CHAPTER 11

Claudia dropped Russ off at the station and picked up Dominic. It would have been easier to take Russ to the post-mortem, but with two detective sergeants she didn't want to be seen to be favouring one over the other. People might have expected the favoured officer to be her father, but in fact it was Russ, the guy who had always been on her team and with whom she already had a working relationship. Not the guy who was grieving and who she shared grief with. That actually made it more difficult than anything else.

'How did it go?' asked Dominic as they strode down the corridors of Sheffield Medico-Legal Centre towards the mortuary.

'About as you'd expect.' Tension ran through Claudia's body. They had fifteen minutes to kill before they were due at the PM. Now was the perfect time to talk to her father about the phone call she'd received.

There was a knot of anxiety in her throat stopping her spitting the words out.

'What is it, Claudia?' There he was again. Noticing the personal stuff with her. She never had this issue with her team.

She ground her teeth together and pulled in a deep breath.

'Talk to me.'

If he'd just give her the chance. She slowly let out the breath.

Dominic stopped still. A woman behind him nearly walked into him, and a loud tut echoed in the corridor as she skirted around him.

'Sorry, sorry.' His hands were up in defence as the anger flared from her.

Claudia could hear the woman muttering about idiots as she marched onwards, out of view.

Dominic moved to the side of the corridor and looked at his daughter. Claudia huffed and side-stepped with him.

'I received a phone call this morning.'

'Oh.' He was going to make her tell him everything.

She was dreading his reaction and had no idea what it would be. Rage would be a good guess. 'It was from Samuel Tyler's solicitor.'

There was an awful silence as the words sank in. She could practically see his mind fumbling with the sentence, trying to rearrange it into something else other than what it was.

Eventually he spoke. His jaw tense. 'What did he want?'

The next bit was even worse. 'Tyler wants to see me.'

She held herself still, waiting for the explosion. Her father was furious, as expected, at Samuel Tyler for the murder of her step-mother. Any time Claudia mentioned his name, even in relation to work and the prosecution, he struggled to hold himself together. That was one reason Claudia thought he had returned to the office too soon.

There was no explosion, though. Dominic's face paled. He leaned back on the wall he was standing next to, as if his legs had given way beneath him. A hand held him against the wall, still and steady.

'For what reason?' It was barely a whisper.

Claudia checked her watch. Ten minutes. They needed to get through this, but her dad looked dreadful. Worse than she had imagined. How had she believed she could do this in a gap in their work schedule? She should have waited until the end of the work day. But the truth was, she wanted to talk to her dad about it. She wanted his opinion. Talking to Tyler was a big deal. Especially with him dangling the promise of it being worth her while in front of her. Like there was something he wanted to say that she would want to hear. It tugged at her curiosity, and her father was the only other person who would possibly understand how she felt. The urge to sort it out sooner rather than later had led her to bring the subject up when they didn't have suitable time to discuss it.

She'd suspected her dad would not deal with it well, and all indicators were that he wouldn't.

The hushed voices that were the soundtrack of the Medico-Legal Centre melted into the distance, and Claudia and her father were the only two people standing here at this moment in time. It was like the world had stopped.

It reminded her of the previous hour with Louise Kennedy. How that must have felt for her.

'What does he want?' her father whispered again.

She stepped closer to him. 'I don't know, Dad. His solicitor didn't have an answer. All he has said is it will be worth my while.'

His eyes widened. 'You can't go!' There was so much vehemence in those three words.

'I haven't decided yet.'

'You can't go.' He was demanding, as though he could control her. A prickle of obstinacy ran up her spine, but she kept her mouth shut. He would be emotional about Tyler. He'd killed his wife. She wouldn't get the conversation she'd hoped from her father.

She checked her watch again. 'We should go.'

Dominic straightened himself and ran a hand through his hair. 'He's poison, Claudia. You can't trust anything that man says. Why would you even consider going to talk to him?' His eyes were hooded and the case visibly haunted him.

'I need to think about it,' was all she could offer him.

Dominic stared at her then walked off down the corridor towards the morgue. Not another word passed his lips on the subject of Samuel Tyler. Claudia trailed behind him. Regretting telling him of the phone call. Wishing for a simpler life.

Wishing Ruth was still here. Ruth could always talk sense into Dominic. She was kind and warm and funny, and her dad could never say no to her.

Tyler had ripped their world apart.

CHAPTER 12

Dominic couldn't think straight. Samuel Tyler was safely locked up for multiple murders, including the murder of his wife. A murder he himself had committed and then framed the serial killer for. It had been easy enough because he'd been the detective who had attended most of the crime scenes. He could copy them well, knowing everything about the killer's MO. Even details not released to the public. *Particularly* details not released to the public. It was these details that made Ruth's crime scene all the more believable that it belonged to the Sheffield Strangler and no one else.

So when they caught that serial killer, and it turned out to be Samuel Tyler, victim support officer, it was easy enough to add one more body to his tally.

Only now Dominic was afraid of the reason Tyler wanted to see Claudia.

Of course Tyler had denied killing Ruth. He hadn't done it. But no one had believed him. They presumed his fear of admitting her murder was because she was a cop and that he didn't want to be treated badly by her fellow officers and by prison officers. Not that it was a thing. Not nowadays, anyway. Maybe in years gone by.

But what reason could he have for wanting to speak to Claudia?

He pushed open the door to the morgue and tried to focus on the task ahead. They were here to do a job. Claudia had dropped this bombshell on him though, and his heart raced. Adrenaline coursed through his body. His thoughts were scrambled. He needed time to figure out what his response should be to what she'd said. But there was a sense of everything moving around him too quickly. How could he gain control?

Samuel Tyler held Dominic's future in his hands. No, Tyler didn't know the identity of the man who had really killed Ruth, but he knew with certainty that he hadn't murdered her and he'd already tried to tell Claudia this. When Ruth initially went missing Tyler had met up with Claudia. Dominic had rushed to their meeting place to put a stop to it, but under the guise of protecting his daughter. He'd gotten away with it. She'd been angry with him, but he could take it. He'd take anything to protect his secret.

Protecting his secret, protecting his life, his career and everything he held close.

He wasn't a cruel man. He was capable of love. He loved his daughter dearly.

And he'd loved his first wife, Claudia's mother, until he'd met Ruth and been swept away with the joy of her.

It seemed to be a fault of his. Other women. Becoming distracted by them. Turning away from his marriage vows and loving another.

No, he wasn't a cruel man, but Ruth had threatened him when she had found out about his affair with Hayley.

Claudia followed him into the morgue. He couldn't bear to speak to her and silently went to change in readiness for the PM.

His mind continued to whirr. Ruth had threatened to take away everything important to him. His career, his standing at work, his pension, his home. She had threatened to tell Claudia he'd cheated yet again. She had threatened to tell everyone at work about what he'd done with Hayley. He would have lost everything. His anger had bubbled the more she had spoken until eventually it had cracked.

And afterwards he was alone with a body. The body of his wife. The body of his daughter's step-mother and friend. The body of a cop.

He was terrified, but he'd seen a way out. No one would understand she had driven him to it. Yes, there were arguments in some court cases of self-defence. But he couldn't see that argument flying here. In fact, he didn't even want a case to go to court. He didn't want to be the subject of gossip. He'd had to take more drastic action.

The fact that both he and Ruth were working on one of the most vicious cases of their career at the time was the perfect get-out clause for him. He knew the MO, that the killer left a lipstick at each scene. And in disguising her body this way, Ruth was counted, as he'd hoped, as one of the Strangler's victims. It helped that when he'd killed Ruth, Dominic had used his bare hands and strangled her. He hadn't premeditated her murder. But it had been a streak of luck that he could hide her death this way.

The net had closed in on the killer, and when they caught him, Ruth was tallied in his body count, and they remanded Tyler in prison for his crimes.

This was where Dominic's life became a little difficult. More so now Tyler wanted to speak to Claudia.

Dominic needed to find out what Tyler wanted. But there was no way he could. He couldn't allow his carefully created world to crumble around him. He was not prepared to lose everything. Not after all the work he'd already put in.

When he was ready, Dominic stalked into the post-mortem room and found Claudia in there with Nadira Azim, Smithy the morgue tech and a photographer who would record the entire process. They were standing to the side, chatting.

Oliver Kennedy was laid on his front on one of the tables in the centre of the room, the blade still embedded in his back.

'Hey, Dominic.' Nadira smiled at him, unaware of the tension between him and Claudia.

He returned her greeting as everyone moved towards Oliver.

'Okay, I've done the body mapping already.' With a pen, she tapped the clipboard in her hand, which held a sheet of paper with two outlines of a human shape. One represented the front of the body on the table and the other represented the rear side. A pathologist had drawn in all the marks, scars and tattoos visible on the body they were examining. 'Nothing particularly stands out. He has a couple of tattoos. One on his back of an eagle and the other on his upper arm of Harry Potter.'

'Harry Potter?' Dominic queried.

'He'd have only been a boy when the first book and movie came out,' Claudia said.

'But still,' said Dominic, 'he was a grown-arsed man by the time he had the tattoo done.'

Nadira laughed. 'It really did speak to a huge generation of people, Dom.'

'But Harry Potter is a real man. An actor, yes? He has a tattoo of . . .' He looked blankly at the pair of women.

'Daniel Radcliffe,' said Nadira.

'Exactly. He's just a guy playing a part.' Dominic stared at Nadira. 'You're a fan?'

'I love the Potter films. Though I didn't read the books. And Daniel is a great actor. Each to his own, Dom.'

Dominic sniffed and returned his attention to Oliver Kennedy.

'Anything else?' Claudia asked.

'There's no obvious sign of injury other than the blade. I'll have to complete the post-mortem to give you more.'

They gathered round the table.

'Have you seen a blade like that before?' asked Nadira.

It was pretty special as far as knife handles went. This was the first time Dominic had seen it, other than in the crime scene photographs.

'I don't know much about daggers, but it's intricate. We must be able to locate where he picked it up.'

'Unless it's passed down in his family,' Claudia said, standing close to look at the detail of the handle.

Dominic ground his teeth.

The rest of the post-mortem ticked by with very little of note. Oliver Kennedy was, other than the blade dug deep in his back, a very healthy young man.

'Cause of death,' said Nadira when they were done, 'was exsanguination from the dagger in his back. If he'd have lived he'd have more than likely been paraplegic, paralysed from the waist down,' she explained. 'The blade hit between the T8 and T9 vertebrae, damaging the lower spinal cord.' She pulled off her gloves and bagged them in an exhibit bag and signed the attached label. 'We'll get toxicology results in a couple of days to find out if he was drugged.'

'You can't think he got on that bed voluntarily?' Dominic asked.

'Stranger things have happened,' Claudia replied.

'But we won't know until the results are returned,' said Nadira. 'He died sometime last night. Between 11 p.m. and 3 a.m.'

'We'll have to find out what he was up to before eleven,' said Claudia. She turned to Dominic. 'We have a busy time in front of us, we should get going.'

Dominic was finding the afternoon more and more difficult. 'I'll meet you outside.'

Nadira looked at him and then at Claudia. Claudia shrugged, but Dominic walked out and heard nothing that might have been said between them. No doubt Claudia would mention Tyler and the solicitor's conversation.

He wondered how others would view the proposal. Maybe that was something he should consider. Though wouldn't they, no matter their thoughts on whether Claudia should go or not, understand Dominic's reluctance to engage with him? After all, Tyler had supposedly taken his beloved wife.

CHAPTER 13

Claudia listened to the *bring bring* of the Skype call rattle through the old speakers of her work laptop as she waited for Audrina Post to pick up the call.

When it was answered Claudia thought she'd got the wrong number. The woman on the other end of the video call looked no older than eighteen. Though she had to be at least in her twenties to be doing what she did. Claudia couldn't help but compare herself and came away feeling ancient, plain and dowdy.

Audrina Post, from the head-and-shoulders view Claudia had of her, was slim, classy and stylish. Where Claudia was wearing a blouse that was obviously supermarket-rack quality, the sleeveless number adorning Audrina flowed from her shoulders gracefully and in such a way you could practically feel the luxuriousness of it. Her hair was cut pixie short. Her face shining with health, whereas Claudia imagined herself looking dull and worn out.

Worrying about the way she looked wasn't something she usually did. Especially in work hours, but then again she wasn't usually faced with a woman who looked like Audrina Post.

'Detective Inspector Nunn?' the agent asked. Her voice sing-song and as beautiful as her whole outer appearance.

Claudia refrained from rolling her eyes. Some women were just lucky.

'Yes. Thank you for taking my call.'

'You said it was about Oliver Kennedy. I do hope he's not in any trouble?'

It was never easy breaking a death message, but doing so over a screen was one of the modern era's worst problems. It was so impersonal. 'I'm sorry to have to tell you, Ms Post—'

'Do call me Audrina.' She smiled. A genuine relaxed smile.

Claudia had to break that easy calm. Her words would crash through Audrina's day and wipe the smile from her face. 'Audrina,' she said, 'I'm sorry to have to tell you this, but Oliver is dead. He's been murdered.'

It was as if the screen had frozen. The image of Audrina Post stilled on the laptop as the agent absorbed the information.

'Murdered?' The word was stuttered and said as though it could turn around and hurt the speaker herself.

'I'm sorry, yes,' Claudia confirmed. 'I believe you were his agent for modelling contracts?'

Audrina visibly tried to gather herself. 'Oh, yes. Yes, I was. Oliver was a client for about . . .' She paused as she considered her response. 'About ten, eleven years.'

Then something occurred to her. 'You don't think his modelling had anything to do with his murder, do you?' She clapped her hands to the side of her head.

'It's what we're trying to find out. We're investigating Oliver's life, and obviously this was a part of it. What can you tell us about his modelling jobs of late? Was there anything that caused you concern?'

A hand went from the side of her face and up through her perfectly brushed hair, ruffling it. Making her look less well-maintained. Even the beautiful blouse no longer had the appearance of wealth and luxury but looked more tired and worn, just from a few sentences from Claudia.

'Everything has been running as usual. He isn't a high-flyer by any means. You know he has to keep working a day job as he can't guarantee a constant wage through modelling?'

Claudia nodded.

'Though he could make good money when the jobs did come in. He was a lovely-looking lad. Perfect for the boy-next-door booking.'

'What about the last couple of weeks or so? Anything suspicious that you were worried about?'

There was a large diary sitting in front of Audrina; she flipped through some of the pages. 'Give me a minute, Detective Inspector.'

Claudia waited.

Audrina's hands were shaking as she worked. Then she looked back at the camera. 'Oliver told me he had been approached directly. Through his social media accounts. It was for a small booking. An artist who said he needed a model for a shoot he was doing. I couldn't find any details of the artist online and told Oliver we wouldn't take it, but Oliver told me the guy was desperate and he'd hit it off with him, so he was going to help him out.'

'When was he going to do this photoshoot?'

'Oliver phoned me yesterday and said he was doing it late evening yesterday because the light would be good with the sun sinking below the windows of the installation the guy had picked out. He was actually quite excited by it.'

Tears pricked at Audrina's eyes. 'When was he murdered?'

Claudia hated to tell her the truth of the matter but she couldn't lie. 'He was killed last night, maybe yesterday evening.'

'You think it has something to do with this shoot?'

Claudia couldn't answer. 'Do you have the guy's details?'

Audrina looked horrified. 'Like I said, I don't think they were legit, but I'll give you what I have. Anything to help. I just wish I could have prevented Oliver from taking the assignment.'

Once Audrina provided her with the social media details that Oliver was using and the username of the person who had approached him for a photoshoot, Claudia thanked her and ended the call. Now she understood how Oliver had been tied to the bed with no defensive wounds. He'd believed he was there for a photoshoot, when he'd been there to have his life taken away in some bizarre game.

CHAPTER 14

He watched the news report with a hot flush spreading over his skin as the reporter on the screen talked about the murder earlier that day.

So many details were missing. The crucial detail, the information that he had sent to the police before the key event, was absent. He had spent so long trying to get that image right. It was a part of the installation and they couldn't see this. If they failed to share his whole exhibit, then he'd have to do something about it.

They couldn't be allowed to silence him this way. The same way he'd been silenced by the galleries and museums.

This was his time.

He'd show the world his art. The critics would talk about him. His exhibit would be famous. As it deserved to be.

No one had thought to do anything like this before. He was a pioneer in his field.

If they refused to give him the limelight he deserved he would have to put his mind to the test and come up with something even better. Something they really couldn't ignore.

The world would see him for what he was. They would adore his artwork and swoon over it. His name would be synonymous with great works of art. The strange and the beautiful. The unusual and glorious. His name would be whispered in hushed tones in brightly lit halls, with the same awe reserved for Pablo Picasso and Ron Mueck.

They would say his name with wonder.

Yes, the next exhibit would have them talking.

CHAPTER 15

'Sorry to interrupt your weekend,' Claudia began the next morning. 'Thank you as always for working through. These early days are always important and typically fall when we're due some time off. I'm sure DCI Sharpe will make it up to us.'

Someone laughed. Claudia didn't see where it came from. She understood the sentiment. Time off tended to be a luxury.

'I spoke to Oliver's agent, Audrina Post, yesterday. She said someone booked him for a shoot through social media and that she tried to advise him against it, but he must have attended anyway. I've requested a Met officer take a full statement from her as soon as possible. This means we have social media accounts and usernames to investigate. It gives us some lines of enquiry to follow up on. I'm heading out of the office this morning. I'll have my mobile with me if you need to make contact. Let's make some inroads in this.'

With the briefing over and everyone provided with actions for the day Claudia teamed up with Russ and headed out to Oliver's regular place of work. The coffee shop. It wasn't a task she would usually engage in. As detective inspector of the team, she should be behind her desk making sure everything was running smoothly. But as this was their first case, she wanted to be involved at a more detailed level. She wanted to go through it step by step herself, afraid to leave anything to chance. It wasn't that she didn't trust her team. She did. It was more to do with the fact that she was a control freak.

Coffee Roast was a boutique coffee shop in a world of chain stores that soaked up the majority of coffee drinkers. It was warm and welcoming, and immediately Claudia was assaulted by the scent of fresh coffee and baked goods. Her stomach rumbled and she wondered if she'd eaten breakfast that morning.

A barista stood behind the counter. His face widened into a smile when Claudia and Russ approached.

'Good morning.' He looked to the door of the store and back to them to confirm what he was about to say next. 'And what a gorgeous one! What can I get for you today?'

He was rather jolly. He either hadn't yet heard about Oliver's death, wasn't that close to him and didn't care or was just good at his job. Claudia needed to find out which it was. She whipped out her ID and matching him smile for smile identified herself and Russ.

'I'll have a tea with milk please and . . .' She looked to Russ, who nodded. 'A flat white.'

'To takeaway or stay in?'

'Drink in, please.' She retrieved her debit card from her pocket as the barista prepared the drinks.

The name badge on his shirt read *Thomas*.

'Thomas, are you on your own today?'

'Yeah, Oliver's supposed to be here, but he hasn't turned up. It's okay now, but it was bedlam earlier. I could have killed him. It's always busy in the morning, even on Saturdays,' he added. 'He'd better have a good excuse.' He pushed a takeaway mug onto the counter. 'That's the tea. Milk and sugar are over there.' He nodded towards another smaller counter to their left.

Claudia looked around her. The coffee shop was quiet at the moment. This wasn't an ideal situation in which to interview Thomas, but it was the best they had. They'd have to deal with it. Luckily, there were no customers waiting behind them. 'Look, I'm sorry to be the one to tell you this, but Oliver was murdered yesterday.' His name had yet to be released on the news as the press were careful to wait for next of kin to be informed. His name would be all over it today, though. Oliver, who wanted fame as a model, would now obtain fame in death. It wasn't the way he would have chosen. Not the way anyone would have chosen.

Thomas dropped the cup he was holding. Steaming hot coffee splashed across the floor behind the counter. He yelped, stepping back from the boiling fluid. 'Oh my God. No. He's not. Oh God. I didn't mean what I said.' His hand flew to his mouth to cover the words that had already escaped.

The bell over the door chimed and a woman with a pushchair fumbled her way through the entrance, trying to hold the door and push the baby through at the same time. Russ stepped forward to help her. The woman gushed her thanks at him.

'Thomas, is there any chance we can have a conversation with you?'

Thomas looked at the woman who had entered. Confusion running through him. 'Can I serve this lady? Then I'll put the closed sign up.'

Claudia agreed, grabbed her tea and moved to an empty table. Thomas looked like a startled rabbit. The mess was still behind the counter, a cop was still without a drink and a new customer was waiting to be served.

'Take your time,' said Russ, noticing the panic on his face. Then he joined Claudia at the far end of the coffee shop, out of the way of listening ears.

Thomas apologised to the woman for the lack of staff and cleared up the spilled coffee. He poured Russ a fresh one and took the woman's order, serving her a decadent looking, cream-swirled hot chocolate before grabbing Russ's drink, flipping the closed sign on the door and moving over to sit with the two detectives.

The smell of fresh coffee from Russ's mug wafted under Claudia's nose. She loved the scent of coffee, like a warm hug, but she never drank the stuff, preferring a good cup of tea. She could definitely see the appeal. What niggled at her more was the desire to have a muffin with her tea, but she knew it would look unprofessional. She clamped down on the desire and got on with her job.

'Thank you for your time, Thomas.'

His leg was bouncing up and down beside her. The woman had selected a table at the other side of the store and was pulling an infant from the pushchair and sitting him on her lap. He looked to be about a year old, from what Claudia knew of children, and he was smiling happily at his mother. How the two sides of the room contrasted this morning.

Thomas waited for Claudia to continue. He had no words. Claudia was sure she had shocked and terrified him in equal measure.

'How was Olivier these last couple of weeks?' she asked.

Thomas looked surprised. 'He was fine. Came to work. Did his thing and went home again.'

'He didn't talk about any problems he was having?'

Thomas scratched his chin. 'No. Oliver wasn't like that. He didn't have problems. He was great. No one fell out with Oliver. He got on with everyone. He was murdered? Why would someone do that?'

'That's why we're here. To try to find out. You can't think of anything?'

Thomas looked across at his customers as if they would hold the answers — the woman with the pushchair and a single man in the centre of the room eating a bacon sandwich with a huge mug at the side to wash it down with. 'You checked with his agent?'

'Yes. We got her details from his mother.'

Thomas fell silent a moment. 'She must be heartbroken.'

That was an understatement. 'She has support.' What support was good enough to hold someone up after losing a child?

'Was Oliver at work on Thursday?'

Thomas stared at the floor a moment and then back to Claudia. 'Sorry. Yes. It was me and Oliver again. We work together quite a lot. He's such a good lad.'

'What time did he finish?'

'When we closed. We both did.'

'And that was?' asked Russ.

'Oh, erm, six.'

'What happened at six?' Claudia asked.

Thomas furrowed his brow. 'We closed.'

'What did Oliver do?'

'I presume he went home. He mentioned something about having another job later that evening, but it wasn't until later . . .'

The child squawked. His mother was wiping his hands. He'd been eating something child friendly she'd brought into the shop with her and obviously didn't like being cleaned up. Thomas brought his attention back to the conversation. 'So I presume he went home.'

'And you?'

'I went home.'

'Can anyone verify that?

'I live alone. Do I need to?'

'Not at the moment.'

Concern flashed across his face. A hand went up to his mouth and he chewed at a nail.

'When you left the shop did you see anyone hanging around? Anyone following Oliver?' Not that there would be if they had planned to get him to the location voluntarily.

Thomas shook his head.

So far he was the last person to see Oliver alive, but it was hours before his death. The house-to-house enquiries around Oliver's home had not been fruitful. No one had noticed him leave or seen anyone visit him. They were a closed-off bunch who kept to themselves. The killer had been clever in managing to get Oliver to drive himself to the kill site.

Claudia offered Thomas her card. 'If you think of anything . . .'

Thomas nodded.

'Please do get in touch.'

* * *

It took a couple of days for the forensic results on the drawing and envelope to come in. Claudia was in her office when she received the email. There were no fingerprints or DNA on either the drawing or the envelope.

She was disappointed but had expected it. So many criminals nowadays were forensically aware. So many crime dramas on TV highlighted the ways in which police could potentially identify an offender, and it made them take precautions of their own. They wore gloves and used self-sticking envelopes so saliva wasn't an issue.

Further analysis of the paper disappointed Claudia even more. The forensic scientist explained that it was common drawing paper that would be available in any art shop, in store or online, with a GSM of 120 and a surface that was cold pressed. All very usual for art paper, apparently.

Claudia rose from her chair, discouraged by how the investigation was playing out. She had the morning briefing to do and she had nothing to offer. She was nearly at the door when her phone rang. She turned around and picked it up. Tyler's solicitor. Did she want her putting through?

Did she?

It was pretty much all she'd thought about over the last couple of days. That and the current murder they were investigating. Could she face him? What could he possibly offer her that she would want to know? She'd thought about the problem endlessly but hadn't come up with an answer.

Something he'd said when she met him, once in the cemetery and once at his arrest. That the reason he hadn't killed Ruth was that she didn't have children. All Tyler's victims had one or more children. This niggled at the back of her brain. It battled up against the fact that Ruth was found in the same circumstances as Tyler's other victims. In a way no one else could possibly know about. They'd kept details to themselves to prevent random people from admitting to a crime they didn't commit. A rare event, but one that happened, nonetheless.

'I'll take the call,' she said into the handset.

And then she was there, in her ear again. The solicitor from the last call. 'Thank you for speaking with me this morning, DI Nunn.'

Claudia's words stuck in her throat. For someone who was a determined, forward-thinking woman, she was not behaving that way when it came to Samuel Tyler. She needed to get a grip. Claudia cleared her throat. 'What can I do for you today?'

Claudia could imagine the smile on the solicitor's face in the quiet before she spoke again.

'Samuel Tyler has asked that I relay to you the importance of his request.'

She'd made her mind up. It had always been made up. But acknowledging that was another matter. And now, here, to the woman who was defending the scumbag, it was an altogether even more difficult task to accept. 'I said I'd think on it.'

'Mr Tyler has charged me with passing along a further message, if you'll permit me?'

A shiver took over Claudia's body. 'What is it?'

The smile seemed to widen and Claudia began to hate the solicitor. 'Mr Tyler has said that his offer to discuss why he did not kill your step-mother is time-sensitive, and if he does not receive a response by the end of today then he will have to withdraw it and never speak of it again until it goes to court.'

Then she would have no ability to question him over whatever he said. 'I'll see him,' she said, before she could stop herself.

'We'll send you a visitor's order, DI Nunn. And please allow me to pass on Mr Tyler's regards.'

Claudia shuddered. She did not need Samuel Tyler's regards. She needed to know why he wanted to speak with her and why it was so important. Anything other than that was irrelevant.

The incident room was alive with activity when Claudia walked in five minutes later, after she'd spent a little time gathering herself.

'Shall we get started,' she shouted over the din, stalking to the front of the room.

Silence settled, and the team focused in on her. She updated them on the email from forensics and a low groan rumbled through the space. Disappointment palpable.

'How are we getting on with the dagger?' she asked.

'We've taken a photograph of it to a couple of dealers in an attempt to identify where it came from or to glean information on it,' said Krish. 'They've said it's a decorative dagger that you could pick up for less than a hundred quid in stores or online. We don't know where it's from yet.'

'So not a good lead,' Russ replied.

'Have we identified Oliver's friends?' Claudia asked, hoping to progress the inquiry at least a little.

'Yes, we've curated a list from his mother. It took a few days as she struggled through her grief, but the FLO sent one over last night.'

'Good, we can get on with visiting them today. Find out about Oliver's life. The people he hung around with. If there was anyone new in his orbit. Anything he showed an unusual interest in recently, or if anyone strange showed an interest in him. There are still plenty of results pending from forensics — from the crime scene, Oliver's vehicle, his body and his home address. Though his home looked pristine. It didn't appear as though there had been a struggle there.'

'To be honest, boss, it didn't look like there'd been a struggle at the crime scene either,' said Russ.

Claudia had to agree with him. 'After talking to Oliver's agent it appears he thought he was there for a photoshoot. It might be that he was asked to get into that position for a shot and . . . well, we know what happened from there. We have a lot of work to be getting on with though, so let's not hang around. I'll catch up with you all again later today.'

CHAPTER 16

The case was going frustratingly slow. Time was slipping past with no forward momentum in the investigation and Claudia was growing increasingly discouraged. A feeling of abject failure sniffed at the edges of her psyche. She pushed it away and focused on what they had, but once the first forty-eight hours of the job were down they were fighting a losing battle. One Claudia refused to accept. Though they were well past their first forty-eight hours now. They were two weeks down and getting nowhere.

She was at her desk when she received a call from Maxine informing her that Sharpe wanted to see her at the smoking shed immediately.

Claudia rolled her eyes but headed out to Snig Hill police station's smoking shed. The sun was blazing down. The summer had been an unnaturally good one so far.

Sharpe was already there when Claudia arrived.

'I thought I'd make the most of the nice day,' said Sharpe as Claudia approached. 'Besides, I was desperate for a smoke.' That was the real reason they were standing outside in this heat.

Claudia stood with Sharpe but kept her distance as she wasn't a smoker and hated the scent of cigarettes lingering on her clothes. She was too young to remember the days when people smoked in pubs, when you went home from a night out stinking of the stuff — her dad had told her of those days, and she was glad it was over. Smoking was a disgusting habit, but she wasn't one to stop others doing as they wanted. It was a free world, after all.

'It's been two weeks, Claudia. I want to know how things are progressing.' Her tone was firm. 'You're supposed to be showing me how good you are with this new task force.'

'We're not suddenly magic because you give us a fancy name.' Claudia wasn't sure where her bravado came from.

Sharpe peered down the cigarette between her lips, then blew out a smoke ring into the air above her.

'That's very true, Claudia, but people are watching what you do. You must have some news.'

'It's an investigation like any other. Nothing has come from forensics. There were no fingerprints on the crime scene and no DNA other than that of the victim. We had no luck when we tried to identify where he bought the dagger from. It might be that he had it in his family already, or he bought it online so we couldn't trace it.'

'Toxicology?'

'Toxicology on Oliver came back clear. He wasn't drugged, so it appears he did climb on that bed of his own accord as we believed from talking to his agent.

'We seized Oliver's car from the industrial site, but there's nothing of evidential value on it. The killer didn't go near it. It looks like Oliver transported himself there and that was it. No fibres were gathered from Oliver's body and no fingerprints were picked up. It appears that our guy is very aware of his actions. We're up against it.' She let out a sigh of exasperation.

Sharpe flicked her cigarette to the ground and stubbed it out with the pointed toe of her shoe. 'What about the guy who booked him for a modelling job that night? He's our killer, right?'

'It looks like it. But we can't get a hook in on him. The username Audrina Post provided got us nowhere. There was nothing in Oliver's home for us to follow up on. We couldn't find his phone, so presumably the killer took it. But we checked with his phone provider. They didn't make contact by phone, so we checked his email address after Audrina gave us the details. The killer originally contacted Oliver through his social media account but then moved to email to thrash out the details. It looks like he created an email account specifically for this and he used a service like Hide My IP or something, so we couldn't locate him that way.' Claudia let out a long breath. 'The same goes for how he used the urban exploring website. He really did seem to think of everything, so it's incredibly difficult to track him. We talked to Oliver's friends but got nowhere with them. It wasn't unexpected, not once we knew he'd been approached online for the supposed modelling job. He could easily have been targeted by searching on model agencies' websites. They all have headshots online. The friends were never going to give us any extra insight. It's wearing the team down, but we're not giving up.'

The sun was beating down on her and she felt like a wasp stuck in a jar. Her clothes were sticking to her, and she wanted more than anything to get back inside where she could hide from the glow of the orange ball of gas that was turning her to melting jelly.

'So, it's difficult then,' Sharpe said in an understatement.

'You could say that.' Claudia wiped at her brow with her palm. Sharpe on the other hand didn't look in the slightest uncomfortable. She looked like she was stood on her own personal glacier in the middle of the desert. Not a strand of hair was out of place, or a stitch of clothing ruffled or clinging where it shouldn't be.

With a change of subject Sharpe lit up another cigarette. 'Have you decided what to do about Samuel Tyler yet?'

Claudia shuffled on feet that were burning like she was on hot coals and cursed Sharpe silently. 'As it happens, I'm visiting him today. I should have gone last week, but being early in the current murder investigation it wasn't the right time. He moaned about it, through his solicitor, but it's not like he's going anywhere.'

'Be careful, Claudia.' Sharpe tapped the end of her cigarette with a perfectly polished fingernail.

Claudia wasn't used to such a show of concern. All she wanted, though, was to get out of this blazing sun.

'I won't allow him to play games with me. Don't worry about that. I'm no mug.'

Sharpe smiled. A strange affliction on her face. 'Oh, I know you're not. What does your dad think about it?'

That was a loaded question. What *did* her dad think about it? How could she answer? She wasn't sure herself. He'd been angry when she first told him and then . . . Then he'd tried to talk her out of it. For her own safety, he'd said. Tyler would mess with her head. Hurt her emotionally. Her dad didn't want to see her go through that. He'd pleaded with her not to go. When that hadn't worked, he'd given her the silent treatment. Now there was an uneven truce.

'He's not particularly happy, to say the least. But it's not his decision. Even though it hurts him, I have to hear what Tyler has to say. Something is niggling at me. It won't let me rest until I've heard him out. Hopefully it'll be a pile of shit and I can settle and forget all about him. Allow the court system to do its thing and send him down for a very long time.'

'There should be no doubt about that. The evidence is overwhelming. And as far as Dominic is concerned, he'll get over it. Grief is a difficult emotion to process.' She tapped on the end of her cigarette again and eyed Claudia over the top of it. 'As you well know. But with time, and with the trial ongoing, Dominic will work his way through all the stages. You're probably at different stages than each other, and that's why it's so awkward between you. Give yourself room to breathe, Claudia.'

Sharpe was rarely kind, but when she was, she dispatched some decent words of wisdom, and Claudia was grateful.

'Do you have any sense of what he wants?' Sharpe asked.

Claudia stared off into the distance. The heat rising from the asphalt, shimmering like silver in the air. 'No. The solicitor says she has no idea, just that it'll be worth my while.' She sighed. 'I can't imagine anything worth my while with that scumbag. He's already caused me no end of pain with Dominic, never mind the business that got him there in the first place.'

Sharpe finished her cigarette and stubbed it out on the ground the same way she had her initial one, ignoring the cigarette bins that stood like silent defenders on either side of the smoking shed. The construction was called a shed, but in reality was a wooden three-sided contraption, wide open at the front so people could gather and inhale the fumes with which they were slowly killing themselves. 'If you need anything from me, don't hesitate to ask.' And with that she strode away, heels clacking, towards the building that housed the control centre of South Yorkshire Police.

CHAPTER 17

Doncaster category B prison, also known by the inmates and locals as Doncatraz, was one of a few privately run prisons in the country. The overcrowding problem caused a high-level tension to run through the prison. Claudia would have to keep her wits about her.

Booking in was a lengthy process. The smell of decaying meat and sweaty feet caught at the back of Claudia's throat every time she visited a prison. She hated the places. Men locked up for hours a day. Desperate for anything new to enter their world. Leering and goading.

As you walked through corridors, all eyes were on you, determined to know who you were. These men made Claudia's skin crawl. She could imagine the thoughts running through their heads as she strode alongside the prison guard, he in his familiar uniform and her in jeans and a T-shirt, with a jacket over the top.

She'd dressed down for today so she didn't stand out as a cop as much as usual. In a suit they'd have her pegged as a cop straight away. In jeans it was nearly as bad, but there was room for doubt. They hated cops, and a female cop gave them reason to leer at her body and offer violent thoughts all at the same time. It was vicious.

The heat of the day meant the T-shirt was clinging to her more than she'd wanted it to, but whatever clothing she'd gone with, she'd have the same problem. Claudia wriggled her back in an attempt to loosen the material, to no effect.

She cursed the warm weather and dreamed of a colder afternoon where she could cover up in a woollen sweater. She had kept her jacket on for this purpose and it was unbearable. Her body did not embarrass her, but neither did she want to flaunt it in a place like this. A place where men wished nasty, evil acts upon you. Where all that separated you was a thin layer of metal bars in some corridors. If they so wanted to, arms could reach through and grab out at her. Corner her, like an animal. When the reality was, they were the ones locked up like animals in the worst conditions. It really was no wonder they lauded any power they could get when they saw the opportunity.

Claudia held her head high and strode on through until she reached the room she needed.

Tyler's solicitor was with him already. The solicitor had secured a private legal room for the occasion. Claudia wasn't sure how she felt about this. There were no cameras and no microphones on the grounds of legal privilege. It didn't feel very secure to her, but she wasn't about to back down and act all scared and give him the upper hand. She'd get this over and done with then walk out on him and never have to see him again.

The solicitor held out her hand and introduced herself. Claudia was so focused on Tyler that she was incapable of taking anything else in, and the name completely passed her by. As they sat around the table Claudia noticed the solicitor had a prosthetic leg. She was wearing a regular-looking navy pencil skirt and beautiful ballerina pumps, and as she crossed her legs, the material of the prosthetic shined under the strip light of the prison room.

Claudia looked away quickly, not wanting to be seen staring.

The solicitor, whose name Claudia hated herself for not remembering, smiled to herself. It didn't matter — she deserved that.

So far Tyler had said nothing. He was sitting quietly on the chair on the other side of the table.

'Mr Tyler has asked that I be present for this meeting,' said the solicitor, pulling an A4-sized notepad from her briefcase.

Claudia agreed. She had nothing against her being here. She just wanted this to be done so she could then get out of there. 'What do you want?' she growled at Tyler.

The solicitor stared at Claudia, surprise showing on her face at the rudeness shown to her client.

Surely, thought Claudia, she knows what he did to Ruth and doesn't expect anything else.

Tyler looked to the solicitor, who gave a curt nod and allowed him to speak. 'Thank you for coming, DI Nunn.'

At least he'd addressed her correctly, though after a period in prison he would become institutionalised and call her Miss, as with all female members of staff in the building. It became entrenched. When interviewing offenders at work, you always recognised the ones who had done time because they called you Miss.

'Get on with it.' She had no patience.

'You know I'm not contesting the charges that have been laid against me for the murders of the women over the last year.' He spoke well. He wasn't a common criminal. He was a man who had supported families before his downfall. He had been a victim support officer. Victim Support was an independent charity, but one which worked alongside the police. They had taken his arrest and charge badly and had put out a statement disowning him.

Claudia ground her teeth. Hearing what the women had been through, coming from his mouth, made her stomach ache.

It was obvious that Tyler took her silence as acceptance to continue. 'What I do contest however is the charge that I murdered the police officer, Ruth Harrison. I didn't kill Ruth Harrison. I never met Ruth Harrison. You won't find any of my DNA on Ruth Harrison.'

They didn't need his DNA, they had enough evidence against him. Her murder matched the women he was pleading guilty to. Including part of the MO that was not released to the public. There was no way it could have been anyone else, because no one else was aware of the facts. Claudia stared at him and crossed her arms tight across her body, tensing her fingers into a fist in her armpits.

Tyler returned her look. He waited for her response, but when one was not forthcoming, he spoke again. 'I'm sorry for your loss. I truly am. The murders I committed benefitted the children of the women I killed, so they could have better lives without having those women as mothers. You see that, don't you?'

The solicitor didn't move other than to scribble notes in the pad, her pen moving silently over paper.

'But Ruth didn't have children. I told you this when you arrested me. I needed you to hear it again. And this time I'll tell you why. My own mother was a failure. Look at my hand.' He held out his left hand, and Claudia looked down at the vivid scarring. Soft pink skin and red ridges, a visible memory of a painful past.

'What happened?' Claudia whispered, shocked at the violent-looking skin. She'd caught a glimpse of his hand when she'd arrested him, but he'd quickly been whisked away into a police vehicle and she'd thought no more of it.

None of the Strangler's victims had been burnt in this way. How did this link to his murders?

'When I was a child, my mother left me in the house on my own. She hadn't fed me before leaving, so I thought I'd make a bacon sandwich.'

Claudia winced. The solicitor continued writing.

'I'd seen how she made them, so I put a pan of fat on the hob to do it myself. Only I was too small to do it properly and when I was trying to turn the bacon I tipped the edge of the pan and the whole lot came over onto me. My hand caught the majority of the fat as I tried to catch it and stop it making a mess of my mum's kitchen. I didn't want to be in trouble.'

He stared straight into Claudia's eyes. 'She'd told me to be a good boy.'

A shiver ran down Claudia's spine. The words thousands of mothers uttered to their children every day. What effect was it having on them? She still didn't see how this was related to the killings. To Ruth not having children.

'Do you know where my mother had gone, DI Nunn?' He spoke quietly, as though the memory were right there in front of him. Vivid and clear and cruel in its clarity.

This time the solicitor looked at Claudia. It was as though she were under some kind of test. One she really wished she knew the answer to. Because failing this test could mean any number of scenarios would be played out. She shook her head. Hoping this wouldn't go against her.

'My mother had gone out on a date and left me alone to fend for myself. She'd left me alone and hungry and in a dangerous situation because she wanted a fuck.'

The last word pierced the air and hung there in front of them. Angry and vulgar. The way he thought of the woman who bore him. Little shocked Claudia though, especially language. But Tyler's face was puce. This was where his fury had come from. The reason for his killing. He wanted to protect the children of women who just wanted to date. Women who were nothing but lonely, whose children were actually old enough to be left alone or were left with responsible adults. Only Tyler's mind was so warped by his past he could see no further than the concept of a mother dating, and he'd wreaked his own revenge.

'Your mother is dead?' Claudia guessed.

Tyler nearly spat at her in response to this psychoanalysing of him. The solicitor placed a calming hand on his arm and he sat back in his chair.

A heavy quiet filled the air.

Claudia ran through what Tyler had told her. Ruth didn't have children, though her undercover profile did. But, when she'd been taken, she'd been taken from her own home, not from a prearranged meeting place from the dating app they'd been using. Whoever abducted her knew enough about her to know her home address, would most likely also know she didn't have children of her own. Claudia was an adult step-child. A fully grown, functioning, police step-child. If the killer was Samuel Tyler, then he wouldn't be interested in Ruth.

'You were killing your mother every time,' Claudia said.

Finally, Tyler spoke again. 'On the nose, Detective Inspector Nunn. On the nose. And if that is true, then why would I choose Ruth Harrison?'

CHAPTER 18

Dominic returned from his walk to the home where his wife had been murdered. People, he knew, silently wondered — and it was silent questioning, because they never dared ask him to his face — how he could continue to live in the same place Ruth had been killed. He could see it in their eyes whenever he mentioned going home or what he'd been doing on his rest days.

But for Dominic, it wasn't the space they all imagined it was. To them it was now a home that a stranger had entered and had fiercely taken the life of one of them. To Dominic, it was his home. A home that had seen an argument flare up, admittedly. But it was his business and no one else's. He saw no reason to run and hide from it.

Today he was anxious, though. Claudia had been to visit Samuel Tyler, and he had no control over what the conversation would contain. What Tyler would say to his daughter or how she would react.

As he waited, the images of that night replayed in his mind. The argument where Ruth had threatened him. The potential loss of all he knew. Ruth at the kitchen sink. His decision as she stood with her back to him. The anger with her gradually manifesting itself and growing until he could no longer ignore it. And there was the feeling of his hands around her throat. The life as it slowly slipped from her. Her eyes losing focus until there was nothing left but a plan ahead of him.

Now Claudia was returning from visiting the very man who could bring him down. His brain wanted to explode.

Eventually there was a knock at the front door and he heard it immediately open.

Dominic took a deep breath, shuddering as the walls closed in on him. Claudia was here.

He walked from the kitchen, where he'd been pacing, to greet her.

'Hey, Dad.' There was a gentle smile on her face.

That wasn't the smile of someone who wanted to wipe the earth with you. He let out some air, the tension leaving his muscles.

'You're back.' It was all he could offer. He could barely speak to her. He was still furious. She was putting his life at so much risk. Little did she understand that.

Claudia moved past him towards the living room and he followed like a lost puppy. He had no choice. He needed to know what had been said. He studied her face as she passed. It was neither angry nor upset.

He had loved his daughter her whole life and had witnessed a whole gamut of emotions from her in that time, but at this moment he had no idea how she was feeling.

'What happened?' He couldn't hold it in any longer.

'Are we having a drink?' she asked.

Dominic clenched his teeth. He just wanted to get on with it. Was she dragging this out to punish him?

'Wine?' It was what she drank.

'Half a glass. I drove over, but I could really do with one.'

He stomped to the kitchen and returned with half a glass of white, as requested, and a can of beer. If she needed Dutch courage, then he definitely needed it. He slugged back a mouthful and waited for her.

Claudia took a sip of her wine and swilled the rest around the glass. 'It was difficult seeing him, Dad.'

He supposed it was. After all, she believed he had murdered her step-mother and best friend.

'Tell me about it?' He sat on the sofa. Attempting not to show his anger or his fear. To be the caring father she needed. To show their unity in grief.

Claudia was still standing. Her shoulders tense and her jaw tight. 'He told me the reason he killed those women.' She'd been staring into her wine glass but looked up at Dominic now. 'You saw his hand?'

'I saw it.' Dominic had met Tyler before he'd been identified as the Strangler.

'It's all to do with that and his mother. When he was killing the women, he was ultimately killing his mother. Each and every time.'

'It must have been hard to hear.' So far he hadn't heard anything about Ruth. He'd go along with her.

There was silence. Was she expecting more from him? He didn't dare speak in case he said something that would trip him up. That had been his problem when talking to Claudia about this before. It had been close to unbearable when Sharpe and Connelly had instructed Claudia to interview him when Ruth went missing.

Their tactic that Claudia would be the one to unnerve him if he'd done anything wrong was the right move to make. So many times he'd been on the edge. The slightest extra push and he'd have tumbled over. But something had always saved him.

The fact that Claudia was there to unsettle him had also had the opposite effect. He was her father, and she could never push as hard as she would any other suspect. She had even taken him to the crime scene after he had planted the idea in her head, and it was there he had managed to show her how human he was.

Yes, Sharpe and Connelly's plan was so close to working. So very close, they just didn't realise. But now he had to keep it up. Now it was Claudia who was unaware she was keeping him on the knife edge. His every word, his every emotion, he had to hold them in check, terrified they were going to leak out and the net would close in around him and take his life away.

'Dad?' Claudia had been speaking to him.

He focused on her. 'I'm sorry. I was a world away. Did you say something?'

'Do you think there's a chance he didn't kill Ruth?'

His nerves jumped, and it took all his power not to fly at her in fury for even following this train of thought. Dominic slid his free hand behind his back and closed his fist. 'No. No, I don't, Claudia. Samuel Tyler is guilty of killing all those women. The evidence backs it up. Don't fall for his games. I don't know why he's doing this to you, but don't allow him to do it.'

Her face twisted in confusion. 'He said Ruth didn't have a child, so he couldn't kill her in the same way he killed the others. It kind of makes sense.'

Dominic's voice turned to stone cold concrete. 'We work with evidence, Claudia, not whimsy. It's evidence that's going to put Samuel Tyler away for a very long time. Don't forget that.'

Claudia stared at her father. She wasn't a weak woman, Dominic didn't expect her to simply back down to him. She had her own mind and could argue her point very well. In fact they'd had their fair share of stand-up rows, as many families, parents and children, had. But Claudia looked at him for a long time, then necked what was left of her wine, walked the glass into the kitchen, placed it on the counter and thanked him for the drink.

'You're leaving?' He hadn't known what to expect, but this wasn't it.

'This is something I need to resolve myself. I'm sorry if I upset you.' And with that, she left.

Dominic stared at the closed door she had exited through. This was worse. By the sound of it, she was going to continue down this path. In what way, he had no idea. But it wasn't something he could allow to happen. Samuel Tyler had to be convicted of Ruth's murder or his own life was at risk. He had to stop Claudia, and he had to stop Samuel Tyler.

CHAPTER 19

The following morning Claudia was in early as she hadn't slept well, worrying about the friction between her and Dominic over Samuel Tyler, as well as the visit to Tyler itself. She put the kettle on and waited for it to boil.

She had no idea what she really thought of what Samuel Tyler had said to her and had hoped to talk it through with her dad, but he'd put paid to that with his anger at her visit and her broaching of the subject.

Had she been heavy-footed with him? Of course they had charged Tyler with killing Ruth. It was only reasonable Dominic would be angry whenever Tyler's name was mentioned. It was why Claudia had backed away last night. She had recognised her own error, and without wanting to make things worse, she had left. She only hoped they could put it behind them at work today.

With tea made, she sauntered down the corridor into her office. The incident room was quiet. Only a couple of staff were in at the minute. She liked this time of day. The quiet before the storm.

Not that there was a storm. They were getting nowhere with the investigation. The top brass were getting annoyed, and the pressure was bearing down. It wasn't that murder investigations never took this long, but they'd created this magical task force as they saw it, and they expected answers within a much smaller timeframe. How could the brass show them off as the cream of the crop if they couldn't solve a simple homicide?

Claudia let out a breath. They had to make a dent in this case soon or heads would start rolling.

She watched Kane stroll in and lifted a hand in acknowledgement. Right behind him was Dominic. He refused to look up at her, so she watched his routine as he sat at his desk, logged on to his computer and said his good mornings to the rest of the team as they ambled in. But at no point did he raise his head her way.

She would have to deal with it. She couldn't allow Tyler to infect their working relationship. Walking out on him last night had been to protect him and their family. How could he not see that?

Claudia placed the now cooled mug of tea on her desk and walked into the incident room. A few voices welcomed her with 'morning, boss'. She gave a generalised 'morning' in response. Her primary aim was to get to Dominic and resolve this issue before it bled into work anymore than it already had.

'Can we have a word?' she asked over his shoulder.

He turned and looked up at her. 'I'm a bit busy.'

'I need you.' She would brook no argument from him.

He tried not to scowl, but the intention flickered across his mouth. She let it pass.

'We can go to my office or take a walk?' she said.

Dominic looked around. 'I don't particularly want to be dragged into your office like a naughty little school boy.' The frustration was oozing from him.

'Let's walk.' She strode towards the door expecting him to follow and he did. 'What is it?' she asked as they moved out of the incident room into the corridor.

'What do you mean?'

'Don't play stupid. This sullen attitude you're giving me this morning. What did I do to deserve it?' She felt like a child herself for asking that question, but they had to hash it out between them. It couldn't be allowed to fester. Not in a work environment.

They reached the top of the stairs and Dominic made his way down. Claudia followed.

'I don't understand why you're chasing your tail with this Tyler stuff,' he said, eventually.

As she knew he would. How to get past it? How to close it down as a subject between them but keep her own counsel? She didn't have the answers. It would have been easier if the tossing and turning that had occurred through the night had provided some, before she found herself in work and facing this problem. Of course she didn't trust Tyler entirely. There was the possibility he had targeted Ruth because she was getting too close to the case. But that didn't sit right because the logical person to kill would have been Dominic or Kapoor, his DI at the time. No, there was more to this that she needed to think about and it would help if she could talk to her dad.

They reached the next floor down and Dominic continued going down the stairs. It was an unusual building in that it was built on a steep hill, and so there were more floors on one side of it than the other.

'I left last night because I didn't want to fight with you, Dad. I didn't mean to upset you. It was wrong of me to come to see you straight after seeing him.' She purposefully refused to use his name. Anything that might trigger her father.

'But it felt like he sucked you in with his lies.'

Claudia couldn't make out the tone in his voice. Some level of distress, but there was an underlying issue there. Not that it surprised her.

How could she deny what Tyler had said intrigued her? 'Can we agree not to talk about him with each other?'

Her father's shoulders stiffened in front of her and he lost his step, stumbling down a couple. She reached out and grabbed his elbow. He shrugged her off, stabilised and continued his journey downwards.

'I'll only be happy when you walk away and leave that bastard to rot, Claudia. He deserves nothing less. He certainly doesn't deserve your time.'

She couldn't make that promise. Something about what Tyler had said was under her skin, irritating her and needling away at her. There was no way she could ignore him.

They reached the bottom of the building, coming out into the front foyer.

Dominic turned to look at her. She hadn't responded, hadn't made the promise he needed. Disappointment was etched on every line. He stared at her a moment longer then turned on his heel and walked out the station, throwing over his shoulder the words, 'I'm going for a quick walk, I'll be back for the briefing.' The early morning sun glinted on the glass door as it swung closed behind him. They were in for yet another hot day. Claudia wondered how long this weather would hold. It had to break at some point.

Her own disappointment clouded her mind, disappointment that she could not resolve the issue with her father. But it wasn't rare that they didn't see eye to eye on things. She'd deal with this as she dealt with every other issue they'd had. The only problem this time was the sensitivity of Ruth's murder. The loss and pain of it. For all concerned. She would have to step carefully.

'Hey.' A smile from the front counter.

Claudia raised a grin of her own at the warm greeting from Steve, who was on duty this morning. He'd been here years. Longer than she had. She'd moved around the force during her service. As a front counter staff member, Steve would have got his job here and settled.

'You want to take your post up to the task force while you're down here? Saves them going through the mailing system,' he asked, holding out a stack of white and brown envelopes.

Claudia stepped forward and took them from him. 'Thanks, Steve.' She flicked through them. There were a few for her and a couple of others for the team. 'Have a good day.' She waved at him as she turned and pressed the button for the lift, using her ID card to access it. This was a public area, and the lift would spit her out into the bowels of the building.

There was no way she was walking all the way up the stairs she'd just descended.

Once in the incident room she distributed the post and took her own into her office and sorted through it. There was nothing of great importance.

That was until she got to the last one.

The last one grabbed her attention.

The last one was a drawing of a crime scene.

CHAPTER 20

It was as intricate and strangely beautiful as the first one she had received.

As with the first one, there was no letter. It was simply a drawing with a clock and a day attached to it.

But it was different to the first one.

The crime scene was different.

Claudia stared at the drawing, awestruck by the complexity of it. The delicacy of the pencilling and shadings bringing the image to life. The beauty of it. But at the same time, the horror of what it represented.

Sitting in her chair, drawing still in hand, terror clawed inside Claudia's chest.

She had to get a grip. She let go of the paper and allowed it to waft down to her desk.

Forensics were unlikely to recover anything from this, but she had to go through the procedure.

First she took several shots of the drawing with her phone, next she dialled the crime scene unit and requested a CSI attend immediately if they had one available, then she put in a call to Sharpe. She'd leave it to her to update Connelly.

Sharpe was, as expected, furious. What was unexpected was that she was marching her way down to the incident room. She wasn't usually one to get involved in the day-to-day work, usually sitting in her office, overseeing the process from there, attending meetings only when necessary and snapping out emails when she had something to say. Being in attendance was not her wheelhouse.

Claudia needed to inform the team quickly.

She emailed the photographs she'd taken of the drawing to her work account, then sent a global email to the team with the images attached, pressing send as Sharpe pushed her way through the incident-room doors.

There hadn't been a lot of time to reflect on what was happening. It had been a matter of immediately reacting to events. There was still the drive of adrenalin surging through Claudia's veins as she printed out the images she'd photographed, so they had a hard copy to work with.

Through her open door she shouted at Krish to collect the printout from the copier as Sharpe elbowed her way past into her office. The scent of cigarettes wafted under her nose. It had not been long since Sharpe had been out for a smoke. Claudia turned away and tried her best not to wrinkle her face in disgust, instead moving towards her desk to show Sharpe the original mailing.

Sharpe was an excellent detective, even if she only managed from a distance now. She stood away from the desk as she peered down at the paper. 'It's not one that's already been called in?'

Claudia moved to her office door again and looked out at the incident room. It was a hive of chatter. Everyone had seen their emails. Krish handed her the printed image. She thanked him and he returned to his desk. She spoke to the team. 'You've seen the image in your email. I want to know if we've had a murder reported that matches it. Let us know immediately.'

She turned to Sharpe. 'You were informed as soon as I saw the drawing. We know nothing about it. We've had no time to do any work on it.'

Sharpe was still staring down at it. 'It looks grim. If there'd have been a murder that looked like that, I'd have heard about it.'

This was true.

Again the victim was male. But this time he was hanging from a small bridge over water, his arms above his head, wrists bound and holding him up. The muscles in the tops of his arms were stretched to their limit as the weight of his body pulled him down. There was a breeze block tied to his feet, pulling and stretching and causing the male so much agony. A scream was etched on his face. This was a drawing, a snapshot, done before death had set in. Did this mean they could find him before the crime occurred and stop it this time?

A pulse flickered in Claudia's temple. 'You think we can stop it before it happens?'

Sharpe held out her hand for the paper Claudia was holding. She handed it over. 'It says Wednesday next to the clock. Eight a.m. That's only one day to identify the victim and the location. The press are going to have a field day, but we need to use them to our advantage with this. We have to stop this murder or we'll be toast, Claudia.'

Claudia was well aware of how this would be perceived if they allowed another man to die at the hands of this killer. Not that 'allowed' was the right word. But if they failed to stop him being killed . . . They could not fail.

This man on the bridge, whoever he was, could not afford for them to fail.

'I'll update Connelly, and obviously we'll have to inform the PCC.'

Claudia rolled her eyes. The Police and Crime Commissioner. A civilian elected to the role, who only worried about how crime looked because how it looked to the citizens of Sheffield determined his tenure. And he was quite happy in the role. Though Claudia couldn't imagine being dictated in your job by what the public thinks of you. Even if it was how policing was pretty much run nowadays, anyway. At least in a task force like theirs, they could simply react to the cases as they came in. Do their job and let others worry about the problems of perception. Claudia realised that as someone on the fast-track promotion scheme, this would at some point be her world. She had to start paying attention. Get used to the political side. The concerns of how policing was perceived. There was a push in the current climate for officers to be aware of proactive policing. To prevent crimes happening rather than just being reactive. Though it was difficult with murders, it wasn't altogether impossible. Just take domestic murders, for example. And here was another case in point.

The whole policing strategies thing was a worry for another day. Right now they had just over twenty-four hours to stop the murder of an unknown man at an unknown location.

Claudia looked up from the drawing that had mesmerised her.

Sharpe tapped her fingers on the desk. 'This is where the task force has to come into its own, Claudia. There's no free run with this. All eyes are on you. You have your actual job. Get stuck in and resolve it.' Her tone forbade any argument. She turned her back on the drawing and marched out of the office and through the incident room, nearly bumping into Dominic as he walked back in. 'Nice of you to join us, DS Harrison,' she sniped on her way past.

Claudia couldn't help but smile behind her door. Giving herself a second of freedom before the hard work of this investigation took everything from her.

'What did I miss?' Dominic asked in the incident room.

Claudia strode in with the drawing in her hand. 'We've had another drawing delivered, and this time we're going to stop him before he kills again.'

CHAPTER 21

He was exuberant. He'd posted the invitation yesterday and the reason for his joy today was that the envelope containing his drawing, his invite, would be delivered this morning.

The police would open it and unlike last time they would understand the significance of the image.

The prospect of their faces sent a flurry of tingles across his skin. The thought of them recognising the drawing for the invitation it was.

He could imagine them working with the drawing, trying to figure out the location.

But he wasn't stupid. Of course, part of the thrill of creating these exhibits was the risk of being stopped before he could complete it. It was as though there was an electric current running through him.

He was alive.

Surging with energy.

The cops wouldn't stop him. There were several bridges it could be. He was a precise artist, though, and there were tell-tale signs within the drawing if you looked hard enough. Even if they did identify it, the clock was out by several hours. He'd be long gone by the time they got there. Even if they arrived early in an attempt to catch him in the act.

No, he wasn't dumb. He needed the audience, but he also needed to play this out again.

This wasn't the end of the line. There was plenty more to come. His mind was ready to play.

The first work of art, the installation at the industrial estate, that had been all about the art. Creating the sculpture and performance piece for his audience in company with the working invitation had been all the thrill he'd needed. After all, he was an artist. One whose work would be recognised for years to come. But he had to admit that following on from that first piece, having the police involved, choosing them as his invitees, choosing DI Claudia Nunn, had turned up the thrill a notch. And in doing so he had changed the effect of his actions a little. He'd chosen DI Nunn after seeing her in the press. She'd gone after her own father, it had eventually been reported. She was hardcore. If anyone was worthy of being invited to his installations it was her. He was now as enthralled by the game as much as by the exhibits themselves. The game, creating the invitations, was intertwining into the final piece for him. Becoming a part of the exhibit. The need for the chase. The hide and seek within the invitation. Making his heart pound. He couldn't separate the game from the installation. It was now part of the performance piece, he realised.

And he was looking forward to the adulation that would come from such extreme work being out there.

CHAPTER 22

They didn't usually pin things to the wall in the incident room. This wasn't a television programme where the evidence was stuck up around them for all to see. But this image, this drawing, it was a different matter. Everyone needed to see the drawing and keep their focus on it at all times.

So, with that in mind, Claudia had the drawing enlarged and tacked to the wall in a prominent position where everyone could see it.

She stood, peering at the pencil work like everyone else in the room. The low brickwork bridge was over what looked to be a canal rather than a river. The water was settled and smooth. Greenery overgrew at the edges and a footpath ran alongside the water. Further in the distance, some buildings added their angles to the skyline, edging out of the bushes and trees and general green area that the image depicted.

The victim's dark hair flopped over his forehead. What Claudia thought of as a new beard lined his face. One that wasn't long and in need of a brush, but rather close to his face. Shaped to his jaw. The drawing was so well done you could nearly see the individual strands of hair growing to create the overall effect. When not close to death, the man in the image looked to be a good-looking male. One who enjoyed his life. Looked after himself.

He was shirtless in the drawing, and his body was well defined. Likely spent time in the gym. Claudia looked at his hands, trying to peer closer at his fingers to see if he was married. She stared at the image. His hands were twisted as the rope looped his wrists and pulled his hands tight together in the centre above his head and up to the top of the bridge wall. It was not possible to see his ring finger clearly. She wondered if he was missing yet, if a loved one had reported him missing and was at home begging for his return. Or was he still walking free, not knowing what was about to happen to him. Living his life, attending a career, a home, with people who loved him, oblivious to the pending horror that was steamrolling its way to him.

It was this prospect that stressed her more than any other. The thought that he was out there free and happy with a clock hanging over him and he knew nothing about it, and they could do nothing to warn him. 'Does anyone recognise the victim or the location for starters? Is he well known in any capacity? Are there any identifying marks in either the victim or location that stand out to you?'

She was met with a wall of silence. Solid and ominous. This wasn't the start she wanted.

'Nothing?' she pleaded with them. 'This is your city, and no one recognises the bridge?'

Again the silence pushed back at her. But this time the team had the cognizance to look guilty about their lack of answers. She could hardly scold them as she didn't recognise it herself.

'Okay,' she said in response to the quiet. 'We don't know who or where he is. We have to move on and zoom in on the details on the drawing. The artist has an eye for detail. Having received the first of his artworks and been to the accompanying scene, I can guarantee they match up particularly well. So, with that in mind, we need to work on what he's given us. It's not often we get the chance to stop a murder, in this task force, before it's committed.'

She clapped her hands together, the sound loud in the unusually quiet space. 'Let's work this.' She faced the drawing again. The image of the man hanging by his hands from the bridge, pulled down by the weight of the breeze block, was gradually being imprinted on the inside of her eyelids. 'Let's start with what we know. What we can see. Who wants to get this going?'

She needed to kick off a discussion. An engagement of minds. To get a free flow of information running. This was how they worked best.

Russ spoke up. She could always trust him in a difficult situation. 'There's no visible injury. How do we think he's killed? Can you be stretched to death?'

She looked to Dominic, who was staring sullenly at the wall. His mind was in a dark place, and if he didn't pull himself into the here and now, she would have words with him about it. There were more important issues at this point in time.

Russ had a good point. 'I have no idea. We'll have to get in touch with Nadira and find out. If he can't die from his positioning, then we need to examine the drawing for any other signs of what might kill him. I don't imagine this guy is hanging here for us to find and take to the hospital.'

Russ scribbled a note in his pad.

'What else?'

'He looks to be a white male.' Krish put forward. 'Between twenty to thirty.'

'Still a large part of the city's population.' She hated to be down on suggestions, but they had to be realistic. She needed more from them. 'How many bridges are there in Sheffield?' she pushed.

Again the thunderous silence blanketed the room.

Claudia ran a hand through her hair, frustration gnawing at the back of her head. 'Look, we can't work like this. It needs to be more dynamic. Okay, if you have nothing on the specific questions I throw out, jump in with something else. Keep the ideas flowing. This silence is driving me insane. We can't solve a crime without words. We have a man who is about to lose his life, and for once in our lives we have the chance to stop his murder before it even happens. Not turn up after the event and chase down his killer. Who here isn't up for that?' She glared at them all. It was a genuine question. 'If you don't want to stop this murder, then you can walk. Get up and leave and I can attach you to another team where the work is familiar. But if you want to stop a murder, then what I need from you is more. More than you're currently giving me. More than you're giving of yourself. More for Oliver Kennedy, because he deserves that much more. If you're staying, you put in everything you have to offer and then some.'

The glare continued as she waited for anyone to climb out of their chair and walk from the room.

No one moved.

'Okay. You're all staying. That's good to know. Now you know what I expect. Let's get to work on this.'

Claudia returned her attention to the drawing. 'It's not a large bridge. Not a well-known structure. Our killer has done this on purpose. It's smaller, brick-built, looks to be over a canal rather than a river. How many of those in the city?'

This time there was an immediate response. They'd heard what she had to say. Lisa spoke up, her voice loud and strong. 'I've no idea, but we could contact the Canal and River Trust, which used to be British Waterways, plus we could contact Highways England. It would be a start. See how they could help us.'

She pointed at her. 'Good job, Lisa. Get on it ASAP.' She thought back to her earlier musings. 'We don't know if he's already missing. Check to see if we have any mispers who potentially match the description of the male in the drawing. We need an ID of the lad in the image. Maybe we'll get lucky.'

Russ spoke again. 'Kennedy wasn't recorded as a missing person because he lived alone. If our killer goes by the same playbook it's unlikely our victim is missing yet.'

'Do you think he's going to be another model?' asked Krish.

'Who's prepared to model that scene?' Dominic scoffed.

Claudia wished that if he didn't have anything helpful to say, he would keep his thoughts to himself. Of course, what he'd said was likely true, but it was the way he went about it. He had difficulty in reining in his thoughts since Ruth's murder. His mood was erratic and everyone was stepping on eggshells around him. Not just her. Krish was part of Dominic's old team and he simply scowled at his old DS, leaving his face to portray what he very likely wanted to say. Claudia was glad it hadn't blown up into anything more. It wasn't what they needed.

'Okay.' She kept the team focused on what they had in front of them. 'What I want to do is split the team into two. Half of the team work the Oliver Kennedy murder and half work on this image. The work on the Kennedy murder might be a help in this new case. We'll keep both cases fluid. Everything out in the open. That way one side might hear a snippet that helps them. Of course the Kennedy case is important, but the priority is the recent case. I've never once in my career been in a position where I've been able to stop a murder like this. I doubt any of you have. We're in a unique position. Let's not waste it. Let's stop a murder.'

CHAPTER 23

Dominic understood the urgency of the investigation in front of them but he had his own urgent matter to contend with. And on his walk the fresh air had given him some ideas on how to potentially deal with it. There was no way Claudia could be allowed to continue on the path she was on in believing Samuel Tyler had not committed Ruth's murder. It led to nowhere but trouble. Trouble for him.

He'd tried asking her to back off, but she was as stubborn as he was. Of course he'd passed that trait on to her. He couldn't go to her mother and ask her to speak to Claudia because . . . well, they hadn't exactly left it on the best of terms when he'd left her for a younger woman. She wouldn't do him any favours, and she'd want to know why it benefitted him so much. Like a small ratty dog with a bone she'd shake at the information he was feeding her until she got something she vaguely believed. No, Claudia's mother was not his escape.

The incident room around him was a buzz of activity. He had to look like he was involved while at the same time working on his own problem.

Typical of Claudia to demand they work this as a team, then glide out of the room all serene and queen-like.

Urgh. He hated working for her. It had always niggled him that she had powered past him in promotions, but to have it so close and personal that she actually lorded it over him by having him on her team, it was nearly too much to bear. Of course he loved her, she was his daughter. Nothing would take that away. But his feelings rampaged through him. Sometimes suffocating him.

Russ Kane, the other DS on the team, stood in front of the image, his hands on his hips. Claudia relied on Russ more than him. Obviously because they'd come from the same team before this task force had been created, Dominic could accept that. But she could at least make an effort to include Dominic more and not make it look like he was just one of the constables.

'What can you see?' Graham asked Kane. Graham was an ex-soldier who, like Claudia, did everything by the book. 'Anything stand out, mate?' He called everyone mate. Something else that grated on Dominic.

Why was it that everything seemed to grate on him recently? Something to do with grief, Claudia would say, if asked. Something to do with secrets, he acknowledged quietly.

'Just trying to analyse it, but no, nothing coming to me yet,' said Kane.

Dominic woke his computer up. Made it look like he was working, but what he was doing was something altogether different.

What he'd thought about on his walk was Samuel Tyler and how to get to him from out here. How to manipulate him into not talking with Claudia. Not telling her he was innocent. It was a difficult ask. Tyler had nothing to lose. And no reason to do as Dominic asked of him. Yes, they'd been friendly before Ruth's death, when Tyler was a victim support officer, before he was identified as the Sheffield Strangler. But he was charged with her murder now, and it wouldn't be good for Dominic to be found on his prison visitor's log if anyone questioned anything about Tyler's activity. And because of that, Dominic couldn't really get to speak with him.

No, he had to get around it a different way.

He needed to find out if Tyler had a cellmate. And if he did, then he needed to find out all he could about that cellmate and then pay him a visit. If he couldn't get close to Tyler he'd do the next best thing.

'Hey,' shouted Kane.

Dominic raised his head. 'What is it?'

'There's what looks to be a pile of clothes on the tow-path. Maybe if we can enlarge the image we can get something from them.'

Dominic was impressed. If the killer didn't want them to get at least a little close to his crime, then what was the point in this charade? He turned to Krish, who had been a part of his old team. 'Can you see about getting the drawing enlarged, Krish?'

Krish jumped from his chair, eager to move this job along. The clock was ticking.

Dominic returned to his research. They didn't have access to prison records, so he couldn't immediately find out who Tyler's cellmate was, but there was a cop embedded within the prison as a liaison. He emailed her to ask the question. Once he had his answer he would do some proper research on him. Find out what he wanted or needed. How he could wrap this guy around his finger to do his bidding.

The email returned within a few minutes. Yes, she was well. She was sorry to hear about Ruth and of course she could help him out with Tyler. As long as he didn't plan on breaking any rules, *haha*. He rolled his eyes at that.

What on earth did she think he wanted the information for?

Anyway, Craig Lawton was his cellmate. Had been since Tyler was remanded. Currently on remand himself awaiting trial for killing the guy who had raped his daughter. *Anything else you need, let me know.*

Dominic typed up a quick response thanking her for the information, letting her know she'd helped a grieving man with a problem, and got to thinking about his next step. He was one step closer to Tyler. Now, how to close Tyler down and stop him ruining his life.

CHAPTER 24

Instead of leaving it to the team to find out, Claudia picked up her phone once she was in her office and dialled Nadira herself. She couldn't wait for her officers to do the work while she sat on her arse twiddling her thumbs doing the crap paperwork. They were on a tight clock, and she was not going to let this guy die on her watch.

Nadira picked up on the second ring. She must have been sitting at her desk.

Claudia said hello and asked if she was busy or if she had time to talk through a problem.

'If you're calling then it must be important.' There were other voices in the background. Nadira told whoever it was that she was taking this call. Claudia was grateful to her.

'It is, Nadira. There's a clock on it as well.'

'You have another drawing?' It was the only logical conclusion bearing in mind their last case together. They weren't disclosing the fact of the drawings to the public, but Nadira was not the public. She was as much a part of the team as any of the detectives. She saw the horrors of the case as much as any of them, and Claudia had informed her during Oliver Kennedy's post-mortem that they had received a drawing prior to his murder.

'We do. Delivered directly to me just like the last one.'

There was a hiss of air down the line as Nadira expelled her shock from her lungs. 'Why are you being targeted?'

'I don't know, but that's not the important question, Nadira. We can analyse that later. I need to ask you about what's depicted in the image.'

'Okay, go ahead. What do you have?'

Claudia explained the man in the drawing. The pain and horror on his face, the stretch and bulge in his upper arm muscles, the breeze block dragging his body down. The terror in his eyes. 'Can he die from this, Nadira?'

There was a quiet pause. Claudia was getting tired of hearing silence today. She waited for the professional to process the information.

'I'm afraid he can die from the positioning, especially with the breeze block attached. It adds extra strain on his chest, and that's the problem. He's going to be suffocating with the pressure on his chest. Air just won't be able to flow through properly. As well as that being the main problem, his shoulders would dislocate or break, even his hips with the added brick tied to his feet. It's a form of crucifixion. It sounds very much like a form of torture used in medieval days called *strappado*. You couldn't hang anyone long this way because death was the likely outcome.'

Black spots danced in front of Claudia's eyes and the noise from the incident room seemed to invade her space. She blinked hard to ground herself. She had never heard of anything so grim. 'How long would it typically take to die in this position?'

A chair creaked. 'I'd say you have thirty to sixty minutes to find your guy once he's been strung up. But . . .' Nadira brightened. 'You have longer than that, don't you? You can find him now you know the image is real.'

Claudia had never felt so defeated. 'It's a drawing, Nadira. It's not a photograph. There's less detail. Though, to give him his due, it's a pretty good drawing. We're doing the best we can, but it's not going to be easy.'

'I'm sorry, Claudia. I didn't mean to pile on the pressure. I know you'll work hard to locate the victim. If there's anything you think I can do, get back in touch.'

Claudia thanked Nadira for her help and hung up the phone, sinking deeper into the swivel chair behind her desk. Shoulders heavy, weighing her down.

What a horrifically awful way to die. And for what? What did the killer hope to achieve? What was behind this? There was no way they could give him the freedom to taunt them like this and then get away with the murder. It didn't bear thinking about.

So far the drawings had been kept out of the press. Sharpe had mentioned releasing them to the public now they knew they were actually advance warnings. But to who? Who did they tell to be cautious? White males between the ages of twenty and thirty? And cautious of what? How were they to live their lives for the next day? Afraid to go out of their homes? It was ridiculous. You couldn't ask a whole swathe of people like that to hide. For one thing they wouldn't do it. Especially in that age bracket. They would refuse. They'd stand tall and say they wouldn't be frightened into hiding away. No crazy person with a pencil was going to dictate their life.

Claudia ran a hand through her hair.

There was a knock at her door and Russ and Krish pushed their way in. Krish waved an even larger printout of the drawing in his hand.

She looked at the pair of them. A giddy excitement pulsed from them.

'What is it?' She didn't dare have her spirits lifted yet. She tempered them and waited the pair out.

'We went through the mispers, and there haven't been any males between twenty and forty reported missing in the last forty-eight hours.'

'So we've still got a chance to find him,' said Claudia. 'What do you have?'

'We've spotted something else on the drawing that might be able to help us,' Kane said.

Claudia leaned forward, her interest piqued. 'Well?'

'There's a bundle of clothes on the towpath at the side. Obviously belonging to the guy hanging from the bridge. It looks like he's definitely chosen his victim beforehand.'

'And does the enlargement help us any?' She tapped her fingers on her desk.

Krish bounced on the spot with the paper in his hands. He laid it out on Claudia's desk, shoving a pile of folders out the way. She tried not to tut at him and lifted the pile out of his way and moved them onto a set of drawers. Krish smoothed the paper out so they could all look down on it, then planted his stubby finger down in the middle where the pile of clothes did indeed sit below the bridge on the footpath.

'Okay, I see them. Move your finger.' Claudia tucked a strand of hair behind her ear so it didn't fly in her way as her head leaned forward over the image. 'What's so interesting about a pile of clothes?'

'Obviously not the clothes,' said Kane. 'There's no way to know what a person is going to wear before they dress themselves. But look at the trainers.'

Claudia trained her eye on the pile of clothes and on top of them a pair of trainers. One upright, one on its side. 'What about them?'

'Look at them closely. They look identifiable and they look pretty special for a pair of trainers. We might have a way to identify our victim.'

CHAPTER 25

Claudia peered down at the enlarged sheet of paper, crinkling her eyes so she could focus in on the trainers which rested on top of the clothes folded on the ground.

Either she was getting old and her sight was failing, or the image wasn't quite clear enough.

'He's taunting us,' she spat out in fury and frustration. Her blood boiled in her veins at being so close and yet so very far away.

Krish leaned in closer, his dark curls pushing her out of the way. His woody aftershave tickled the back of her nose. 'I thought enlarging it would help,' he said, disappointment clear in his tone. 'Does anyone have a magnifying glass?'

'A magnifying glass? What century do you think we're in?' Russ teased.

Krish didn't take it very well. He jolted upright and stared at his supervisor, a glint of his frustration at the job now directed at his boss. Claudia watched them. Krish was obviously loyal to Dom having come from his original team. He might feel Kane was taking priority because Claudia leaned on him more. She recognised that and needed to actively change it. They worked well together, and he'd been a rock when they'd had to investigate Dominic. By her side the entire time. None of this task force could even comprehend what that had been like. But she had to include them more.

'I think if we can get our hands on a magnifying glass it might help,' she said. 'It certainly can't do any harm. We'll be able to see the image more clearly, at least. Anyway, it's not like we can scan and enhance the image using these archaic computers. And sending it to the computer forensics department will take too long. Let's give it a shot.' She turned to Krish. 'Try to source one, will you, and we'll have another look at it and see if we can figure out where these trainers are from.' She smiled at him. 'Good shout.'

Krish glared at Kane again and stalked out with a nod to Claudia.

'That went well.' Russ turned his attention back to the drawing.

'You asked for a punch in the face.' Claudia grinned at him. 'Really? I'd have punched you if you'd have mocked me like that.'

Russ had the good grace to look shamed. 'It kind of slipped out. Do you think he's okay?'

'If he's not, he's in the wrong career. We don't need babies in this department, but it warranted a right hook is all I'm saying.'

'Yeah, and with your by-the-book approach to everything the poor guy would have been out, regardless of whether you agreed with him.'

Claudia laughed at him. 'Then it's a good job he had the sense to keep himself in check.'

Russ returned his attention to the drawing again. 'A magnifying glass, though?'

'It can't hurt to try, can it?'

Russ shrugged. His broad shoulders like shifting boulders under his work shirt. 'You think we can do this?'

Claudia dropped back into her chair, the question a punch to her abdomen. All the air in her lungs was expelled with the bluntness of the query. She grabbed for her breath and clambered for an answer that didn't sound as if she was reading a greeting card. All sweet and sickly promises of what they could do if only they tried hard enough. This was her second in command — if you didn't consider Dom. If she couldn't be honest with Kane, then she couldn't do this job.

'We're fighting an uphill battle. But at least it's a battle we're in. We usually turn up when it's all done and dusted and the body is on the ground. This time we have a chance to stop it before it happens.' She let out a long breath. 'If we can't do this, if we can't make it work, we're going to make sure we did the best job we could have done — there'll be no room for second guesses.'

Russ tapped the drawing with his fingers. 'What's this all about?'

She considered the question. 'I don't know. We'd need a profiler for that. Maybe something to consider? The case is unusual enough to warrant one. But if I was to guess, I'd say he was playing some kind of game. He wants our attention.'

'He's certainly got that.'

Claudia leaned back in her chair. 'He has indeed. I spoke to Nadira before you came in. If we don't get to this guy in time, our hanging man is not going to make it if he's left up there too long.'

'This is definitely a murder?'

'It's definitely a murder.'

There was another knock, and this time Lisa stuck her head around the door. 'I've been in touch with our GIS team and they can help with the bridge issue.' She was as excited as Krish had been by the trainers in the drawing.

The team was making inroads, and it was great to see.

'What exactly is a GIS team?' She should know, but there were so many small teams that functioned within the force she couldn't possibly be aware of them all.

'The Geospatial Intelligence Systems team.' Lisa had stepped fully into the office now, peered at the enlarged drawing on Claudia's desk. Her eyes sparkled at having found someone to aid with identifying the bridge.

'This team can help, how?'

'They're going to get us a list of all the bridges over canals in the city. We can visit each one and see if any match the drawing.'

'Good work. Thanks, Lisa. That'll prove to be extremely helpful. What with the trainers in the drawing and the GIS team, we might actually be in with a chance of stopping this before it happens.' A small flutter made itself at home in Claudia's chest at the prospect of preventing a murder before it was committed. They'd never been in this position before, and it was a good feeling. One she could definitely get used to. If only all criminals gave them a heads-up first.

Lisa bounced back out of the office, her excitement visible in her walk. Claudia smiled.

She peered out through the windows into the incident room. Krish was back and appeared to have retrieved a magnifying glass from somewhere. A small group of the team were standing with him around the enlarged image on his desk. Krish bent right over, his nose practically on the paper. He was shouting at the team to get off him and to shut up, he couldn't focus with all the noise.

They dutifully shut up.

Claudia jumped to her feet. She couldn't wait in her office for the news. She strode into the incident room, took up position behind the huddle of cops currently all showing her their covered backsides.

'Got it!' screeched Krish. 'I've got it. Look at the way they're fastened at the top. The laces go all the way down the side of the trainer. Not many can look like that.'

Claudia stepped forward. 'How does that help?'

Krish bolted upright, not realising she had been behind him. The magnifying glass in his hand clattering to the desk.

'Yeah, I think I recognise those. That's it: Adidas Human Race NMD Pharrell x Chanel,' said Graham, reading from the website. 'Came out in 2017. An expensive brand that not many guys on the street can afford.'

'Something you buy?' asked Rhys.

Graham gave a quick look at the drawing. 'Not for me, mate. But when I was in the army, there were some young lads who were into that kind of thing. It kind of got me interested. We weren't paid enough to kit ourselves out in that gear, but they'd rave about the brands they liked. The stuff they'd wear when they were either higher ranking or had left and got some cushy civvy job that earned them a hell of a lot more.' He scratched at his jaw. 'Like I said, they were young lads. But when someone talks enough about something, it's hard to forget.'

'Any way we can chase down who owns these trainers?' Claudia asked.

'It's worth a try, boss. They're expensive, at five to six grand a pair. Whoever owns these has some spare money to throw around and loves his footwear. But even at that price, there will still be plenty, maybe hundreds of them, out there to make our job difficult.'

'Hundreds narrows our victim pool from what it was. Make contact with all the places who sell these trainers and find out if they shipped to Sheffield. That way, if we focus on the Sheffield buyers, we might be able to ID our victim and stop his murder.' She would not give up. She could nearly reach out and touch their next victim.

CHAPTER 26

Claudia hadn't been part of the team that headed out to check out the bridges. As a detective inspector, it wasn't her job to do the legwork like that. Neither was she calling all the footwear distributors and attempting to identify the victim.

Because of this, she was a ball of anxiety. Her skin was clammy and her nerves shredded.

She paced from her office into the half-empty incident room. A low hush quivered through the air as the few officers left in the office space made the required calls to locate the trainers — to no avail so far or she'd know about it.

The other side of the team weren't having much luck either, as she hadn't heard from them.

She wanted to lash out at something. Take her pent-up rage out on an inanimate object. Release the energy that swirled around within her.

Instead, she stormed out of the incident room and out of the building, finding herself in the smoking shed again. A place that was of no use to her as she wasn't a smoker, but it was a place the smokers gathered, regardless of rank. You could have a conversation with anyone in headquarters down here on the flats of the grey concrete that headquarters towered over. Maybe someone could soothe her furrowed mind.

The shed was empty, the heat of the day searing up from the ground, making Claudia hot and sweaty and uncomfortable.

She kicked the side of the shed and cursed as her toe throbbed in her shoe.

'Whatever did the shed do to you?' a voice behind her asked.

She didn't recognise the voice and turned to see who it was. A male in a suit stood behind her, which, because of his suit, meant she had no idea of his rank. He could be a DC two ranks lower than her own or any rank higher.

He was tall and filled his suit well. And had the most twinkly blue eyes she had ever seen. They stood out because his hair was dark and his eyes sparkled below his eyebrows.

'Sorry about that. It's a tough day.'

'I can see that.' He smiled. 'Anything I can do to help?'

She had no idea who he was. Headquarters was so huge you didn't know everyone inside. It was easy to never meet other colleagues in there, to only head into your own part of the building and out again and not engage with the rest of the staff.

This was the reason she had come to the smoker's shed, to look for help, wasn't it?

As he waited he pulled out a pack of cigarettes and a lighter from his pocket, offered Claudia one.

'I'm sorry, I don't smoke.'

He raised an eyebrow.

She laughed.

'So you don't smoke . . .' He lit his own cigarette and inhaled. 'Yet I find you in the smoking shed. Not only in the smoking shed, but assaulting the poor structure. What on earth could it have done to offend you so much?'

Claudia brushed a strand of hair behind her ear. She looked a little ridiculous. It would never sound sensible if she tried to explain herself. 'I wanted . . .' She thought about her next words. 'I wanted . . .'

He waited patiently.

She actually wanted to kick him for his patience.

'How about you tell me about your day?' He tried instead.

That was easier. It was unlikely he was Press wandering about within the confines of the outer limits of South Yorkshire Police grounds.

'I'm waiting for my team to identify a male, who, if we don't find him, will become a victim of murder.' She ran a hand through her hair. Some pent-up pressure was being released in the conversation.

He nodded. 'Ah, the drawing victim. That's your job?'

How did he know about that? 'Yes, but how—'

'Did I know?' He swapped the cigarette he was smoking into his left hand and held out his right hand. 'DCI Adam Blackwood. I'm the new Intelligence DCI. Taking over from Jennings.'

It all clicked into place. 'Oh, I'd heard Jennings was leaving. I hadn't realised she'd already left. I would have popped by and introduced myself.' She tried to prevent herself from blushing. A thoroughly female thing to do and a bodily function she had no control over. But he didn't seem to notice. She was annoyed at herself for not being on the ball with the new mover in the intel department. She should know better. She took his hand. Although the sun was beating down on them, his hand was not hot and clammy as expected but cool, and he held hers in a tight grip.

'Jennings had some leave due, so she took that to start her retirement early. Her retirement do is still planned for next month if you're going to be there?' He smiled. It was crooked. Like someone had fitted his teeth in his mouth incorrectly. 'Plus, don't worry about not coming by. From what I hear, you have a hell of a lot on. I wouldn't be welcoming the new boy if I was dealing with what you're sorting through.' He let go of his grip on her and Claudia withdrew her hand.

He walked past her to the bin and stubbed out his half-smoked cigarette. She watched him.

'I'm trying to stop,' he said by way of explanation. 'I've not got there yet, but I keep trying. For every half I don't smoke I class it as a win. So, anything I can do?'

She frowned.

'The victim you're chasing.'

Talking to him, coming down here, it had done what she had hoped it would, and she had calmed considerably as the stress ebbed away.

'We've got two lines of enquiry going at the minute that I don't think your team will be able to help with. But it's really useful to have met you. I'm glad I came down here. Thanks.' She smiled at him.

'You never gave me your name.'

'Claudia Nunn. DI on Complex Crimes.'

'Ah, the new task force. And you have a crazy sending you drawings. You're off to a fast start.'

Wasn't she just.

'You'll get in touch if we can help at any point?' DCI Adam Blackwood said.

'I will. Thank you. And thank you for . . .' She waved a hand in front of her and then around at the smoking shed.

Blackwood laughed. A loud, hearty laugh. 'You're more than welcome. It was refreshing seeing someone give this old piece of crap a kicking. I just wish I could be more helpful. I do hope you find your victim.' And with that he turned and headed back towards the building.

But not before Claudia had clocked that he had not been wearing a wedding band.

* * *

The day dragged on and the team gradually returned to the incident room looking dejected one by one. Each time one of them entered, Claudia leapt from her chair to be met by a shake of a head, to which she slunk back to her own office, completely deflated.

The section chasing the trainers had got nowhere either. They'd had to stop searching hours ago when the working day finished. But the unit looking for the canal bridge had stayed out into the late evening as the daylight worked in their favour.

It was no good, though. In the end, they had to call it a night. There was no way they could look for the bridge in the dark.

'We'll start again in the morning,' Claudia said with as much enthusiasm as she could muster. 'We have some hours left on the clock. As long as we find the location, we stop the murder. Don't give up, guys.' She had to push them onwards. She could sense their despondency, the pending grief in their body language. It was in her own body, like a still lake waiting to relinquish its goods from the depths.

At home, she allowed the grief to take over. She grabbed her PJs and, childlike, curled up on the sofa with a blanket around her while she tried to lose herself in a book, but it was no good. Her mood wouldn't allow her to focus on the words.

Somewhere out there, a man was living his life, and while she tried to read a book, he was oblivious to the fact that this might be his last night.

CHAPTER 27

It had been a long day, but Dominic trailed the car in front of him for about a mile. Watching every junction taken, every indicator used, every stop sign halted at and every speed limit broken. He couldn't stop the vehicle because he didn't have blue lights as he was driving his own car, and more importantly, because he wasn't in uniform. You could only do a traffic stop if you were in uniform. You could use a plain car, but you did have to be in uniform.

He looked at the clock on his dashboard. It was 11.10 p.m. He needed to get this done and get some sleep as they had an early start again in the morning and he was no spring chicken any more.

The roads were quiet at this time of night. It was obvious where the driver was heading. He'd been to his girlfriend's and was driving home for the night.

With one last click of his indicator, the driver pulled over and parked in front of his home.

Dominic pulled in behind him.

A young lad climbed out of the driver's side, unfolding himself as he was tall and willowy. Under the street light his face was pasty, a grey hue to it. His wide eyes stared in panic at Dominic, hands at waist height in case he needed to defend himself.

'Hunter Lawton?' Dominic asked as he took a couple of steps towards him.

The boy stepped back the same amount. 'Who's asking?'

He was a good kid. He wasn't into drugs or theft as far as Dominic knew, so wouldn't be expecting trouble from any quarter. Dominic shoved a hand into his pocket and pulled out his leather wallet and flashed his ID. It was quick. Too quick for the kid to see any details other than the police crest. 'Police. I need to speak to you.'

The boy went rigid.

Dominic moved closer to him. He could see acne scars on his cheeks and chin now. Some were deep. They'd trouble him through his life. Dominic and Claudia had both been lucky in that respect and had not suffered badly with teenage skin.

'I haven't done anything.' He waved his hands about in the air as if to dismiss something that might be floating around him, pointing out his flaws.

Dominic took the last couple of steps so he was closer to the boy. He didn't want to have to shout his business in the street for the neighbours to hear. This was between him and the boy. 'Your driving, Hunter. I couldn't pull you over as I don't have my uniform on. I had to wait until you stopped.'

His jaw slackened.

'You know why I want to talk to you?' It was so easy.

'I . . . I . . . might have gone a little . . . over . . .'

'You were speeding.'

The boy's neck vanished as his head sunk into his shoulders, like a tortoise going into hiding.

'You're going to give me a ticket?'

Dominic thought he could see tears glistening in the boy's eyes. 'No, I'm not going to give you a ticket.'

The boy lifted his chin. His chest puffing out.

'You're going to remember there's a speed limit on the road in future? Even at night when there's little on the road?' Dominic kept his voice stern.

'I . . . I promise.' Like a nodding dog.

'Okay then.' He made a show of registering the vehicle's details but in reality he already had them. There was no need to write them down again. But he needed the kid to be afraid that he'd be stopped in the future and have his licence taken from him. 'You know as a new driver you're on thin ground with your licence, don't you?'

Again, the nodding dog.

'Which is why I'm giving you the benefit of the doubt today. I don't want to have to see you again, do you hear me?' He made to move away, back to his own vehicle.

The boy agreed wholeheartedly. Dominic just wanted to get out of there before any nosy neighbour intruded and butted in. Or, God forbid, his mother came out to see what was happening.

He grabbed his car door handle and turned back to the boy, 'Oh, Hunter, do tell your dad I said hello.'

CHAPTER 28

Wednesday came at the most sluggish pace. Claudia was showered, dressed and out the door before it had even barely lifted its own eyes.

She wasn't the only one with the same idea. The rest of the team were trailing in and grabbing drinks around her, feeling the same need to find their victim before he was hanged from the bridge and the life drained from him.

Someone shoved a tea in her hand. She gratefully received it.

Claudia held the morning briefing at six thirty. The earliest she could remember them starting in a long time. It was brief. A recap of where they were yesterday. Claudia tried not to focus on the day as a failure, but as a step closer to finding their man and the spot they needed.

'Today we locate that area, even if we don't find the owner of the trainers. That way we can camp out there and catch our killer in the act of stringing the victim up before he dies. Get him the help he needs and make the arrest — for the murder of Oliver and for the attempted murder of this new male.' It was all positive energy pumping from her. This was the way she wanted to send her team back out into the world.

‘We only have a few hours left. Let’s get this done, guys.’ She clapped her hands together.

Chairs scraped on the floor as everyone rose from their desks, ready to go out into the brightening day, to search for the location shown on the drawing. This was their last chance. They were well aware of that. They couldn’t fail.

The call came in at 8 a.m.

Claudia’s heart plummeted when the control room called it through to them.

A stunned silence filled the room. They hadn’t been able to find the bridge in time. They had failed the man in the image. They had failed to arrest the killer taunting them. They had failed.

The air in Claudia’s office was suffocating.

She rose. ‘We have to head out and process the scene.’ Her voice was thin.

‘You want me and Dom to deal with it?’ Russ asked.

She whirled on him. ‘No, I bloody don’t. Yes, we failed, but this is still my team. As long as I’m head of the task force then I’m in charge, I’m SIO and I’m heading out to deal with it.’

Russ recoiled as if she had actually whipped him. ‘I’m sorry.’

Claudia consciously relaxed her shoulders, which were hunched up to her ears. ‘Me too. I shouldn’t have reacted that way.’ She moved towards the door. ‘Shall we go?’

The Bacon Lane Canal Bridge over Sheffield and Tinsley canal was a Grade II listed building. Claudia hadn’t realised a bridge could be listed until one of the crime scene techs had advised her on her arrival.

She knew he’d informed her so she’d be aware no damage should be committed against the bridge, but all she cared about was the man attached to it. It was his life that had been ruthlessly taken, long before he was ready. A bridge was of no concern to her. Though that little niggle of needing to follow the rules played on a loop in her mind as she approached.

The scene was exactly as the image had depicted. It was no surprise, considering the accuracy of the last drawing with Oliver on the bed. The only difference was the body was no longer hanging from the bridge as it had been depicted in the drawing. Emergency services had pulled him down to check for signs of life. Life trumped crime scene in every single case. And unfortunately, in this case, the male in question had been found to be life extinct when he'd been examined. He'd been strung up too long.

'This is the reason we couldn't find the bridge. There are just so many that look like this. He knew what he was doing.'

The sun glistened off the canal water as it glided gently under the small footbridge. A beautiful day, if not for the body lying on the footpath. Nadira bent over him, working. Crime scene investigators in their high-vis white Tyvek suits scurried over the scene, brightly lit by the sunlight bearing down on them.

Claudia and Russ walked steadily up to the tape cordoning the vicinity. A uniformed officer was taking details of everyone who entered and exited, and preventing unwarranted entry.

'Who found him?' asked Claudia.

The uniform pointed down the track some way, where a huddle of officers stood. Between them was a slim figure.

'What's he say?' Russ asked.

'That he was out running before work when he found him. Apparently this is his regular route.'

'Easy for someone to know there are regular runners on this path,' Claudia murmured.

And it was at that point more blue lights joined the party and an ambulance pulled up further down on the road. 'That'll be for the witness, I take it?' said Claudia.

'We decided we should check him over before we subjected him to anything else. He's pretty shaken up.'

They were good guys, thought Claudia. All she wanted was the evidence. She was desperate to get her hands on this killer, and here was a shift of uniforms who were taking care of their witness. She was glad of the fact. 'Thank you,' she said.

He grinned at her and allowed her entry.

'We'll get to him shortly,' said Russ, understanding how she was feeling. 'First step is our victim.'

Claudia turned to the uniformed officer. 'Once he's been checked out and cleared that he's okay, can someone take the witness to the station, please, so we can get a statement from him? We need to get it all organised today. No letting him run off home.'

The cop nodded. 'Consider it done.'

She thanked him. 'Russ, can you call one of the team and get them prepared, please?'

They walked towards Nadira and the body. Russ made the call.

Nadira turned as their heavy footsteps thudded on the dried soil pathway behind her. 'Sorry to see you here today.'

Claudia looked down at the body. She didn't want to address their failure again. 'Any identification?'

'The CSI has dealt with his clothing on the footpath, you'll have to ask them if they recovered anything.'

'How long has he been dead?' There wasn't much room here. The towpath was narrow and Nadira was crouched over the body and needed all the space to work. Claudia and Russ stood to the side and out of her way.

Nadira let out a loud sigh.

'I'm sorry.' Claudia apologised for the question. Her anguish at his death was making her pushy.

'I wouldn't say it's been very long, but I can't be precise.' Nadira sighed again. 'Look, I know you tried to stop this one. I'm sorry you couldn't get here in time.' She twisted so she could look up at them. 'Don't beat yourself up about it. He was always going to be one step ahead of you. This is his game. And when someone else is making the rules, you're never going to beat them.'

Nadira was right. But it didn't help the sinking rock that was dragging down Claudia's insides.

She turned her attention to the CSI who was conducting a forensic search of the man's clothing to see if he could find any identification or other items that would be of interest to the investigation team. She saw the expensive trainers they'd identified prior to his murder. A much-loved item she imagined, at the cost of them. But she had to move on now and focus on the task at hand. 'Is there any ID in there?'

He peered up from below his Tyvek suit hood, which was pulled so far over his forehead it obscured the view above him. He twisted his neck at an unnatural angle to get a better look at who was talking to him. 'I'm quite surprised to find a driving licence. Obviously the offender didn't care if you ID'd the victim.'

'The details are?' Claudia snapped in her excitement. It was always the most important step — identifying the victim.

The CSI flicked through images on his camera until he came to the one he wanted. 'Brendan Carter.'

She thanked him and asked him to email her a photograph of the driving licence as soon as he could, providing her details so he could do this.

'What do you think he wants?' asked Nadira from below them. 'With the drawings and contacting you beforehand?'

This, of course, wasn't the first time she'd been asked this question, and it wouldn't be the last time she didn't have an answer. Claudia wished to hell she knew what the nutter wanted from them. But she was as lost as everyone else.

She turned to Russ. 'Now to dig into Brendan Carter and find out if anyone had anything against him. See if there was a reason for this or if he's choosing his victims randomly. We must also inform his next of kin.' A task she didn't relish.

Standing over the dead was an undertaking she had come to see as part of the job. Bereaved families were another issue altogether. Their grief didn't stay within the family member's neat little human cubicle. No, it infected everyone within reach. That meant the cops who were informing them of the death. When the grief was at the most raw. When disbelief and anger rampaged through the body and fought for dominance. And for all the emotion spilling about, they never taught you how to deal with it in police training. Just that it wasn't your pain, and you had to remain professional.

Easier said than done.

Of course, it became something you schooled yourself in the more you did it. But you were one hardened son of a bitch if the heartbreak of another didn't touch you at all.

As Claudia looked down at the victim her heart ached for his family. His loved ones.

She drew in a slow and steady breath and tried to control herself at the thought they'd failed to identify the location in time.

Nadira had said he hadn't been dead long. Professional guidelines dictated she couldn't provide a time of death at the scene, but Claudia had to push her fists into her pockets to hide her emotions, her fury that they'd had a chance to stop this and they'd failed.

She would find this guy and she would lock him up for the rest of his life.

CHAPTER 29

Brendan Carter had lived in a luxury apartment on St Paul's Square. A concierge directed them to the floor they needed. The door was opened by a lovely-looking man in shorts, T-shirt and bare feet. Dressed for the warmth of the day. How Claudia wished she could dress for the heat rather than in the suit she was currently wrapped up in. Sweat ran down her back. There was nothing she could do to make herself more comfortable, so she did her best to ignore it.

Claudia ascertained the man's name. In front of them was Obasi Chuke. Brendan's husband. Claudia introduced herself and Lisa and showed him their identification, asking for entry to his home.

Fear flashed across Obasi's face and he stepped back, providing access. Claudia and Lisa crossed the threshold. Claudia was pleased to note the inside of the home was cooler than the day outside. The floors were laid with wood and the walls plastered and painted cool shades. Large, colourful prints were hung artistically around and the windows were open, allowing the air, what air there was, to circulate through the apartment.

Claudia had a moment to recognise that this was a warm, loving home, and a monster had ripped it from its moorings. She and Lisa were about to do that monster's bidding by passing on the news to Obasi.

When they were all seated in the living room, Obasi anxiously wrung his hands, waiting for the information that brought the officers to his door. Claudia informed him in as calm a way as she could of the terrible loss that would break his world apart.

He crumbled and broke in front of them. His love for his husband clear and obvious. No words were possible through the tears. He tried for questions, but Claudia could see his throat was closing up as Obasi kept swallowing away the pain, but it just cut him off.

They quietly waited as the tears subsided and his throat loosened on him. 'What happened?'

How to explain the horror of what had occurred to Brendan? It wasn't the reason for these home visits. Attending to see loved ones was to relay the information of the death and to show there was a point of contact for the investigation. That there was a senior investigating officer in charge. That everything was under control. Causing pain and distress was not the intention, but honesty was important.

'We don't know exactly what happened,' Claudia began. Which of course was true. 'We'll need to ask you some questions, learn as much as we can about Brendan from you, if you'll allow?'

Obasi nodded. His voice still strangled by the grief that was wrapped around his throat. He scrubbed at his face with his huge hands. Then his voice broke through again. 'You say he was killed. How?'

It was no good. They were going to have to give him enough information that he felt involved. But all the details were not for sharing at this point. Not least because they weren't aware of everything themselves anyway. It also felt wrong that he be told something so brutal. Wrong or not, Claudia gently informed him of the bridge. It would be reported on anyway.

Obasi quietly sobbed into his hands. 'What kind of monster is he?'

'This is why we need to ask you some questions,' said Claudia. 'We need to know about Brendan's life. Find something in there that could catch the attention of a killer this way.'

Obasi stood, walked out of the room and returned with a handful of tissues scrunched up in his hand. He shook his head, continuing the conversation he'd just broken from. 'We were photographers. We didn't have a life that would antagonise anyone. We ran a business together.'

'You were both photographers?' asked Lisa.

'Yes, quite successful. We have a small shop in the city. There's me and Brendan and Sean, who handles reception, sales and accounts stuff.'

'We'll need to speak to him, if you can give us the address of the shop, we'll pop by and see him tomorrow. That's if you're opening tomorrow. Or his home address if you're going to close.'

Obasi dictated the shop address and checked his phone for Sean's personal details.

'When did you last see Brendan?'

Claudia could tell that the memory of having seen his husband for the very last time had shaken Obasi further as his lips parted and tears streamed down his face.

'I'm sorry. We have to ask these questions.' It was always difficult. They were not only here to break the news of a loved one's death but to ask the most difficult questions to aid the investigation. It was never the best time to do it for the one left behind. All they wanted to do was grieve, to deal with their shock. But for the investigation it was vital and they couldn't leave without asking the questions they needed to. Claudia softened her tone. 'It'll help narrow down a timeframe for his abduction and help us identify where he was taken from so we can target our search.'

Obasi rubbed at his eyes with the back of his hand. The words were reaching him, but Claudia wasn't sure how much was actually going in. It was usually the case. A FLO would go over everything again in the days following the initial death message and questions.

'He went to the gym last night and never returned. I phoned you guys and reported him missing. Someone came out and took details.' He bent double and sobbed into his knees. 'But he never came back.'

Claudia paused and allowed Obasi to grieve some more and then gather himself before they continued. They'd checked the missing person register yesterday when they first looked for the victim, but must have looked too soon, before Brendan was taken. 'Did he attend the gym with anyone?'

Obasi shook his head. The grief was taking all his energy out of him.

'He never met up with any friends there?'

Again Obasi shook his head. 'He did his workout with his music plugged in and came home again. It was his release after a busy day. Said it helped his creativity.'

Lisa noted the details of the gym. They'd follow up. Talk to clients and see if it had any CCTV.

'What time did he leave home?' Claudia asked. They needed the timeframe.

Obasi looked broken. They were nearly done with their questions — all they had to do was finish up and make arrangements for Obasi to attend the mortuary and identify his husband.

'He left about 8 p.m.'

That gave them a timeframe to work with.

Claudia informed him that a FLO would be in touch with him and would keep him updated with the investigation as well as interview him for continuing information on Brendan.

'He was the kindest man you could meet. I really don't understand who would do this,' Obasi repeated, grief tearing down his face.

Claudia wouldn't make him a promise she couldn't keep, so she didn't tell him she would catch Brendan's killer. Instead, all she could do was tell him they would do everything in their power to bring him to justice. It wasn't enough.

To Claudia, it was as though they were giving the killer free rein to put fear in the heart of Sheffield.

CHAPTER 30

He flicked through the news channels, waiting for the report on his exhibit. On his work of art.

It had all gone as planned. The clock on the image, the short time frame provided, was treated by the police as it was intended, as an invitation. Not a random drawing to be ignored. He needed to be prepared, and he was. The clock was the time that the exhibit was ready for them. It wasn't a time where they could meet him, the creator of the work.

This was about his art. Not about him.

Eventually the report came. Bland and boring. Reported as a crime.

A murder.

Could there be anything more pedestrian?

It was so much more than how they were depicting it. They were missing the entire point of the installation.

He had to wonder why.

Why would they report it in such a way?

It was usual for the media to embellish a story, not cut it down to the bare bones of what it was, as they had with this.

There had to be a reason for doing so.

He paced, staring at the photographic printouts he'd created to savour his work. They were now pinned to his spare room wall, out of the way should someone, very unusually, visit him.

If the press had attended the scene — witnessed his glory, compared it to the invitation — they would have been salivating over him.

He knew this.

That was the problem.

They hadn't been informed of the invitation, let alone seen it.

The police had withheld information about the invite. The reporters were unaware, so could not do the job to the best of their ability.

This was something he could rectify. And switching on his laptop, he printed out the photographs he'd taken, typed out a brief letter of explanation to go with them and folded them into yet another envelope, wearing his gloves.

This was his exhibition.

This was his story.

And he would control the narrative.

No one would change the direction of what he had planned.

He had complete control.

Shame on Detective Inspector Claudia Nunn for thinking she could take it from him. He'd be watching her.

The game is on, DI Claudia Nunn. Let us play.

CHAPTER 31

The following morning Claudia was again in work early. This time Sharpe was in her office. Waiting for her.

Sitting in her chair.

Claudia was a little flummoxed. She stood in the doorway, hovering like a new probationer without a backbone.

'Oh, do come in, Claudia. This is your office.'

Her rank and knowledge snapped into place, and Claudia stepped further into the space. 'I wasn't expecting to see you so early. Is there a problem?' She threw her bag onto the floor in the corner and placed her phone on the desk, for when she managed to get her desk back.

'You could say that.' Sharpe's face gave nothing away. It was like a mask. Still and void.

It was then that Claudia noticed the newspaper between them. A knot curled in her stomach. 'What is it?' She inclined her head in the paper's direction.

Sharpe picked it up. Waved it at Claudia. 'He's written to the press. They're having a ball with it, and they've named him. They've given him a bloody name. I hate it when that happens, Claudia. It gives them some kind of perceived power when the press gives them a name. They've fuck all power.' She glared at Claudia. 'Do you hear me? Fuck all. He does not have any power.'

Claudia nodded. Ice had run down her spine. 'What's the name?' She had no idea what it could be. He hadn't been consistent in his MO. Other than both being young males, there had been nothing similar at all between the victims, and they were miles apart. She couldn't even contemplate what the press could come up with.

Sharpe wrinkled her nose and unfolded the newspaper to show the headline: 'The Artist'.

Claudia reeled, taking a step back. She twisted and slammed her door shut, facing Sharpe with fury of her own. 'How the hell do the press know he sends us drawings? I'm going to have someone's head on a stake.'

'Calm down.' Sharpe seemed to sink into the chair. 'It's not one of your team. Apparently our friendly little artist contacted them himself.' Venom tinted her tone.

'Why would he do that?'

Sharpe threw the paper back on the desk. 'For this. For the media frenzy that he's whipped up. He's the talk of all of them. Even the television stations. He's got fame and glory in his eyes. And a shiny new moniker.'

Claudia dropped into the chair opposite Sharpe. Uncaring now that it wasn't her own. This was a revelation too far. 'This wasn't supposed to get out.'

'He believes otherwise.' She prodded the paper with a polished nail. 'It gets worse.'

'In what way?' Claudia didn't want to consider how it could be worse than this.

'He sent them photographs of the crime scenes. He photographed them after he killed them.' Her voice was like stone.

Claudia jumped to her feet. Her body twitchy and unable to get to grips with all the information that was being thrown at it.

'They're not showing them to the public, are they?'

Sharpe let out a sigh. 'They agreed not to. It wasn't in good taste. They contacted us late last night. But they ran with the name and informed the public of everything he sent them.'

'What do you want to do?'

'I want you to pull your finger out and make an arrest. Can you do that?' Sharpe stood. Her perfume wafted across the desk under Claudia's nose. Sweet and floral. In complete contrast to her tone and stance.

Claudia agreed the task force was on this and would not let up until they had identified their offender and brought him in.

This seemed to appease Sharpe somewhat, and she moved around the desk — Claudia's desk — and towards the door. 'Don't let me down, Claudia. Connelly is watching as well as the chief constable, and above him the PCC is paying attention. Those who hang on to his coat-tails want to know when this will be resolved, and he doesn't like not having an answer for them. It makes him feel stupid, was the phrase they gave me.'

'God forbid we make the PCC feel stupid.' Claudia retook her chair in a show of dominance, juvenile as it was.

Sharpe had her hand on the door handle. 'We may not like the politics of the office of the PCC, but it's a role we have to respect, regardless of our thoughts.'

Claudia was suitably scolded.

'But, saying that—' Sharpe opened the door to the incident room, letting a low thrum leak into Claudia's office as team members came in for the day — 'our attention should not be on what the PCC is saying, but on the evidence we are following. Do not be distracted by the politics. Do not allow them to distort the investigation. For you, the PCC and even the chief are not important.'

Sharpe was deadly serious.

'We have someone who thinks it's incredibly clever to kill people. We know he thinks it's clever because he sends us drawings before he commits the crime. We cannot allow him to continue on this path. Anything other than that is not worth your time or energy. Leave everything else to me to worry about. I'll be your gatekeeper.' She turned to walk out and then looked back. 'Just do your job, Claudia, and catch this bastard. "The Artist" indeed.' She huffed. 'We don't need a mad man with a stupid name roaming the streets and etching his way to his next murder.' And with that, the door closed behind her.

Sharpe stalked across the incident room and through the outer doors. Not a word was said to the staff who had come in early this morning 'to catch this bastard', as she'd so succinctly put it.

Claudia followed Sharpe as far as the incident room. Her team were waiting for her. She jumped straight into it. 'There were no witnesses to the murder of Brendan Carter. Just the jogger who found him and called the police.' This wasn't helpful to the investigation, it was like wading through mud on a foggy afternoon. Hard work and with no ability to see anything.

'The press are having a field day screeching about the murders, and social media channels are alight. But what I want to know is if there's anything useful on there. Anyone hiding out behind their keyboards instead of coming to talk to us?'

Lisa's face puckered. 'Do they have no respect for the dead? They're like a pack of dogs. Especially now the press has provided the killer with a ridiculous name.'

'I think someone's had a little too long staring at Facebook and Twitter,' said Rhys. 'Maybe come off for a while. I don't think the Artist is going to show himself on there, anyway.'

'You're calling him the Artist, are you?' Lisa snapped. Claudia could see she was tired from analysing social media channels and agreed with Rhys that she could probably do with a break.

'It's something to call him, in lieu of his name.' Rhys scratched at his head.

'It gives him far more kudos for what's happening than he actually deserves,' Lisa moaned quietly. The anger was seeping out of her. 'He doesn't deserve to be known like that. I imagine him preening to it.'

Claudia could imagine the same thing, but the welfare of her staff was paramount. 'Lisa, Rhys is right.'

Out of the corner of her eye she watched as Rhys opened his mouth to speak then closed it again.

'Have a break and go back to it later.'

Right now Claudia needed to go to the photography shop and speak to Sean.

CHAPTER 32

Claudia and Russ turned up early at the photography shop. They wanted to get a head start on the day as there was a lot to do. The PM was booked in for the afternoon.

Though the shop was closed for the day, Sean informed them he had decided to go in and use the free day, as it were, to tidy and order the place, so they had all agreed to meet there.

Sean unlocked the door and checked their IDs thoroughly before allowing them access.

There was an air of barely contained excitement about Sean, as though the murder and the subsequent enquiries with him this morning were some top-secret, high-level conspiracy case rather than the sad and barbaric killing that it was.

'How can I help?' He really was trying to contain the grin on his face, but it ended up being a twisted contortion from one cheek to the other.

'You know why we're here?' Claudia tried to level him out.

Sean straightened himself and pushed his hands deep into his pockets. 'Yeah. It's awful. Really awful. I can't believe it. Brendan, he was a great bloke. A really great bloke. They both are. Or Brendan was.' He looked at both Claudia and Russ. 'You know what I mean.' His body bounced. Energy flowing with nowhere to go.

'Have you noticed anything different in the shop the last week or so?' Russ asked.

Sean looked around the space as though it would speak to him and tell him what he needed to know.

The walls were clean and bright white, and hung in groupings to show off various different themes were photographs taken by Obasi and Brendan. There were stunning black-and-white images of the city, the buildings shot from ground level up. The sky looming overhead, the structures solid and every single one with a story to tell. And colourful shots grouped together of life, of people, smiles, laughter, tears, distress. It was all captured with a beautiful sincerity. Claudia was awed by the imagery, and if she hadn't been here on a case, she would most definitely have been be drawn to a number of photographs for her wall at home. Though she imagined they'd be well out of her price range, looking at the place.

'No,' said Sean. 'No, there was nothing. They were working on a new batch of images which they wouldn't tell me about. But that was usual for them. They liked to be secretive while they were drawing up a new feature.'

'Nothing out of the ordinary from buyers, anyone who came into the shop? Problems with customers?' Claudia pushed.

Sean shook his head. His excitement wearing off slightly, it was obvious he had nothing of substance to offer. 'Everything seemed to be ticking along as normal.' A hand went up very dramatically to his chest. 'I can't believe this has happened. They were such a lovely couple.'

He tried for grief, but there were no tears in his eyes. For him, this was about being involved in the investigation. As soon as they left, he'd be on his phone to his friends telling them he'd been 'questioned' by the police about the murders, no doubt. People like Sean really got under Claudia's skin.

She continued her professional front, though. She would not stoop down to his level.

'What about Obasi and Brendan?' she asked.

He looked puzzled. 'What about them?'

'Have you noticed anything different about them? Between them? Have they been fighting at all?'

'Oh my.'

He should have gone into amateur dramatics.

'I didn't even consider Obasi for this. You think it could have been Obasi? You think he could have had something to do with this? Oh no.' The dramatics were well done. Just enough shock to show it hadn't crossed his mind.

'No, that's not what we're saying. In an investigation like this we try to get a feel for the victim's life in all areas. That includes their relationships.' She closed him down.

He looked suitably deflated. 'I get you.' He attempted to keep the ground he had.

'Well?' Claudia prompted.

'They were fine. More than fine. They were who they always were. They had a great relationship. I've never seen a couple who were in each other's pockets — you know, living together and working together — be as strong as they were.'

Again, it was as though he had an insight no one else had. One the investigation team should be grateful for.

Claudia would not give him what he was looking for. The gratitude he needed to soak up.

The door rattled as someone tried to enter. Sean snapped to attention to check it was locked. It was. It stayed closed. He took a couple of steps closer so whoever was on the other side of the glass partition could hear him and shouted that they weren't opening today and that the police were currently here.

Claudia couldn't help but let out a sigh. There was no need to say they were there. It would have been easy enough to inform the potential buyer that they were closed for the day, but Sean needed the added drama.

She wasn't going to allow him any more of their time. She looked at Russ and shook her head. He shoved his pen away and flipped his notebook closed in agreement.

Sean had had all the attention he was going to get from them for the day.

CHAPTER 33

Next stop was the gym that Obasi said Brendan frequented and had attended the night of his disappearance.

Fab and Fit gym on Arundel Gate wasn't far from their apartment, which meant Brendan had walked there.

It was quiet when they entered. Empty but for a couple of women. Claudia presumed they were mothers who had dropped the children off at school and were getting a quick hit in the gym before a busy day took over. Maybe single women hitting the gym before a day at the office. People lived many a varied life.

Immediately Claudia was overwhelmed with the smell of rubber and body odour along with a slight whiff of anti-bacterial cleaner trying to hide the stale sweat.

A male in baggy shorts and sports vest was behind a tall desk. Behind him was a glass product display case holding exercise bands, supplements and various other small items you could fit in the cabinet. He smiled as Claudia and Russ approached. 'Morning, how can I help you guys? Want to book in a complimentary tour?'

Claudia and Russ both pulled out their identification and pushed it in front of his face. 'DI Claudia Nunn and DS Russ Kane,' said Claudia. 'We'd like to talk to someone who can help us with information on a client and whether he attended the gym last night. Preferably someone who was here and saw him.'

This piqued the receptionist's interest. 'I was here last night.'

Behind them a bell above the door pinged and an older man walked in, towel draped around his neck. He raised his hand to the receptionist who lifted his own in response. Then the man wandered past and into the gym proper.

'Do you have a few minutes?' Claudia asked.

'I can't really take time away from work, but if you don't mind me working around you, I can talk,' he said.

Claudia looked around again. It was quiet enough. She was sure they could manage. If he had anything of evidential value to say then they could organise a statement when he finished his shift. 'Sure, that sounds fine. What's your name?'

'Great. I'm Angus.'

Claudia thanked him. The music in the gym was beating hard through the building and throbbing through Claudia's bones. She wasn't a gym-goer. She preferred to get her exercise out in the fresh air rather than being trapped in a building with other sweaty bodies and with a beat you potentially weren't going to like. Though of course most people took their own earphones.

'Who is it you're after?' Angus asked. He picked up a bottle from under the desk and took a slug.

'Brendan Carter.'

Angus's eyes widened. 'What's happened?'

It was always difficult, getting cooperation without giving too many details away. Brendan's family had been informed, which made this an easier conversation. 'Did Brendan come into the gym last night?' Claudia attempted to sidestep the question for the time being.

'Yeah, I remember speaking to him. He was pumped because they, he and his husband, were working on a new project. He was pretty excited about it. Loves his work. I've seen some of his shots. He's pretty goddamn amazing.' Angus stopped talking and stared at the detectives. 'Has something happened to him?'

'I'm afraid to tell you that Brendan has been murdered.'

'Shit.' Angus took a step back. He reached out a hand and found the glass of the display cabinet behind him, his palm leaving a print on the smooth surface. 'Fuck. No.'

'I'm sorry.'

'And you think it was on the way home from here?'

'It appears that way. What time did he leave?'

Angus looked at his watch, even though it wasn't going to tell him the time from last night. He shook his head. Claudia didn't know if this was in shock at their disclosure, or because he didn't know what time Brendan had left. She waited him out.

He shook his head again. 'I didn't see him leave. I had a new client. I was tied up last night while he was here and didn't see him leave.' He sounded hurt.

'You said you spoke to him about his new project,' said Russ.

Angus looked at him surprised, as though only now noticing Russ was there. 'Yeah. That was when he arrived. We said hello. Spoke for a few minutes. Then he went and did his workout and my new client arrived. I didn't see him from then. Oh God, I'm so sorry.'

'Were there any arguments in the gym last night?' asked Claudia.

Angus ran a hand through his hair and frowned. 'No. We don't have many of those. It's a pretty laid-back place.'

'What about Brendan? Has he had any run-ins with anyone recently?'

'Like I said, it's a laid-back place. And Brendan's a great guy. I've never heard anyone say a bad word to or about him. I can't believe he's gone.'

Claudia looked across at the treadmills, where one of the women she'd noticed earlier was now looking pleadingly at the trainer standing beside her. He was waving his hands in the air, encouraging her to keep going for a while longer. Her face said she wanted to do anything but keep going. Claudia longed to walk over and tell the woman that running outside in the fresh air was so much better, with the air in your nose and the breeze on your skin, people to watch or rivers to run alongside. Your view was entirely up to you. But she kept her counsel and focused on what she was doing.

'Did Brendan mention anything he was worried about that he might not have mentioned at home?' Claudia was desperate for anything.

'I'm sorry. We chatted, yes, but I didn't know him that well. It wasn't like that. He came here to train. Not to get a coffee and make friends. Gyms are quite isolated places. Most people like to be left in peace generally, other than a welcome when they come in. We provide them with what they need.'

Claudia looked around. She couldn't see any cameras but she asked the question anyway. 'Do you have CCTV?'

Angus rubbed his jaw. 'I'm sorry. The only CCTV we have is in the entryway and carpark. No one wants to think we're watching them train.'

Claudia looked hopeful but wondered why Angus was looking so forlorn. She questioned him with a look.

He continued. 'It's currently down. It's been down for a week. We're upgrading it, you see. It's a really old system, and though no one wants it, what we have needs to be reliable. And what we had just wasn't.'

Claudia took a deep breath, then thanked Angus and gave him her card. 'If you think of anything else, please do get in touch.' She didn't hold out much hope. It was as though Brendan had disappeared off the face of the earth to then appear again hanging from a bridge over a canal. And only the killer knew what had happened to him.

CHAPTER 34

The post-mortem was a grim affair. It had indeed shown that Brendan Carter had been suffocated by the weight of his own body. There were more tests that Nadira had to send off, but from what she could see from his body she gave Claudia a preliminary report.

Claudia wasn't sure if she could think of anything more grim than suffocating because you had a brick attached to your feet and the weight of your body was too much for your lungs to bear. The thought made her shudder.

This killer was inventive, and he needed to be brought in quickly before he took the life of anyone else.

Graham had managed to trawl Arundel Gate and seized the council CCTV as well as CCTV from private premises. It had all fitted together to provide snatched glimpses of Brendan as he made his way from Fab and Fit towards home.

Brendan had had a sports bag slung over his shoulder, and Claudia wondered where this bag was now. Brendan looked relaxed, as if he didn't have a care in the world. Strolling home to his husband in his beautiful apartment, little knowing these were his last moments alive before a crazed killer would scoop him up and make him part of a scene that would have the country talking.

Again, grim.

The incident room watched on in silence as Brendan turned the corner and disappeared out of sight.

'So we know he was safe when he left the gym,' said Claudia. 'He had his gym bag with him and he made it along Arundel Gate. What we don't know is what happened next. I find it difficult to imagine you pick up a fit guy like Brendan from the street against his will. So was it someone he knew? The problem with that is our circle of friends is wide. We're not just talking about friends we see regularly, but acquaintances, people you come into contact with and know by sight. I want you to attempt to create a list and interview all of them, though I recognise this is a long shot. Obasi isn't likely to know everyone Brendan knew in passing. For instance, he won't know his gym acquaintances. So go back to Fab and Fit and get a list of all clients with active memberships and visit those. There are people who came into the shop. See if Obasi has a record of regular customers and find out what other pastimes Brendan was into. We talk to as many people as we can and find out their whereabouts at the time Brendan walks around that corner.' Claudia looked at the screen again.

It was a lot of work, but that was the nature of the beast of a homicide investigation. Murders weren't the thrilling cases that were depicted on television dramas, but a dull slog of enquiries, often going on for weeks at a time as officers tirelessly worked their way through them for the smallest lead. But when a lead came through, it made the slog all the more worthwhile.

But right now the team were staring down the barrel of a long and tedious line of enquiry.

'We don't think it's the husband?' asked Rhys.

'I don't believe so,' answered Russ. 'But when we speak to Brendan's friends let's get a feel for the relationship between Brendan and Obasi. We need to rule him out in any case.'

'He's obviously got no alibi,' said Lisa scratching a pen on her scalp through her hair. 'He was at home waiting for Brendan to come home.'

‘Let’s be as discreet as we can.’ Claudia remembered the sobbing man in the apartment. Now alone. ‘He’s grieving for his husband. I know this has to be done. Just tread carefully.’

Murder affected not only the victim but those left behind. It was of course their job to investigate the death, but Claudia wouldn’t have her team lose sight of the fact that these were real people at the heart of the investigation. No matter how monstrous this killer was. They would follow him with integrity and care for those he was leaving behind.

CHAPTER 35

Dominic lined up with everyone else to enter the prison and go through the security procedures. He was of course taking a risk in visiting Samuel Tyler's cellmate, but it was a better course of action than visiting Tyler himself and having a big flashing sign above his head showing he was interfering with the case.

No one was paying attention to the cellmate, and Dominic had to keep it that way by making sure Craig Lawton didn't speak to anyone he shouldn't do.

His mobile phone was taken from him and boxed securely away. He was then seated in what was called a boss seat. This was a chair that scanned you for any items you might have secreted inside of you. Once cleared, Dominic was moved on to the visitors' section of the prison.

He hadn't identified himself as a police officer. He was in the main visiting room with everyone else. This wasn't a work task. In fact, questions would be asked if anyone found out he was here.

A row of visitors, single men and women, and women with children hanging off their hips, shuffled into the visiting room.

It was a risk coming into the open prison this way as a visitor. If any of the other prisoners recognised him as being a cop, they were extremely likely to kick off and attempt to attack him. Cops were really not popular within these walls. To try to prevent this happening, Dominic kept his head bowed. Refusing to make eye contact with anyone. Hoping they were all focused on their own visitors, their loved ones. After all, they were locked up so long that the joy of seeing a loved one should distract them long enough for Dominic to get in, say what he needed to say and get out again.

Dominic looked around. He'd never met Lawton but had seen his custody photograph. He'd been a little surprised when Lawton had agreed to add him to his visiting order. Maybe the guy didn't get many visitors and was glad of the request.

The room was filled with the expectant faces of the occupants of the prison.

Dominic's first concern was that Tyler would be in here, but a couple of seconds scanning the room put paid to that concern.

Next he had to identify Lawton.

The man sat in the corner with hopeful look on his face. Lank hair down to his shoulders. A grey sheen on his skin. It was the hope that was different to his police photograph, where Lawton held a look of arrogance. Now hope shone out. Someone from outside wanted to see him. Prison tended to strip the hope away from you, but it had wheedled its way onto Lawton's face.

Dominic almost pitied the man waiting for him. Being inside should have taught him better.

Dominic approached.

Lawton lifted his chin in acknowledgement. He half raised himself from the plastic chair pinned to the floor, then in his half-crouched position decided this didn't warrant him standing for his visitor, especially when he caught the look in Dominic's eyes. He dropped back to the plastic chair with a thud.

'Dominic Harrison?' he asked.

Dominic seated himself opposite and gave a curt nod.

'Do I know you?' A puzzled frown crossed Lawton's face as he tried to place his visitor.

'You don't know me. I'm DS Dominic Harrison from Snig Hill police station in Sheffield.' He allowed the silence to play out as the information sank in. The police didn't normally visit this way. For starters, they were up front about who they were and didn't request to see you. They came and pulled you out of your cell and interviewed you at their demand. This was, Dominic knew, highly unusual.

'I don't understand.' Lawton looked around the room as though a group of cops were going to jump out at him, obviously afraid this was some kind of sting operation.

'Calm down. It's just me.'

His head stopped rotating, but his eyes flickered around him still. Not sure of his visitor's honesty. 'What do you want?'

'To have a chat with you.'

'About?' He scratched at his upper arm. He was a thin man. There was no bulk on him at all. But he was wiry. Dominic suspected he could probably hold his own if he got into a fight. Something he'd be nervous about if any of the occupants in the visitors' room recognised that he was talking to a cop.

'Look, I've had a look around, I don't recognise anyone. You can relax.'

'You still haven't told me what you want. It's a bit strange, isn't it?' The room was loud with the excited noise of people who were pleased to see each other, but Lawton's words were low and quiet.

And he was right. This was not by the book at all. Dominic needed to play this extremely carefully. 'You might be in a position to help me.' He mirrored Lawton, keeping his voice low. He didn't want to draw more attention to them than was necessary.

'Why would I do that?'

Dominic ignored the question. 'Your cellmate is Samuel Tyler, isn't it?'

Lawton stiffened.

Dominic waited for a response.

None was forthcoming.

In here Lawton had learned to play the long game. The silent game.

If Dominic wanted something, he had to speak. He had to say what it was he wanted from Lawton rather than expecting Lawton to figure it out alone. 'Do you know who I am?'

Lawton looked around the room again. Trying, difficult though it was, to make it appear as though he really wasn't keeping an eye on his fellow convicts. 'You're the cop whose wife Sam says he didn't kill.'

Dominic took in a deep breath. They were already halfway there.

'That's what he's saying, is it?'

Lawton shut his mouth. A solid, thin line on his face. His eyes steely.

Dominic leaned forward and lowered his voice even more. 'I need for you to tell a different story.'

'And why would I do that for you, filth?' Lawton leaned back in his chair and crossed his arms. A look of defiance.

Dominic found he was looking forward to this next bit, even though he had been in two minds about whether he would actually use it. 'Have you spoken with your son recently? I hear he's doing pretty well in college. It'd be awful if anything stopped his dreams in their tracks.'

Lawton tipped his head to the side. Narrowed his eyes. 'What d'you mean?'

Now was the time to play the cards in his hand. See how Lawton reacted. He had to be careful. He didn't know Lawton, other than the fact he was a family man. Family meant everything to him. It was the reason he was sitting right where he was.

Some goon had tried it on with his daughter after a date. Hadn't known what the word 'no' meant, had taken what he wanted and raped her. His daughter had run home in floods of tears and talked to her parents. Lawton's first reaction had been to explode out of the house and find the male in question. A beating had gone too far as his temper and anger at his daughter's distress fuelled him on, and the man had succumbed to his injuries.

Craig Lawton would do anything to protect his family. It was why Dominic had decided to take the route he had. But Lawton had been locked up for a while and could clearly flare up if provoked. Dominic wasn't protected. The screws didn't know Dominic was a cop. Of course they'd protect him as they'd protect anyone. But they weren't paying him particular attention, and that was because he hadn't wanted them to. It was swings and roundabouts, the game he was playing.

'Did you hear he'd been stopped in his car recently?'

Lawton lifted his chin and tightened his jaw. Colour streamed into his face. 'What d'you know 'bout that?'

'I asked him to say hello to his dad. Did he mention it?'

The hand that was on the table curled into a rigid fist, but very quickly Lawton yanked his arm from its position and back into his lap.

Dominic allowed himself the smallest of smiles. Not too much. He didn't want to gloat and antagonise and put Lawton too far offside. No further than he obviously had. But this had to be done. Gloating on top of the threat was a step too far.

The visitors' room continued the loud buzz, everyone unaware of the table at the end where the two men were in a silent standoff. There was no movement to give away the animosity and violent threats that were passing from one to the other, but they were clearly heard between the two present. One had the upper hand, though. Circumstances gave him all the cards, and he knew how to play them.

'What the fuck?' Lawton hissed.

'There's no need to be like that.' Dominic tried to calm him down. It really would do him no good if Lawton flew off the handle. 'I just needed to give you a little nudge in the right direction, is all.'

Lawton's eyes bore into Dominic. 'For what?'

'Like I said, I need a little something from you. It won't be too much trouble.' He had no idea how much trouble it would actually be.

Lawton hardened his stare and Dominic carried on. 'As I mentioned, Tyler . . .'

A pulse flickered in Lawton's jaw.

'I need for you to tell someone of importance, a screw or suchlike, that Tyler has told you that he did in fact kill Ruth Harrison.' He leaned back a little, not knowing what reaction was coming.

Lawton paused. Took in what Dominic had said. 'Your wife, yeah?'

Dominic nodded.

'And you want me to say Tyler admitted to me that he offed her?'

Dominic nodded again.

'But he didn't.'

'Samuel Tyler has killed multiple women, and my wife was murdered in the exact same way they were killed.' No reason to make Lawton suspicious as to his reason for the request. Make it sound reasonable. Like a grieving husband wanting justice.

'So you think he killed her too, no matter what he says?' He tilted his chin again.

'Can you do what I asked?'

'What if I don't?'

'How many points on your son's licence is going to affect his chosen career? Does he need to be able to drive?'

Lawton leaned forward. His eyes like coal. Flat and dark. 'You can't do that.'

'I didn't see anyone stopping me the other night. Did you?'

The bell rang, alerting the room that visiting was over. Dominic looked up at the ceiling as though he could stop the bell or extend the limit they'd been provided. 'I expect you to do this within the next week, do you hear me?'

Lawton rose from his chair and leaned forward in Dominic's face. 'Do you have any idea what Tyler will do to me if he finds out?'

'That's not my problem. You have to decide which is more important. Yourself or your son. I'm guessing your son.'

Inmates said their goodbyes. There were tears. Children bawling loudly as though this wasn't a trauma they were regularly put through.

'You can always request a cell move after you've done it.'

The inmates started to line up at one end of the room and the visitors at the other. 'LAWTON,' shouted a prison officer.

Lawton stepped away from the table. 'You've put a bullseye on my back, Detective Harrison.'

CHAPTER 36

They were weeks down the line and the press were having a field day as they were no closer to identifying the killer, now known by all and sundry as the Artist.

The pressure from above was immense, and Claudia wished she could do something to resolve the case. But this killer was good. He had an awareness of forensics and took steps to avoid being seen by witnesses. There was nothing similar between the victims. Nothing that linked them. They didn't attend the same gym or shop at the same supermarket. They weren't friends with each other online, or even shared friends of friends online. They didn't frequent the same coffee shops or bookstores or any other place people would gather or go regularly. The only link Claudia and the team could figure out was that they were creatives.

Was this the one thing that pieced the puzzle together? Bearing in mind the killer was called the Artist.

Claudia leaned back in her chair and stared at the ceiling.

Russ knocked on the door and entered without waiting for a response. He knew her well enough to sense what mood she was in, and she could tell he was here to chivvy her up.

In his hands was a white plastic fan. 'I thought this might help the brain cells get more comfortable.' He dumped it on the floor near a wall socket and plugged it in. Immediately the blades of the machine whirred and air slowly circulated. Not that Claudia could feel it from behind her desk. It wasn't the largest fan she'd seen, but she was grateful for the sentiment.

Russ saw her face. 'No good?' He frowned. Looked around the room for another socket closer to her.

'It's fine.' She didn't need to be cooler. Obviously it would improve her mood because it was getting pretty unbearable, but the important thing was the case. If anything was going to help her, a break in the investigation was it.

Russ completely ignored her, pulled the plug from the socket and jumped up with the plastic fan in his hands, moving closer to the desk, walking around it, searching for an empty socket to use. Then he bent down and peered under her desk.

Claudia crossed her ankles. She wasn't wearing a skirt, but the suddenness of his action had startled her.

Russ apologised and she waved it away.

Beneath the desk was an extension where her computer was plugged in. There was an empty socket.

'Aha!' He pushed the plug in and dumped the fan on the desk. Again it whirred into life.

Corners of paperwork lifted as if about to take off. Claudia and Russ watched, ready to catch any that whipped off the desk. But they stayed steady.

'Okay,' said Russ. 'That'll help you.'

She stared at him. 'Where did you get that?'

'Oh, Ted, one of the caretakers. I gave him a bottle of whiskey last Christmas, so when I asked him if he had a couple of spare fans, he rummaged around the station until he found some for me.'

Claudia smiled at him. 'How many people did you pay off with gifts last Christmas?'

Russ winked. 'Just enough.'

They both laughed.

'I can see you're going to come in very handy,' said Claudia. 'I didn't know this about you.'

'I don't tell you all my secrets. Where would that leave me?'

He'd cheered her up, as he intended, without even trying too hard. She was grateful for him.

'What was on your mind?' Russ took the chair opposite Claudia now he'd sorted out the fan. 'It was obvious you were deep in thought.'

Claudia scratched her head. 'There seems to be a theme of creativity between the victims and the killer himself. I was wondering why that was.'

Russ looked thoughtful.

The phone on Claudia's desk rang. She picked it up. 'DI Nunn. Hi. Yes. Oh. Okay. I'll be right down.' And with that, she replaced the receiver.

Russ gave her a questioning look.

'The front counter has received what they believe is another letter from the killer addressed to me. It's come with the rest of the mail, but the writing on the envelope is familiar to him.'

'You're going to collect it?' They both rose from their chairs and headed out of the office.

'There's no point getting a CSI to examine it until we know it's actually what we think it is, and we need to see the contents as soon as possible so we can attempt to track down the next victim.' She made for the stairs rather than waiting around for the lift.

She swore. 'I can't believe we have to play this game with him again. I won't let him win this time.'

Russ pulled his phone out of his pocket and dialled the CSU, updated them on the situation and asked that a CSI meet them in DI Nunn's office as soon as possible.

At the bottom of the stairs, Claudia turned to Russ. 'We can't allow him to beat us, Russ. He's providing us a head start with the drawings. We have to identify the victim. We have to do better.'

She spoke to Steve, who was manning the front counter again. She was grateful he was on as he'd been able to spot the envelope.

He bent under the counter and retrieved a white envelope and handed it to Claudia, who was prepared. She snapped on a pair of blue gloves and took it off him. Steve looked horrified.

'It's okay,' she said. 'You'd already handled it. I'm a fresh set of prints that don't need to be involved. Thanks, Steve.'

She headed back to the stairs and Russ trailed behind her.

Once in her office, she closed the door behind Russ and sat behind her desk. 'Can you close the blinds for a few minutes, please?' she asked of her second in command.

He twisted the poles hanging down the sides of the windows, closing the slatted blinds and blocking out the incident room beyond.

Claudia took a deep breath.

Russ took the seat opposite her.

Tension filled the small office space. They both knew what this meant. There was a new victim being stalked. Out there, currently unaware that they were hours away from their own death, that the police were in the fragile position of potentially being able to prevent it. They held all the power. It was overwhelming.

Claudia stared at Russ. 'I don't know how to open this. It should be left to a CSI, but we're on a very real clock where a life is at risk. If we open this envelope, we might be able to stop a killer.' A pained look crossed her face.

'When I made the call to the CSU they said all their staff were out at the moment, but one van was about ten minutes away, if we could hold off.'

Claudia looked to the door as if someone would suddenly walk through on demand, but it stayed stubbornly closed. Then she looked back down to the envelope, which was resting on a sheet of paper on her desk in front of her. 'I don't think we can wait. We have no idea how long, or ultimately, how short the timeframe on this image is going to be. So far, we've picked up nothing forensically from the envelopes and drawings. I'm betting nothing will change with this one. He's not stupid. We should open it carefully, photograph the image and then leave it well alone for when they get here. What d'you think?'

Of course, this was her decision and she would take the fall if there was any blowback, but right now, the pressure was building and she just needed a nod from Russ to dive straight in. He was her right arm.

'You've explained your reasoning well enough.'

Claudia let out a deep sigh, opened her top drawer and selected a letter opener. Tension ran through her shoulders, bunching them up to her ears. She wriggled them in an attempt to ease the pain that was radiating up her neck and into her head.

The victim within this envelope needed them. And they were needed right now. Not in ten minutes.

With letter opener in hand, Claudia inserted the tip into the corner, making sure to hold the envelope over the sheet of paper so it could catch any forensic debris that might fall as she worked, and angled the handle to make the cut. It was better to use the letter opener and slice along the top of the envelope, thereby leaving the sticky folded section intact, as it was possible the killer could potentially have licked it. Though it was unlikely.

The metal blade slid along the fold with ease, and soon the envelope was open, its contents there for the taking.

Claudia peered inside. A folded sheet of white paper. Claudia flexed her fingers and checked the door again. Again it stayed resolutely closed. There was no one coming through to do this the proper way.

There would be blowback, but she was ready for it. This was important.

She flexed her fingers again, then reached in and, very gently with the tips of her fingers, she pulled out the folded sheet, dropping the envelope on the paper she'd placed underneath on the surface of her desk.

There was a loud rap at the door and Claudia and Russ both jumped. Russ gathered himself quickly and opened the door. A CSI waited with a black bag in her hand. 'You have a letter you want me to process?'

Russ ushered her in.

Claudia hadn't moved. The unopened letter, or likely to be a drawing, was still folded in her hand in mid-air above her desk.

The CSI looked horrified. 'You've opened it?'

'It's time-sensitive. A person's life is at risk, and we can't work out who it is until we see the drawing that's in this envelope. I took a calculated gamble. If your supervisor wants to have a word with me about my decision then I'm happy to discuss it with him later, but for now can we please move this along? We have no idea of the time the killer has put on this third image.'

The CSI inclined her head before snapping on her own pair of gloves. She ushered Claudia away from her desk and promised to work quickly.

Claudia placed the folded paper down on the sheet she'd laid out and rolled away from the desk before jumping up and stalking to the other side of the office.

The CSI opened up the piece of paper so it could be photographed and so the team could get to work on it.

Nerves rattled through Claudia's body and fired messages of frustration to her muscles. She paced as the CSI worked. Russ, on the other hand, was patient and still. The opposite to her anxiety.

Eventually she was able to come back around her desk and take a quick photograph of the drawing that had been laid open for her before it was all packed away to be forensically examined for trace evidence.

The CSI said her goodbyes and shuffled out of the office, taking the evidence with her for further forensic examination.

Claudia transferred the photograph to her computer.

They had the image of the next victim and the next location.

CHAPTER 37

As with the other images, it was beautifully depicted, other than the fact that they were looking at the future death of a member of the public.

'What are they?' asked Russ, staring at the image.

Claudia bent closer. Narrowed her eyes. 'They look like wings.'

The victim, a slim white male again, was sitting in a chair with a pair of huge wings flying out behind him. There was no obvious sign of injury, no sign of how he was going to die this time.

'It looks like there's a house or a building of some description behind him,' said Russ, incredulous. 'He's going to set all this up with the risk someone might see him?'

'You think he has to make the wings?' asked Claudia.

'What else can they be?'

Claudia looked at the image. 'So he could be anywhere. There's nothing in this image that tells us where he is. It's so bland. It's even worse than the previous one. There's nothing on the person or at the side of the victim that tells us who he could be.' She turned away from the drawing for a moment. 'How the hell are we going to stop this before the clock runs out?'

The time on the clock was 6 a.m. tomorrow morning. They had less than twenty-four hours to identify and locate the victim before his time was up.

'We can't do it, Russ.' She rubbed her hands down her face. 'This drawing is worthless.' There was a deep urge to drag the laptop across her desk and sling it at the wall. She was sick of staring at the drawing already. The failure weighed down on her.

'It's not completely worthless,' said Russ. 'We could put the image out and ask if anyone knows the victim. The killer sent us the drawing, let's use it to our full capacity this time. Yes, we might get some false positives, but guarding a couple of guys and keeping the right one safe is better than not keeping anyone safe at all and turning up at the crime scene in the morning.'

She smiled at him. 'I knew there was a reason I kept you around.'

He grinned at her. 'You mean it's not my stunning good looks?'

Russ could take this in his stride. He was happily married with a young daughter. His loyalty to his family could not be shaken. The gossip was that women had thrown themselves at him throughout his police service, particularly when he was in uniform. He was good-looking man in a rugged kind of way, and she'd seen him catch the eye of more than one youthful witness or victim of crime. He'd had to very gently put them right and get on with the job at hand, as well as report the interaction to prevent any unfounded allegations coming through the system.

Claudia leaned in closer to the drawing on the screen again. The man sitting on the chair was naked from the waist up. He had long hair flowing down his shoulders. Claudia pointed at the screen. 'Is that a tattoo on his chest?'

Russ peered over her shoulder. 'It looks that way. You're thinking we can follow up on that? With tattoo artists in the area?'

Claudia jumped up. 'Absolutely. Let's bring the team into this and get them working. We don't have a lot of time.'

She pushed her door ajar with force and Russ spun the blinds back open. Faces twisted to see what all the commotion was about. Claudia strode around to her laptop and forwarded the sketch to everyone's email, then stalked into the incident room. Russ followed her.

'Listen up, everyone, we have another drawing.'

There were quiet pings from every machine as the email she had sent arrived. The team, understanding what the sound meant, scrambled to open it. They muttered curses at the sight of the winged, tattooed, seated man. Beautiful as it was, they knew he was dead in this image.

But he was currently alive, and they were the ones who could prevent the image on their computers becoming a reality.

'As you can see,' Claudia said, pacing around the room, 'this victim is tattooed. It's quite unique, a skull with wings. Hopefully someone will recognise their work. As far as I understand it, tattoo artists don't share images. Their work is theirs alone. We're going to use that as our first lead to identify him. Make a copy of the image. Close-cropped, please, I don't want anyone realising what this is about. And make contact with all Sheffield tattoo artists and see if anyone recognises their work. If we fail to make headway with this line of enquiry, we're taking the image to the press.' She let out a sigh. 'We don't have a lot of time. If you notice the clock, you'll see it's set for 6 a.m. tomorrow. We're really up against it this time. Maybe he thinks we were too close last time. I don't know. But it's tight. You get three hours to trace him through the tattoo, then I'm going to the press.'

There was a scurry of movement as the printer whirled into life and everyone printed off the drawing.

'Don't forget to crop the drawing down. I don't want anyone knowing what this is to do with,' Claudia barked. 'And someone find the list of tattoo artists and split them up.' She was talking to herself. They were an organised group and well aware how to work, though this was the first real case they had all worked together. They were good cops individually. That was why she had chosen them when she'd put the team together. But as a cohesive team she had yet to see them meld.

Graham was at his computer, a look of pure concentration on his face. He was the one collating the list. He looked up, shock shadowing his features.

'What is it?' Claudia asked.

'There are ninety-two places this guy could have had his tattoo done in Sheffield. And that's if he even had it done here. What if he only moved here recently and had it done elsewhere? Or had it done at a favourite place in London?'

'We can only go on the information we have and we can't chase down every tattoo artist in the country, so we do the best we can and check with the local ones. Split that list up and you should hopefully get it done within the timeframe. I'll consider extending it if we're close to covering all the artists.'

CHAPTER 38

Claudia spent the next couple of hours sitting in her office going through the case files looking for details they could exploit or had missed.

As the clock ticked on, frustration gnawed at her bones. She was restless, tapping on her desk as she read through the reports, desperate for any piece of evidence that would give them the lead they so very much needed. An email pinged into her inbox. It was from Nadira. Toxicology had come back on Brendan. Diazepam had been in his system. Not enough to kill him, but definitely enough to sedate him and make him pliable enough for the killer to manoeuvre into the position he wanted him.

Claudia sighed. It helped to know his MO, but it didn't provide them a line of enquiry that would help with this new victim. Diazepam was a fairly easy drug to obtain, and you wouldn't need much to make a person woozy. She hit reply on the email and thanked Nadira for letting her know.

Eventually she checked her watch. The hours were moving faster than she'd realised. As she'd been working, staff had been clocking in, advising her that their results were negative with the tattoo artists.

Time was running out.

She looked down at the tally sheet she was keeping. There were ten left to contact with only twenty minutes before her self-imposed deadline. They couldn't do it, but if she mucked in, they might just cover them all. No point stopping the task for only the few that needed contacting.

She needed to do something physical, so Claudia picked up her Airwave radio, headed to the stairs and ran down to her car as she informed the team of the three artists she was picking up to interview in person. They should finish the rest.

The first shop she entered was small, dark and dingy, by the name of Shirley's Tattoos. There wasn't a female in sight, so Claudia had no idea who Shirley was. An enormous bear of a man was sitting on a high stool behind a tall desk. The sides of his legs, in skin-tight black jeans, flopped over the edges of his seat.

'Looking for anything in particular?' he asked, his voice deep and baritone.

Claudia pulled the cropped drawing from her pocket and shoved it onto the desk. 'Is this one of yours?'

The bear of a man peered down. Strip lights above glistened off the skin on his bald crown. Claudia wondered if he polished it, it was that bright.

A thick sausage finger outlined the skull and then the wings, as if this would help decide if it was from this shop or not.

'We can't do it for you if it's not one of ours,' he said eventually.

Claudia then fished out her ID and flashed it at him. 'DI Nunn. We need to trace the man who has this tattoo. Can you help?' She doubted it by the second.

Finally, he lifted his head and shook it. Meaty chops wobbled with the motion. 'It's not one of ours.'

If only he'd said that in the first place.

'But . . .' he said.

Claudia tensed.

'I do recognise the work. It belongs to Textured Tattoo. I'd know their art anywhere.'

Claudia pulled the list of places she was visiting from her pocket and saw Textured Tattoo. 'You're sure?'

'I worked there for a year. Like I said, I'd recognise his work anywhere. He does some unique pieces. This is a classy tat.' He nodded to himself. 'Yeah, definitely Jimmy's.'

Claudia thanked the man and rushed through the door into the brilliant sunshine. He'd managed to cut her job down to just one more premises. She checked the address. It would take her ten minutes to get there. No point calling everyone off until she'd confirmed what she'd been told. But her pace quickened as she walked to the car and had to bite down on a smile at the thought that they might actually be able to identify the victim this time before the killer got to them.

Maybe, just maybe, he'd given too much away in this drawing and the police were going to beat him to his prey. She nearly ran down the street, desperate to get to Textured Tattoo, and prayed that she was right.

Textured Tattoo was the complete opposite to Shirley's. This place was brightly lit and spacious. The walls were whitewashed and filled with the artwork that customers could have etched onto their bodies from the artists within.

Again, Claudia thought to herself, another link to a creative endeavour.

A tattooed woman, slim with a red pixie haircut, lounged on a sofa against one wall. She shifted slightly when Claudia entered.

On the back wall was an archway, through which Claudia could see seating where the tattooing was done. It was akin to a dentist's office.

The tattooist looked appraisingly at Claudia. Not dismissively. For all she knew, Claudia could have a host of artwork covered by the stiff suit she wore for work. It took all sorts to adorn their body with permanent images.

'I've been told I might be able to find Jimmy here,' Claudia said.

The woman's interest was piqued. Her chin lifted. Her eyes sparkled. 'Who's asking?'

Once again Claudia produced her ID. 'It's important that I speak with Jimmy. He might be able to help with a case that could involve one of his clients.'

The woman looked toward the archway, through which Claudia could hear the hum of what she presumed was the tattoo machine working, and shouted for Jimmy.

The hum stopped and a slim man in ripped jeans and white vest, best for showing the tremendous amount of artwork he had across his body, up his neck, and down his arms, appeared. His hair was tied back in a ponytail. It was shaved around the sides but longer on the top half of his head. There was a large black ring through his nose, not dissimilar to a cow ring, and several in a line through one eyebrow. He was wiping his hands on a thin wipe. Claudia could smell the faint scent of disinfectant.

'Yeah?' The man looked her up and down. Not his usual client, she presumed.

'This woman, she's a cop, thinks you can help her with a case.'

The man who must be Jimmy raised his heavily pierced eyebrow at Claudia. Claudia showed her ID. 'I have an image that you might be able to help with.' She pulled the drawing from her pocket, unfolded it, tried to smooth out the creases and handed it over to Jimmy.

He considered the drawing. 'And what if I can?'

Claudia hadn't considered she might have a battle on her hands. 'The man in the image is in dire need of our help. He's in a huge amount of danger, and if you can help us you are in turn helping him.'

Jimmy looked again at the drawing in his hands. 'It's one of mine.'

A flutter of joy bubbled in Claudia's chest. They were one step closer. 'Can you tell us who you did this work on?'

'It took several hours and a few different sessions to complete it. I log clients by time taken because that's how they pay. Plus for the intricacy of the piece they want. But I'm not sure I can identify him for you.'

Claudia wanted to scream. 'You don't keep a log of your clients?'

'We get hundreds of randoms through here a month. A lot of university kids who want something small, usually when they've had a shot of something to steady their nerves.'

Claudia stared at him.

'Don't worry. I don't do the kids if they're legless. I run a professional establishment. There is a consent form they have to sign, but it only contains the bare details. A name and contact number . . .'

Once again Claudia's heart raced in excitement. 'That'll help. We can work with that.' A wide smile was on her face.

'I'm afraid we don't have this guy's. I remember it as being one of mine, but it's old. Older than the time limit we need to keep the consent forms for. What do you mean he's in danger?'

'His life is in danger,' Claudia conceded.

Jimmy whistled. 'I'm sorry I can't help you.'

So was Claudia. She'd been so hopeful the tattoo would lead them somewhere. Now they were three hours down and the victim was three hours closer to his death.

CHAPTER 39

Claudia gathered everyone in the incident room. The tattoo chase had been a bust and she was pacing the room with frustration. She'd put all her eggs in the tattoo artist's basket. Now they'd lost time on the clock and were no closer to identifying the victim.

'We have no choice but to bring the press into this,' she said. 'Yes, they're a pack of vultures who distort and manipulate everything, but we need their reach to ID this guy. They can distribute his face widely, and that way we might be able to find him. Sharpe has organised a press conference for an hour's time.'

The image was again directed onto the wall. The victim's head lolled slightly to the side in death, but there was enough of his features visible for anyone who knew him to make an identification. Claudia looked at the drawing for what felt like the hundredth time and asked inside her mind, directly to the man, who he was. What was he doing right now? And was he even subliminally aware of the danger that faced him? To prevent scaring him any more than he needed to be, the decision had been taken to only show a cut-down image at the press briefing — an image of his face, so he or someone he knew could recognise it. To show the rest of the image, the drawn wings from his body, would only serve to terrify even the most hardy of people, knowing what had happened in the city recently. He'd want to know why wings were floating from his torso matching the tattoo on his chest. Of course they'd explain this when they met him, but for now, he could be identified by only his face. It was the easiest option.

An hour later she filed out with Sharpe to face the curious media. Of course the previous two murders had caught their attention and they presumed this press conference was to do with that.

Sharpe stared out at the sea of faces until they silenced themselves for her. She'd informed Claudia this was not to be a long affair. They needed something from the press, and in asking for it they were also giving. They were giving the press something to run with. It was a fair trade. She would put up with no messing about from them.

Once everyone was quiet, Sharpe spoke. 'You have all been handed a press pack. Within that is a copy of a drawing.'

The room hummed with voices.

Claudia watched as Sharpe waited them out. She knew Sharpe would refuse an attempt to speak over the rabble. Her view was that if they were rude enough to keep speaking then she would wait until their manners kicked in. And it worked every single time. Like trained dogs, the press realised they'd get nothing else until they listened. So silence once again reigned.

'We would appreciate it if you could run this image in your various outlets with a request for anyone who knows the man to come forward.'

The room erupted, understanding what this request meant.

Sharpe was going to struggle to bring them to order. Questions were being shouted, microphones thrust closer, flashes blasting in their eyes. It was pandemonium.

Sharpe was rigid, though. Claudia watched her work. She would not fight with them for airtime. If they wanted their questions answering, they had to shut up. She treated them as errant schoolchildren. Though Claudia wasn't sure Sharpe had children — she kept her private life close to her chest, only discussing work-related issues, and there were no family photographs on her desk — the woman did know how to get misbehaving adults to fall into line.

After a good five minutes the journalists recognised again they were getting nowhere, and those that had leapt up to be heard better returned to their seats. They quietened down and pulled their microphones back, closer to themselves.

Sharpe glared at them. 'I'm sure you have a lot of questions,' she went on as though the last five minutes hadn't just occurred. 'I will take a couple before finishing.' She pointed to the back row.

'Simon Frith, *Sheffield Chronicle*. Does the fact you're asking us to share a drawing for identification mean you have another image from the Artist, that someone else's life is in danger?'

He'd asked two questions but hidden them as if it was all one.

Sharpe narrowed her eyes. Claudia was aware she'd picked up on it.

'Of course it means we have another drawing from the person you call the Artist. Although I see no reason to give him such a name. There is nothing artistic in the murder of another human being. How do you think the families of those he has already killed feel about such a moniker?' She scolded him well.

Frith sank down into his chair.

'As for his life, it won't be in danger if we identify him. And that's where you come into it. With your reach, we hope to locate the male in the drawing. Luckily, the person who drew him is particularly good, and all the drawings to date have been very lifelike. We can trust that this is the same. This person, or someone who knows him, should be able to make an identification based on the image we've shared.'

Sharpe pointed at a woman on the front row.

'Lucy Zhang, BBC. It's obvious you're attempting to identify the victim, but what lines of enquiry are you following to identify the killer?'

Something curled up and died in Claudia's stomach. So far, the killer had evaded every attempt they'd made to ID him. He was cautious, and they had no lines on him. All they could do was hope he'd make a mistake.

'Some elements of the investigation are not for public consumption because we don't want to alert the killer to our methods, as I'm sure you can understand. We provide the press with as much information as we possibly can without causing complications for the case.' And with that she rose from her chair. She had promised only two questions, and she was sticking to it.

Claudia followed her lead and stood. Arms waved in the air, looking for attention. They wanted more, little realising that Sharpe had simply used them for her own ends and would give them nothing else. What she had given them though was certainly newsworthy. An image of the next victim. Before he was potentially murdered. The media would usually pay good money for something that juicy, but here the police had provided it willingly. Claudia had no qualms about walking away behind Sharpe. All she wanted was the image of the man to be distributed far and wide and for someone to recognise him or for him to recognise himself. Preferably before 6 a.m. tomorrow, when, if this failed, he would be sitting on a chair with a pair of wings behind him. Dead. Being examined by a pathologist and a bunch of police officers.

All she could do was wait. Wait for the press to release the image and wait for the results.

They had set up a tip line to go out with the drawing for anyone who might recognise the male and had several detectives drafted in to man the lines.

It would take a couple of hours for them to come to life. Time for people to pick up their papers. To see news reports on local stations. To let the outside world seep into their busy lives. Time Claudia didn't know their next victim had.

CHAPTER 40

The Artist, as he was now known — and he was quite proud of the name, if he'd had to decide on a name for himself he couldn't have done it better — saw the report on the local news channel. A cropped section of his invitation to the police covered the screen and viewers were asked to call a tip line if they recognised the man in the drawing. The number also flashed up.

Why though, had they used a cut-down version of his invitation? Instead of the whole image, they had sliced it down so only the head of his next installation was visible. There was nothing offensive in the artwork. Nothing that would upset viewers. It was quite a beautiful drawing, if he said so himself. Especially the wings. The wings were magnificent. To have found a location in Sheffield that suited the man he'd picked out at his local gym, that paired with the winged tattoo on his chest. It was just so perfect.

The Artist liked to keep himself in shape. It helped him craft his artwork. The heavy lifting needed a steady hand.

Each installation took weeks of preparation. He had to follow his subject around to find out where they lived and how best to get them into the piece he had selected. He had to research and obtain drugs to knock each subject out, as required, so he could do what he needed to. Though drugs hadn't been necessary for every subject, of course. The first one had climbed on the bed voluntarily.

He'd manoeuvred that situation so the guy came to him, and how he laughed to himself at that thought. The fact he'd even managed to get him to lie in position, hands tied, as part of the photoshoot. All before he slammed the dagger deep into his back. The poor boy hadn't known what was coming. But it was by far the easiest piece he had created. The following two were much more intricate.

He turned his attention back into the television, where the reporter was reeling off the tip line yet again and asking anyone who recognised the man in the drawing to call in. Telling viewers it was of the utmost importance.

They had taken notice of the clock then.

Little knowing it was not as straightforward as it looked.

The clock was simply the time he was promising the installation would be found. Not the time the piece would be created.

CHAPTER 41

Claudia decided they'd be working late, so had ordered the team pizza. It had just been delivered. Rhys had been down to reception to collect it. He entered the incident room carrying a tower of boxes. She wasn't just providing for the detectives on the team. She was providing for all. Civilian staff as well. Everyone was working flat out on this job.

'Grub's up.' Rhys dumped the boxes on a desk as soon as he could relieve himself of them. 'They smell divine. Thanks, boss,' he shouted across the room.

Claudia came out of her office and stood in the doorway. There was a mass pile-on of the boxes. Lids were opened and slices of pizza lifted out, cheese trailing behind like yellow tentacles.

There were more groans of 'thanks, boss', but Claudia could barely hear them behind the stuffed pizza-filled mouths. This crowd could always be relied upon to be hungry and to eat whatever was put in front of them.

She wondered if they'd leave her a piece but had faith they'd not empty the box and cut off the hand that fed them that easily. No matter what their stomachs told them.

Eventually the herd thinned and Claudia made her way to the fan of open boxes. She selected a slice and took it away.

It did indeed smell divine. The scent of warm cheese, tomato and pepperoni wafted gently under her nose as she shoved the pointed end of the slice into her mouth. It was only then that she realised how hungry she was. Work had distracted her. She couldn't remember when she had last eaten. Maybe this morning before she left the house.

She was striding into her office with the slice of pizza flopping in her hand when a voice shouted behind her, grabbing her attention with the excitement in the sound. It was loud and high-pitched. Like a squeak. Desperate to get the words out before she disappeared from view.

She turned slowly. Trepidation seizing her muscles.

'Ma'am,' the officer at the back of the incident room shouted at her again.

She looked his way.

'Ma'am.' He was on his feet, the landline phone handset to his face. A finger pressed firmly down on the mute button. 'I have someone on the line who thinks the drawing the press have put out is a picture of himself. He's quite upset and wants to know what the hell is going on.'

CHAPTER 42

Claudia took Dominic with her to the house. She was conscious she'd relied heavily on Russ recently and needed to use Dom more than she had been doing. It surprised her how quietly he'd taken this and got on with the tasks at hand. Maybe he realised how important the job was.

A male Claudia instantly recognised opened the door. He was the double of the man in the drawing. There was no mistaking the guy had correctly identified himself.

The killer was a talented illustrator and deserved the moniker the press had given him in that respect. His drawings were always so true to life. How he could depict exactly how his crimes would go, though, was beyond her. He had an active imagination and an intricate attention to detail.

The man who she now knew to be Zach Williams was wired, as you'd expect him to be after seeing a drawing of himself plastered all over the news.

'My phone's been ringing off the hook,' he said before they could get through the door, and even though mobile phones didn't have a hook, the phrase had still clung on.

'I'm sorry,' said Claudia. 'Can we sit somewhere and explain what's happened?'

Zach was in his gym gear and several times rubbed a finger around the inner neckline of his T-shirt with the energy that was coursing through him.

Claudia and Dominic followed him through to a small living area.

'You live alone?' she asked.

'Yeah, I moved out earlier in the year.' He blushed. 'With a little help from my parents.' He didn't bother to sit, instead he turned on them. 'So tell me.'

The room was sparse. A young lad on his own, still attempting to find his feet, to find out who he was in a space of his own. There were no family photos. No prints on the wall. Instead, the focus of the room was the television in the corner, and to the side of it a bookcase crammed with assorted books. Claudia studied the shelves, trying to make out what Zach was in to. She was always interested in other people's reading habits.

From what she could see he was a sci-fi reader. Old classics like *Dune*, *Fahrenheit 451* and *The War of the Worlds*, smashed up against new releases by authors such as Charles Stross, John Scalzi and Blake Crouch. There was a book, *A Town Called Discovery*, by R. R. Haywood, slung casually on the sofa, a bookmark poking halfway through it. There was an attempt at comfort with cushions scattered along the back of the sofa. Claudia could imagine him curled up here reading his book, not a care in the world.

Zach had his whole life in front of him, and here they were about to terrify the life out of him.

'Shall we sit?' asked Claudia, directing her gaze to the sofa.

Zach huffed. 'Tell me.' He sat down and Claudia and Dominic followed suit.

'You've been following the news?' Claudia asked by way of an answer.

Zach thought for a minute. Obviously there was nothing but negative reports coming through on the news channels, and his mind was too scared to make the very clear link with the drawing. Though she wasn't sure how the press had presented it.

'You don't mean . . .' He struggled to find the right words as his mind stumbled over the answer.

'The murderer we are trying to trace that the press have dubbed the Artist, yes. I'm afraid so.' Claudia was sitting forward, offering her reassurance.

'You must have it wrong.' He clawed at his neck.

'You have a tattoo of wings that go across your chest?'

His eyes widened in shock. 'How can you . . . how do you . . . how?'

'Do you have a bag you can pack?' Dominic asked.

'A bag?' Zach couldn't keep up with the conversation.

'We need to relocate you tonight,' Claudia explained. 'As you can see from the image, it very clearly is you. It's a warning that you're the next victim. We want to put you in a safe place where he'll be unable to get to you.'

Zach jumped to his feet. Spun on the spot. Ran his hands through his hair. Spun around again.

'Look,' said Claudia. 'This is a lot to take in.' She was over the moon they had found Zach before he had turned into a victim, but it was clear he was scared and uncertain and didn't know what to do with himself. Her job was to reassure him and get him to come along with them so she could keep him safe. That was her first step. Once he was safely ensconced in a hotel room, they needed to focus on finding a way to get their hands on his prospective killer. 'If you can slow down and take a couple of deep breaths we'll walk you through everything at a pace you can cope with.' She'd go as slowly as he demanded. Now they were with him, he was safe. She couldn't imagine how terrifying something like this must be. Seeing the Artist all over the news reports for his drawings and subsequent murders and then seeing your own face on the next drawing — it must be totally horrifying. No wonder he was a man on the edge.

'I have a job. In the morning. I can't just . . .' He trailed off.

'I'm sure they'll understand,' said Dominic, 'considering the circumstances.'

'Your safety is paramount,' said Claudia. 'As you can see, the image is of you. That means you're his next target. He's coming for you, and we won't allow that. We need to take you out of circulation. Do you consent to being in our protection?'

Zach quivered. His whole body vibrating. Then he nodded.

'Good.' Claudia kept her tone relaxed. 'Pack that bag. It only needs to be light. We'll get out of here and put you up in a hotel. Somewhere he can't find you.'

Zach looked around the room, then stalked to the corner, where his phone was charging at a plug socket. He pulled the charger out and held it with his phone. 'I'll go and get a couple more bits.' His voice was shaky.

Claudia and Dominic sat on the sofa and waited. They could hear him moving about in the other rooms of the flat. He soon reappeared with a small holdall in his hand and a jacket thrown through the handles. He walked to the sofa and collected the book that was resting there, shoving it into the unzipped bag.

'Let's go then.' Dominic stood. 'We'll get you to safety and go from there.'

The hotel they chose, the Jurys Inn, was not too far away from Zach's flat and it didn't take long to get him booked in to a room on one of the higher floors.

'There are only a handful of us who know you're here,' said Claudia as she inserted the plastic key card into the reader.

She entered first and had a good look around. Nothing was out of place. It looked like any other hotel room she had ever been in. There was a television on a wide set of drawers and a tray with a kettle and a couple of mugs with tea and coffee sachets ready for thirsty guests. Opposite was a double bed, and on the bedside table a couple of pamphlets for things to do nearby as well as a box of tissues and the remote control for the television.

'Looks like you have everything you need,' said Claudia.

It was a nice hotel. Zach looked worried. 'You're paying for this?' he queried.

'Don't worry.' She smiled. 'This is most definitely on us. We have an organisational discount with the company. If you can, try to relax, make the most of this. Order yourself something to eat. Room service, please. Don't leave your room under any circumstances. And do not inform any of your family or friends where you are tonight. Of course, you can be in touch with them. I'm sure your parents are worried about you. Call them and tell them you're safe. Tell them the police have installed an alarm at your address. No need to worry them. But pretend you're at home.' She stared hard at him. 'Do I make myself clear? We do not want this killer to have any possible way of finding out where you are.'

Zach nodded.

'I mean it. No updating your Facebook profile that you're the guy in the drawing and are in a hotel for your own safety. No matter how exciting it might sound. You do anything like that and you alert him to the fact you're not at home. We're going to have officers watching your flat. As long as you do as I tell you and keep your location secret and even the fact that you're not at home a secret, then you'll be safe.'

There was the sound of mumbled voices beyond the door as a couple walked past the room.

Worry washed over Zach's face again. 'You're leaving me here? Alone?'

'You're not alone Zach. There's a marked police car outside the front and someone will check on you every hour or so. It might disturb your sleep, but that's not really why you're here tonight, so you'll have to put up with it. The thing is, the killer will search for you at your home and we only have so many resources, so I'm prioritising your flat. I've risk assessed this decision, and so long as you do as I say and don't leave this room, then you'll be perfectly safe. Do not make me regret trusting you, Zach.'

CHAPTER 43

As soon as they arrived back at headquarters, there was a message for Claudia and Dominic that Sharpe wanted to see them.

Claudia looked at her father and he shrugged.

She popped into the ladies and straightened herself up, spraying herself with deodorant to cover the after-effects of the day's heat and frustrations. Then with Dominic's agreement they selected the lift. Climbing the stairs was too much right now, even though the warmth was lessening as the day died.

Sharpe's PA had gone home and the door was ajar. She must have seen Claudia or Dominic, as she called them through the second they arrived.

Sharpe was standing, face to the window, arms crossed. Without turning she instructed Claudia to close the door. An icy shiver ran down Claudia's back. This didn't look good. She had no idea what it was about, but she didn't have a good feeling.

Eventually Sharpe turned. Her features pinched. Her lips pursed. 'Have a seat.'

Dominic did as he was told, but Claudia didn't want to sit. She had an urge to pace around the office space. This wasn't positive news and sitting still was not what she wanted to do. 'Can I stand, ma'am?'

Sharpe gave her a pointed look, recognised that she herself was still standing and inclined her head.

Claudia let out a silent breath. Whatever was coming, she would control her reaction.

Dominic looked between the two women who were now towering over him and got to his feet. Sharpe let out an exasperated sigh.

'I'll get straight to the point,' she said. 'You're wondering why I've called you here when you're so busy.'

Claudia needed to organise a team to sit up on Zach Williams's address. She hoped this wouldn't take long. All she could do was wait her boss out.

'I've had a phone call today from the prison liaison officer at Doncaster, and apparently a guy by the name of Craig Lawton, Tyler's cellmate, has made a statement saying Tyler confessed to him one night in their cell to killing Ruth.'

Claudia's throat tightened up. The air that was so natural for her to breathe became thick and cloggy. She struggled and choked. Coughed and spluttered. How could this be? She'd spoken to Tyler. He'd been adamant he hadn't killed Ruth. Why would he then confess to someone else he had done it?

Dominic jumped up to Claudia's aid. He grabbed her arm, swung her sideways and rubbed her back, gently telling her to breathe.

Easier said than done.

She grasped for air.

Dominic wavered in front of her.

The heat of the day and the shock of the announcement had affected her, but she could get this under control.

She looked at her father supporting her and steeled herself. How dare she react so badly when this was his wife and the love of his life? She slowed down her breaths, taking them in deep until they were under control again.

Sharpe was peering at her awkwardly and with some degree of concern.

'I'm okay.' She straightened herself up and pulled herself free of Dominic's grip. 'I'm okay,' she said again, feeling more than a little foolish for her reaction.

The news had come from out of the blue. Tyler had only just finished trying to convince her he hadn't killed Ruth. Why would he then blab to someone else and tell them he had killed her? She shook herself and focused on her father. 'How are you?'

He gave her a weak smile. 'It brings some kind of closure, I suppose.'

'I'm sorry to be the one to bring this news to you, especially in the middle of such a difficult case.' Sharpe walked to her desk and seated herself behind it.

Claudia and Dominic were still standing, processing the information she'd imparted.

'You believe the snitch?' Claudia asked to no one in particular.

Puzzlement covered both Dominic and Sharpe's features, and Claudia was a little anxious at having broached the question. It was clear from their faces they'd swallowed the story whole.

'What are you thinking?' asked Sharpe, rather than answering Claudia's question. Ever the diplomatic supervisor. She ruled with an iron fist, but she was cautious and sensitive when the need arose. Especially when it came to the loss of a serving police officer, and having the family of that police officer — both of them serving officers themselves — standing in front of her. Claudia could see that she knew when to be careful.

Dominic's face was darker. Like he wanted to shut her down. Like this was over for him, and she was about to explode a bomb under it all. He wanted it all to be clear cut, she knew. He could grieve and have someone to blame. It made it easier.

Yet, here she was about to, if not explode a bomb under it all, at least light a touch paper. And at the very least, show them an unearthed ordinance.

'I spoke to Tyler,' she turned to Sharpe. 'You know that.'

Dominic's eyes darkened.

'He said he didn't kill Ruth.'

Sharpe leaned forward and steepled her hands in front of her face. 'How many criminals have you known, Claudia? And how many of those have pleaded their innocence to you? It's what they do. But in the dark of the night when they're alone in a tiny space with no one in the world for comfort but some other scrawny guy to talk to, what do you think they're going to do? They're going to talk. They're going to try to make a connection with someone. I'd let what he told you slide, Claudia. We have it in a proper statement from Lawton. He's no reason to make it up, and he hasn't been promised anything in return for making his statement. Those are the best kind of statements, as well you know.'

And she did. She sank into one of the chairs opposite Sharpe and put her head in her hands. 'I'm sorry. I'm sorry, Dad.' What must he think of her, putting her own feelings before his?

A hand landed on her shoulder. 'It's okay, love. It came as a shock to both of us. It was something I hoped for, though. You, on the other hand, have been given the run-around by the evil bastard.'

She looked at Sharpe, who shrugged.

'I suppose I'd better get back to the team and carry on with what we need to do.'

'You're both okay?' asked Sharpe.

'I am,' said Dominic, his hand still resting on his daughter's shoulder.

Claudia stood, shrugging off her dad. 'I'm fine. If Tyler has screwed with me, then so be it. I'll move past it. I've got other things to be getting on with.'

Sharpe gave a curt nod and released the two detectives from her office.

CHAPTER 44

The mood in the incident room was buoyant. They had identified the third victim and had him stashed away in a hotel. There would be no murder tonight. They had stopped the killer in his tracks and it felt pretty damn good. If they could drink on the premises, then Claudia knew they'd be popping a cork or two this evening.

'Let's not get ahead of ourselves though,' she said. 'We've done well with the ID of Zach Williams, but the difficult part of this investigation is still in front of us, and that's catching the guy behind all this. He's been two moves in front every step of the way. I need a couple of volunteers to stake out Zach's address to see if this killer makes an appearance. The rest of you can go home and get some rest, ready for tomorrow. I'll update the uniform night shift inspector about what we're doing, that way if you need backup they'll be there immediately.'

She looked around at her team. 'So, volunteers?'

Lisa raised an arm.

'Thanks, Lisa. One more. Don't leave Lisa out there on her own. You know she'll fall asleep if she doesn't have someone to talk to.'

Lisa objected and the room laughed.

Krish shouted out that he'd join her for the night. If anyone was going to get their hands on the Artist, he would be the one.

'Thanks, both. Keep a discreet distance. Don't put him off coming up close. Allow him to make a move on the property. Keep your wits about you, pay attention. We've got permission from Zach to watch his flat, and all the directed surveillance authority paperwork is in order. Stay safe. I don't want to come in tomorrow and find out one of you has fallen into his hands because he's lost his target. He's not a stupid man from what we know of him.'

The rest of the team gathered their things together. Their day was over. Another long shift finished. But this one had closed on a high note. Exuberance jostled among them. Joy at saving the victim from a fate at the hands of the killer and becoming tomorrow's news.

'I'm having a pint, who's joining me?' asked Dominic.

Claudia looked at him. She wanted the team fresh tomorrow. She didn't want to rub Lisa's and Krish's noses in the fact that the work day was over for most when they were pulling an all-nighter. Yet Dominic had something else on his mind he was probably wanting to soak up with alcohol. She couldn't blame him.

'I'm going to get some rest,' she said.

The look he gave her said everything without saying a word. It said he was disappointed. That she was a spoilsport, a killjoy. That she shouldn't put her mood on everyone else. He wanted a drink and he bloody well was going to have one, thank you very much.

She turned away from him. Glad that he had some closure at last, but she was unsettled. She couldn't in all good conscience pretend she'd taken in the words of one criminal over another. In fact, she needed to research and see what Lawton was inside for, see if that provided her with any clues.

'I'll grab a beer with you, mate, before I head home to get some zeds,' said Graham.

'Just the one for me too,' agreed Rhys. 'Today is worth celebrating. Our first big break in our first case on the task force. I think we should whet our whistles in honour.'

Dominic grinned. 'Better get there before they call last orders then.'

Claudia said goodbye to the team as they walked out the door and then turned to Lisa and Krish, who were packing what they needed for their surveillance of Zach's flat.

'The uniform inspector is aware, as you know, but so is the duty inspector in the control room. You have all the backup available to you at the push of a button. We'd have more resources on Zach right now, but Uniform are tied up with a crowd they have in custody. They did a drugs raid today and closed two houses. It was a good one by all accounts, but it's left them pretty short-staffed. The seriousness of our situation has meant they're stretching themselves thin to help us, but help they will. Use it if you need to. Don't be a hero tonight, either of you.'

They agreed not to be heroic, but were determined to catch the Artist in the act.

'He has to make a move on Zach,' said Krish. 'He has no idea he's at the hotel. You said Zach has no plans for tonight, so there's no way the Artist could be planning to grab him away from home.'

Though Claudia fully agreed with Krish, her stomach still twisted in unease, as though she were missing something. 'Have we missed something obvious?'

Lisa stared at her thoughtfully. 'I don't see how. Zach is safe and we know he wasn't lined up to meet anyone this evening. There's no way we've dropped the ball. It's up to me and Krish now.'

Claudia watched the pair head off before moving to her office. She had something to do before she went home for the night herself.

Craig Lawton.

Who was he and what was he inside for?

She tapped at her keyboard and waited for the screen to load the answers she desperately needed.

The incident room was silent. The whole team had left. Peace should have settled over her, but there was an uneasiness wrapping its way around her.

Lawton's details popped onto the monitor. Claudia leaned forward and read them. He was on remand for murdering a man. She needed more information. She logged into the crime system and searched his name. After his daughter reported being raped he attacked and killed her rapist. An act of emotional anger and rage. Not the same kind of man as Tyler.

Claudia steepled her fingers. Could she trust Lawton? He obviously wasn't a cold-blooded killer. Yes, he'd killed a man, but love had driven him to lose his temper the way he had. If Lawton was telling the truth, then what game was Tyler playing telling Claudia one thing and Lawton another?

Did he think it was funny? Was he trying to muddy the waters? Or was he trying to cause emotional hurt to Ruth's family?

There were no answers within the police system.

Claudia closed it down, disheartened that nothing had popped up as an alert for her.

She headed for home still confused as to what had happened to Ruth and determined to find out the truth.

CHAPTER 45

Dominic entered the Church House. A Grade II listed building that was once a church but was now a public house. He liked the vibe, and the team liked to congregate here in their downtime. What little downtime they had. He'd informed the others the drinks were on him and they'd gone to grab seats where they could gather. It wasn't difficult. It was a weeknight and the hour was late.

He had something to celebrate and was in high spirits, though he couldn't show how high his mood was. When the rest of the team found out about Lawton's statement, they would understand his happiness at the case coming to a natural conclusion but would be concerned to see him overjoyed. It would confuse them. He was still a grieving widow. The man who had killed multiple women around the city had also admitted to taking his wife as his victim.

But he was joyous.

He had finally pulled Claudia off his back.

The bartender asked for his order and Dominic requested three pints.

It wasn't just Claudia, though. She had been a side issue. It was Tyler himself. He'd been the problem, and Dominic had managed to shut him down. He'd never wanted to go head-to-head with his daughter. She wouldn't be involved in all this if it wasn't for that worm Tyler. He had so much to answer for.

Why couldn't he simply accept the extra body on his charge sheet instead of kicking up a fuss? It wasn't as though it would make any difference at all to his sentence. He was going to be locked up for the rest of his life, regardless of whether they added Ruth as one of his victims or not.

How could he not see that? Why did it matter to him? Surely he'd feel good taking the glory for someone else's work. Especially a cop. Dominic had banked on that at the time. It would bring him kudos in prison, being a cop killer. The convicts inside hated cops, and if he entered as a man who had taken one down, his reputation would walk ahead of him.

But no. Tyler wanted everything by the book. If he didn't kill her, then he would not take the rap.

Well, Dominic couldn't have him screwing up his plans.

The bartender placed the three beers in a row in front of him. Dominic paid the man before encircling the glasses in his hands and carrying them over to where Graham and Rhys sat, their heads together, deep in conversation.

Dominic handed out the drinks and sank down on a stool opposite the two men. 'Cheers. Here's to a job well done.' They may have thought he was talking about Zach Williams, but he was talking about Lawton and Tyler.

Graham and Rhys raised their glasses and took a slug of the amber liquid.

'You think they'll get the Artist tonight?' asked Rhys.

Graham took another gulp. 'If those two have anything to do with it, he'll be wrapped up like a Christmas turkey for the boss by morning, mate.'

Rhys grinned at the thought of his colleagues' determination. 'You think he'll turn up, Dom?'

Dominic considered the question. 'He hasn't failed to carry out his kills so far. If he doesn't know we've moved the victim, then I don't see why he wouldn't make his move.

Though . . .' He analysed the situation. 'I still don't understand why he sends the drawings to the police in the first place. Giving us the opportunity to stop him in his tracks like we have with Williams. Surely it was always a possibility for him?'

'Maybe he likes the game,' Graham countered.

'Maybe. It's certainly a strange one. I've never come across anything like it in all my years.'

'How long do you have left?' asked Rhys, referring to Dominic's service.

'I'm fifty. Ten years if I go for the full pension. Or I can take a reduced pension at fifty-five.' He shrugged.

'You wouldn't leave early, would you?' Graham looked appalled. 'I mean . . .' He paused.

Dominic stared at him over his pint.

'I know it's been a tough year, but . . .' Graham seemed to be struggling to put what he wanted to say into sentences. On a path he no longer wanted to travel. But Dominic didn't help him out. He simply waited for him to continue.

'But you're a good copper and you're made for it. I can't imagine you walking away. Not if you haven't done so far, that is . . .' His words hung in the air, heavy, waiting for Dominic to respond.

Rhys watched the two men. He wouldn't interfere.

'Look,' Graham started again, 'this is the first time I've worked with you, but I supported Claudia with the rest of the team during the whole Tyler investigation when you were . . .' He rolled his hand trying to move the conversation forward without the need to say the words. That he'd been part of Claudia's team when they'd been investigating Dominic for killing Ruth. 'It was tough on her. You being her dad and all. But you both got through it. That tells me you're both cut from the proper cop cloth. It's in your blood. If a scenario like that can't take you out then there's nothing that can.' He put his pint glass to his face and supped. A sign that he'd finished his emotional and quite frankly stressful comment.

Dominic waited a beat. Then he smiled.

Graham let out a sigh of relief.

'Look,' said Dominic, 'I'm playing it by ear. You're right, it has been a tough year so far. I'm learning to be a different person on my own. Learning a lot of things, to be honest. But coppering, yes, you're right again, it's in my blood. As it's in Claudia's. But don't tell her I said that or she'll get a big head.'

The three men laughed.

Dominic downed his beer and thought about his daughter and how difficult she made it to keep his secret. If he was to stay a copper, then he had to also keep not only lying to his daughter but actively deceiving her.

CHAPTER 46

The sound broke through the darkness.

Claudia clawed her way through the fog. She must have been asleep for all of ten minutes and here the phone was ringing.

Her arm reached out from under the duvet and grabbed her mobile from the bedside table. She pulled it under the covers and muttered her name into the handset.

'I'm sorry to disturb you, DI Nunn,' a voice with a slight stutter broke through.

She grunted. Her spare hand rubbed her eyes to clear them from the haze of sleep.

'I was asked to call you and inform you that an evening check-in of Zach Williams was conducted, as you requested, and the officer involved . . . well . . . he was unable to get hold of him.'

Claudia bolted upright. 'What do you mean?' She was alert now.

'The officer in attendance couldn't get him to respond to his knocking at the hotel room door, so demanded the hotel staff open up for him. He didn't want to call you if Mr Williams was simply a heavy sleeper.'

Frustration was clawing at the base of Claudia's neck as the story dragged on. 'Do get on with it.' She scratched at her neck.

'The hotel staff opened the room up and the officer entered. He made a search, well as much as you can of a bedroom and a bathroom, and found it empty. A couple of other officers were called in and a sweep of the hotel was conducted and he's still not been found. The decision was then made to inform you, ma'am.'

Claudia rubbed her face. Where could he be? It was made abundantly clear how much danger he was in and from who. Why on earth would he pull a disappearing act in the middle of the night?

'Ma'am?'

'I'm coming in. Check with the team at his house that his vehicle is still in place if you haven't already. And find out what the state of play is there. Tell them to keep their wits about them.'

Shit. What the hell was happening?

'Yes, ma'am.'

She thought about her team. Some had been out drinking, but Russ hadn't. 'Contact DS Russ Kane and tell him to meet me at the hotel. Inform him it's at my direction.'

The effect of sleep had long gone. Claudia was alert and eager to be back in the incident room. Zach was under her care and was missing. There would be hell to pay. Not just from those above, but from the press when they found out, and they would. You could never hide anything from them.

The control room inspector rang off and Claudia checked her phone. It was 12.36 a.m. The clock on the drawing was set for 6 a.m. They had less than five and a half hours to find Zach before he became another crime scene clone of a drawing.

Her first call was to Zach's mobile phone. It was switched off. A sickness spiralled to her stomach. What had she been hoping for? That the cops who had been first on the scene hadn't thought of calling him? That he was going to pick up and tell her he'd gone for a walk to get some fresh air and what was all the fuss about? Or that he wanted to go home? Either would have made her both angry and at the same time utterly relieved.

But there was nothing. The phone was dead. It went straight to answerphone. Not even his voice to listen to, just the automated answerphone that came with the phone.

She ended the call, the sickness sinking deep and leaden.

The next call was to Lisa and Krish. Lisa picked it up.

'How's it going?' Claudia asked, with an open question so she could elicit as much information from her subordinate without giving her the news of Zach's missing status.

'All quiet here.'

'And she's still awake, boss,' Krish shouted down the phone from the side of her.

Claudia smiled. Glad they were bonding during their stint in the car. They'd come from different teams and had been pushed together when she'd created the team she wanted for the task force.

Lisa cursed him and turned her attention back to Claudia. 'Honestly, boss. It's as silent as a church. I don't know what time he's planning on picking this guy up, but he's not here yet. No sign of movement at all. There are still some lights on, in properties on the street, but nothing's moving outside.'

'And you've seen nothing from inside of the flat from the street?' Claudia pushed, wondering if Zach had left the relative safety of the hotel to go back home. That would solve all their problems. They'd have to scoop him up again, but it was a better scenario than the alternative.

'Nope, no sign of activity. Like I said, the street has been quiet and we'd have seen if the Artist had got inside.'

Lisa hadn't realised why Claudia was asking. She'd presumed they were talking about the reason they were there. The Artist. Even though the control room inspector had called for an update. A shiver ran down Claudia's spine. If

Zach hadn't gone home, then the odds rose of the Artist somehow having been involved.

But how?

'Zach Williams is missing from the hotel, Lisa.'

'Shit. How?'

It was a very good question, but one she couldn't answer. 'We have no idea. I'm going to the hotel to see what I can learn. Can you and Krish keep your eyes open for either the Artist—' she agreed with Lisa, she hated using that term for him. The Artist sounded whimsical and not the brutal phrase he deserved — 'or for Williams himself. If Williams shows, phone me immediately. And put your hands on him instantly. I don't want anything happening to him. I'm still hoping he left the hotel of his own accord. Homesick or something.'

'Will do, boss.'

Claudia thanked them and ended the call.

Russ met her outside the hotel within half an hour. She couldn't ask the whole team to work through two solid days without rest. Russ would do this. Of course her team would, but she made the decision that they shouldn't.

Instead of his work suit, Russ was dressed in jeans and a thin jumper. It might be gloriously hot through the day, but the temperature still dropped in the night. There was five o'clock shadow shading his jaw, and though he'd attempted to straighten himself out, his hair was more rumpled than usual, a telling sign that he'd not long removed himself from his bed.

The street was silent. But at gone 1 a.m. what else could she expect? What her eyes searched for were signs of a struggle, though. Something kicked over as the killer pulled a frightened young man into a car, maybe. How else had this occurred? But there was nothing. Everything looked to be in order. If it weren't for the couple of police cars parked up you wouldn't think anything was wrong.

'Shall we speak to the staff then?' Russ suggested.

Claudia ran a hand through her hair. Sure it was as unruly as Russ's looked. Realising this, she then used both hands to pat some of it into place. There was no need to go into public looking unkempt just because of the hour.

They strode through the huge double doors and up to the unmanned reception desk. Again Claudia saw no signs of a disturbance. Nothing askance. The door to the stairs was closed and clean, and the potted plant next to the lift was in position and undisturbed.

There was a buzzer on the reception desk, with a sign propped against it, asking guests to *press for attention*. No doubt the staff would be sitting with their feet up somewhere in the rear. Claudia couldn't blame them. She hadn't enjoyed night shifts when she was in uniform. The 4 a.m. brick wall had nearly killed her, utter exhaustion overwhelming her, limbs that seemed to weigh more than a baby elephant and a mind filled with fog.

Claudia pushed the small white button, and they waited. Barely a word had passed between her and Russ, both of them shocked by the turn of events. They had been so sure that Zach was safe and secure, that they had placed their resources in the correct place. Now Claudia bit her lip as she waited for the hotel staff to appear and tell her where Zach had gone.

The receptionist appeared, a half-hearted smile etched onto his face. Obviously he wasn't a fan of night shifts either.

'Good evening, how can I help you?'

Claudia pulled out her ID and introduced both herself and Russ. 'We booked in a male by the name of James Rogers last night. He's no longer in his room. We'd like to know the last person to see him and we'd like access to his room, please.'

They'd booked Zach in under a pseudonym in case the Artist was clever enough to do a search for him. But with the amount of hotels in Sheffield it would take him the whole night or an incredible amount of good luck to find him quickly by calling the hotels and asking for Zach Williams.

The receptionist looked Claudia and Russ up and down, checking out the relaxed dress code. 'One moment.'

Claudia waited. Not so patiently. She had an urge to tap her fingers on the desk but didn't want to appear rude and annoy the one person who was currently helping them.

'Mr Rogers ordered room service at 10.50 p.m. and it was delivered at 11.06 p.m. The waiter who delivered the food was the last person to see Mr Rogers.' He looked up from his computer. 'I can take you to his room if you would like?' He smiled again. There was no trace of genuine warmth behind the expression.

Russ took out his notebook. 'We'd like the name of the waiter who took the food to Mr Rogers, please.'

The receptionist looked down at the computer screen again. 'Of course. It was Gareth Davids.'

'And is Gareth Davids still on duty?'

'He is. Will you need to speak with him?'

'We will,' Russ confirmed.

'Very well. Would you like to speak to Mr Davids first, or would you prefer to attend to Mr Rogers' room?'

Russ checked with Claudia.

She thought about priorities. The last person to see Zach might have something to tell them, but Zach could equally have left them something in his room that told them where he was going. 'We'll have a quick look in his room and then we'll speak to Gareth, please.'

'As you wish.' The receptionist moved back out of view, most likely to talk to whoever would be covering the reception and to grab the master key card, and then he ushered them to the lift, where they ascended to Zach's room. A journey Claudia didn't think she would be making quite so soon. Guilt ate at her as the small box moved upwards. The walls that confined her like her own personal prison cell for her crimes of not protecting Zach. It was something she'd have to learn to live with. Especially if harm came to him. If they couldn't get to him in time.

The receptionist opened Zach's room and Claudia and Russ strode in, snapping on gloves to protect the integrity of any surfaces they might come into contact with. The Crime

Scene Unit would do a full examination, but time was not on their side and they needed to look round now.

The receptionist waited for them in the corridor.

'Nothing's out of place,' said Russ. 'Not from what I can remember. Obviously he'll have unpacked the few things he brought with him. But it looks tidy enough in here.'

Claudia looked at the book open on the bed, *A Town Called Discovery*, and remembered the shelves of sci-fi he had at home. The hours of escapism he enjoyed. Had he been reading his book before he disappeared? Had this book managed to settle the nerves that had so obviously been on display when they'd last seen him?

Claudia moved into the en suite. Again there was nothing amiss in there. 'What about his phone?' she asked Russ. 'Is it in here?'

He looked around. 'I can't see it.'

'Which suggests he either took it with him when he left, meaning he went of his own accord, or someone else picked it up. We need to figure that out. But what would make him get up and leave? He was terrified when we left him.'

Russ shrugged and rubbed an eye with the back of a gloved hand. 'We'll see if we can trace his phone.'

Claudia shook her head. 'It's off. There's no doubt about that. But of course we'll try.'

With one last look around the hotel room they moved back downstairs and were ushered to a comfortable seating area in front of the reception desk. They were not worried about being overheard at this time of night. Everyone was tucked up in their rooms, oblivious to what was happening within their hotel. That the Artist's next victim had been here for a short time and was now a missing person. That the police were here and concern was high.

It was only a matter of minutes before Gareth Davids was ushered out front to speak to Claudia and Russ.

He was anxious. His hands were clasped in front of him like twisted, gnarled twigs. His shoulders bunched up to his ears.

‘Thank you for coming out to talk to us,’ Claudia said, trying to settle him.

Gareth nodded his head, his lips a thin line in his face.

‘We’re told that you took Mr Rogers’ evening meal up to him last night, is that correct?’

Gareth nodded again.

She was going to need him to speak if they were to get anywhere with him.

‘Won’t you sit with us?’ Getting him a little more relaxed would help. Gareth folded himself into a chair opposite Claudia and Russ. He was tall and lanky and appeared uncertain of himself in the seat. Claudia moved on. ‘He was in his room when you took it up?’

Again, another nod.

Claudia held in the sigh she so wanted to release.

‘Tell me about your transaction with Mr Rogers, please.’ He had no choice but to talk to them.

Gareth opened his mouth, closed it then opened it again, but nothing came out.

‘I know it’s daunting talking to the police.’ Claudia tried to soothe the jittery man in front of her, but time was running out for Zach and she was about to lose her patience if this waiter didn’t start speaking soon. ‘But you’re not in any trouble. In fact, what you tell us could prove really helpful. Mr Rogers could be in real danger and something you say might help us help him. You’d like to do that, wouldn’t you?’ She hoped that small spark of something that people had for being involved in an important situation with the police would kick in and open Gareth up.

Again he opened his mouth. This time sound came with it. It was quiet, but it was sound. ‘I knocked on his door.’

Claudia and Russ both leaned forward at the same time to better hear him. He looked startled and leaned back in his own chair a little. Claudia clenched her teeth together but said nothing. Sensing his boss’s rising frustration, Russ asked Gareth to continue.

'It took a while for him to answer. I shouted that it was room service. He seemed unwilling to open the door. He asked what his order was. I had no idea. It was covered with a lid. He refused to let me in unless I told him, so I had to check under the lid and tell him.'

He paused.

'I'm presuming it was correct and he let you in?' Claudia said, feeling proud of Zach for thinking of his own safety that way. If he'd been so cautious, how then had he gone missing?

'Oh yeah. He let me in. Locked the door behind me while I was in the room. It was all very strange. But now you're here, it kind of makes more sense. He was hiding out, wasn't he?'

Claudia could hardly deny it. 'He was keeping himself safe, Gareth.'

Gareth nodded again.

'Did you see or hear anything unusual in the room?'

Gareth scratched at his face. His fingers long and slender now they were unfurled from the bundle they'd been tangled in not a minute previously. 'I don't think so, other than the guy in the room was jittery. That was what stood out as strange to me. The whole thing with him. Him not letting me in. Having to check his food and him locking the door behind me while I was in there with him. I were only in there a minute while I put it down and yet he locked me in with him. Very unnerving it were.'

Claudia could only imagine the number of strange customers hotels saw through their doors and didn't for one minute believe that Zach was the strangest Gareth had come across. 'What did he say while you were in there?'

'He wanted to know if anyone had asked after him on my way up with his food.'

'And had they?'

Gareth looked surprised. 'No. I picked up his meal and carried it to his room. I didn't speak to anyone.'

'What else?'

'Just the tray and the food on the tray.'

'No, what else was said.'

'Oh. He checked under the food covers. I wasn't sure what he was looking for, but I asked if everything was okay and if I could do anything else for him.'

Claudia waited for him to continue.

Gareth got her point. 'He said he didn't need me and unlocked the door. On the way out, he asked me not to tell anyone he was there. Not to tell anyone his room number. The only people who should know were already aware, he said.'

That would be her and Dominic he was referring to. She was puzzled. What had prompted him to leave his room? He was obviously worried sick after they'd left him.

'Did you see anyone lurking around the hotel that you didn't think belonged here?' Russ asked, as though reading her mind.

Gareth returned to non-verbal communications and shook his head.

Claudia stared at him.

'No, nope. Nothing.'

That was a no then.

She thanked him for his time and gave him a contact card, asking him to get in touch if he remembered anything else. He scuttled away as if the chair he'd been occupying was on fire.

'What are you thinking?' asked Russ.

She sighed. 'I have no idea what's happened here. We had him secured in his hotel room. He was obviously frightened and didn't want finding if Gareth's verbal statement is anything to go by. I don't understand what got him out of his room. And with no one seeing him.'

Russ looked across at the reception desk. 'Well, the no one seeing him part is easy enough. The front desk doesn't look manned unless you ring for attention as we did. Anyone could easily walk in or walk out unseen.'

'The question is,' Claudia groaned, 'did our killer walk in or did Zach walk out?'

CHAPTER 47

Uniformed officers had seized CCTV from the hotel and the surrounding streets. They'd been provided with a photograph of Zach from his driving licence and the timeframe from him last being seen by the waiter to the moment he was discovered missing, so they could search through the footage to see if they could find him.

Claudia wasn't going to wait for a team to search through the hotel CCTV when she could do it herself. The timeframe was reasonably tight for her to view it on fast-forward, and as she did Russ stood behind her, his body tense as they waited for the corridor cameras to show them the truth of what had happened.

Russ's hand flew up. 'There he is.'

Claudia watched as Zach walked down the corridor alone. Hands shoved deep into his pockets. Shoulders hunched. Chin tucked tight into his jacket. Curling himself into as small a ball as he could. Trying not to be seen. By the camera or by someone else? The person he was walking straight to?

They watched as Zach moved through the hotel. Though it had no sound, his stance gave the impression he was skulking through the building as quietly as he could so as not to be seen and stopped. He was flowing through the corridors until he wasn't. Suddenly he stopped still at a door and looked around furtively.

'What does that door say?' asked Claudia.

Russ leaned in. 'Staff only.'

Claudia rolled her eyes. 'Please no.' But then he was gone, through the door and out of sight. 'Check where that door comes out, but my best guess is it's a back exit. He's avoiding the front. The marked car. But how? How did he know to do that?'

'He left of his own volition,' said Russ, grudgingly.

Claudia shook her head, trying to clear the image. The young man had seemingly willingly walked to his own death. 'What would make him do that? He was so scared.'

Russ shrugged. 'We need to find him.'

The on-duty night inspector had been helpful in providing staff to support her with the missing person investigation, knowing what it was likely going to lead to. Everyone in the force was aware of the Artist and wanted to be involved in stopping him in his tracks. Claudia held a mug of coffee. Not a drink she would normally consume, but she needed to be awake and alert, though she was probably overloading her nervous system with adrenalin. There were plenty of natural hormones circulating around her body without the need to add the viciousness of the synthetic component she was ingesting.

Russ was doing the same thing. He was an everyday coffee drinker, and it wouldn't have as much of an affect as it would for Claudia.

'We've got a request in on his phone, haven't we? To locate it the minute it comes back online?'

Russ agreed that they had.

The last place the phone had placed him had been at the hotel. The fact that his phone was off was not good news. People didn't just turn their phones off. Though she had warned him when she left not to use his phone to tell the world about the exciting incident he happened to find himself in. Maybe this was his way of controlling the urge to Tweet or Facebook his situation?

She doubted it. In her experience, when missing persons' mobiles were off it was not because they were protecting themselves. It was usually because something bad had happened. Someone else had control of their phone and had switched it off in an effort to hide their location from police.

Claudia now moved away from the video and paced around the incident room. 'I don't understand what happened.'

She was lost. And she was afraid. For the second time in her life, she was truly afraid. The first time had been when Ruth was missing and they knew the Sheffield Strangler had her — what was it with these monsters' names? It made them almost appealing, and they most definitely weren't. Now a young man was missing, and most likely in the hands of another killer. The clock was ticking, and he was getting closer to meeting his death.

She was not only afraid because Zach was about to lose his life, but because she was at a loss as what to do, and that terrified her.

With her free hand she raked through her loose hair. 'We need to identify the location in the drawing. Immediately. It's the only way we have of saving Zach.'

Russ looked bleak. 'There was nothing in the image that gave the site away. There was a plain-looking house behind Zach and a pair of wings etched onto him. Maybe the killer's created the wings and will attach them to him? But other than that, the image is the blandest he's sent us.'

He was talking sense, but Claudia didn't want to admit it. She didn't want to admit defeat. 'We can't simply stand here and wait for someone to find him in the morning, Russ. We have to be active. We have to save his life. He trusted us to do that for him.' She sank into the nearest chair.

The incident room was silent without all the staff in the space. She checked her watch. It was 3.15 a.m. 'Let's get everyone in.'

Russ put his mug down. 'You're sure?'

'We have a large contingent of uniformed officers working this with us, but it's not enough. I can't sit on my hands while Zach Williams is a hair's breadth away from death. And if getting the team in and putting up with tired faces for the rest of the day is the price I have to pay, then so be it.'

Russ gave a curt nod and pulled his mobile phone out of his pocket. 'I'll get onto it.'

'Thanks. I appreciate it. Leave Lisa and Krish in place, though. We don't know that Williams didn't leave of his own accord because he was homesick. Either he or the killer could still turn up at his home address.'

She walked away and left Russ making calls, waking the team up and getting them in during this desperate time.

Claudia strode through to the viewing room, where a row of uniform cops were glued to the television screens, watching the night and waiting for signs of their victim or their killer. 'Anything?' she asked, knowing that if any of them had found anything they'd have jumped straight up and informed her. She chewed down on her bottom lip, desperate to know something. Anything.

They shook their heads. 'Sorry, ma'am.'

'No sign of Williams?'

'No, ma'am.'

'Or anyone else acting suspiciously?'

'No, ma'am.'

There wasn't a camera outside the hotel, so Zach could easily have walked out without being seen. But to then have disappeared? To not have gone home? The resulting conclusion wasn't good, and Claudia stalked away from the viewing room disappointed with their lack of information for her.

Gradually the team filtered in. Claudia stomped about the incident room, waiting for a lead to break, but nothing happened. They'd had their big lead. They'd placed the image with the press and Zach had come forward for them. Then they'd taken him out of the way to what should have been a place of safety and yet here they were, accomplishing little, with no sign of Zach and a clock that was rapidly ticking down to what looked to be his demise.

CHAPTER 48

The Artist was pleased with himself. He'd watched Zach, the piece he'd needed for his art installation, being taken from his home by the police and had been hit by despair and panic. Panic that he could no longer complete the exhibit. But then he'd put his mind into gear and got back to work.

This was what thrilled him most, when his mind was alert and the thrill of everything coming together made his body thrum.

He of course had Zach Williams's phone number from being in the same fitness club. All he'd had to do was make a call with a mild threat against his parents, and he'd come running out to the car like a meek little lamb, following his directions to the staff exit to avoid the marked police car watching and waiting out front. All thought of his own safety was gone, so long as he, the Artist, promised to leave his parents out of it.

The stupid boy. The Artist had no idea who his parents were or where they lived. Zach hadn't even thought to confirm any of this. The threat had been enough to send Zach scuttling into his arms. Fear drove people to do the most ridiculous things. And this boy was no different.

And now he was as he needed him, in the car's boot. Ready to be installed in the exhibit.

CHAPTER 49

The call came in earlier than the clock had dictated. It was just after five. They'd had no chance, really. She was furious with the hotel staff for not noticing Zach walk out and furious with herself for not alerting them to their precious cargo and not putting someone on his door. Yes, they'd had a marked car outside and had an officer check on him every hour or so, but it hadn't been enough. Someone should have been outside his door. She'd thought her resources were best used elsewhere, that the killer would turn up at his home, not knowing he had been moved. Damn policing cuts and lack of staff. Of course, she'd had to let the majority of her staff leave at the end of the day yesterday, leaving her with critical resources only. They'd been on duty far too long as it was. They couldn't work through two days with no sleep. Lisa and Krish, who stayed to watch the house, would go home to sleep now. But the rest were now back in for another full day. They weren't robots who could do every job, though.

It had been confirmed the exit Zach had left by on the CCTV had taken him to the rear of the building, where there were no cameras and where the marked police vehicle had no line of sight on him. A small CSI team had checked around the exit but not picked up anything of value. He'd slipped out like a ghost, for all the fear he'd been holding onto.

Her mood was leaden as they headed out to Wincobank.

'Apparently,' said Russ beside her as he drove, 'they have a patch of green with multiple fanciful-looking chairs built on it. One chair has wings. It's this chair that Zach's been placed on.'

Her head dropped into her hands. 'So,' she mumbled through her fingers, 'if I hadn't been so determined that the image be cropped to only show Zach's face when putting it out with the press, if I'd allowed the whole image to be seen, someone might have recognised the chair at Wincobank and we could have been there waiting?'

Russ kept his attention on the road. Claudia was grateful for this. She didn't want to see the blame fire up in his eyes.

'You made an investigative decision to only show the part of the image that was needed at that point in time. To not show Zach as a dead body, which would frighten the public. There was no way you were to know it would all end like this. We had our hands on him. Your plan worked.'

She shook her head, regret for the loss of the young man's life welling up within her. She had no idea how she would contain it when they arrived on scene. This would be the first time she'd attended a murder where she had previously met the victim. Where she had tried to save the victim and had ultimately failed.

Russ hadn't sounded like he was blaming her, though. There was that to be grateful for. Though he might not blame her, she had plenty of blame to go around for the both of them.

It was a short journey to Wincobank. With no traffic on the roads at that time in the morning, they made it in fifteen minutes.

A cordon was already in place and Russ parked safely outside. An ambulance and a marked police vehicle were also at the scene. Claudia wondered if someone had been injured or if the person who found Zach's body had needed medical support.

They climbed out the car and immediately pulled on the white Tyvek suits which would allow them to enter the crime scene.

They were parked at the side of a village-type green space. On it, as Russ described, were various whimsical chairs, all made out of different materials. Claudia had seen nothing like it and was surprised she wasn't aware of their existence before. One chair was steel, and the back of the piece was formed into a stumpy wrinkled face. The chairs were scattered over the green rather than being uniform in their placing.

A tent had been erected over Zach and, Claudia imagined, the winged chair he was sitting in. As it was such a public place and Zach needed to remain in situ while the CSIs and the pathologist worked, it was better to cover him from prying eyes.

Gaining access through the cordon, Claudia and Russ made their way to the tent. Claudia's stomach twisted as they drew closer.

'Knock knock,' Russ said, pulling one of the door flaps to the side to gain entry.

Pathologist Nadira Azim turned from what she was doing. 'Ah, good morning. An early one for us today.' She noted Claudia's face. 'I'm sorry you weren't able to stop him.'

Claudia stared at the body in the large, wooden winged chair, as he'd been depicted in the drawing. The boy she had previously known as Zach was now a lifeless corpse. Just another victim, just another crime scene. The boy she had talked to was no longer here. Whatever he had been was snuffed out. Here was a shell that the real person, Zach Williams, had walked about in. Zach no longer had use for this body. There would be no more curling up on his sofa reading a good sci-fi book. Now the body was left for them to determine what and who had done this to him.

Claudia stepped forward, determination spurring her on. 'Me too. But now we do what we can to identify his killer and make him pay in court.'

Nadira inclined her head and returned her attention back to the body. 'You can see he's held in position by rope.' She pointed to his torso. 'There's a piece wrapped tightly under his arms, keeping him upright, otherwise he'd have slumped forward.'

Around her a CSI clicked away on his camera, photographing the scene, the body and the pathologist doing her work. All of it had to be evidenced. Every step logged meticulously.

'That's different to the drawing,' Claudia observed. 'I wonder how our killer feels about having to deviate from his plan. He obviously didn't realise he wouldn't be able to prop the body up.'

'He was able to adapt quickly though,' said Russ.

Claudia peered at the rope, strapped right through the middle of Zach's tattoo. 'What did that do to his mindset? Having to adjust like that. He obviously plans his murders meticulously because he can draw them out in such intricate detail. For someone who makes plans and shares them with the police in such an artful way, this must have really messed him up.'

'You think he's going to be spiralling because of this?' asked Russ.

'It's a possibility. You don't agree?'

He thought about what she'd said. 'He's a details man. You could be onto something. But what does him spiralling look like?'

She shrugged. 'I have no idea, and I don't really want to find out. Whatever it looks like, it's not going to be good news for us.'

Nadira coughed for their attention.

'Sorry.' Claudia stepped closer.

'It's fine. Interesting point about the rope. If you lean in, you'll be able to smell alcohol on our victim.'

Claudia wanted to scream at Nadira that he had a name. That the boy in the chair in front of them was Zach, but she clamped her teeth down and kept her mouth shut, leaning forward as she'd been instructed. 'Yes, I can smell it.'

'He would have had to drink quite an amount for us to smell it on him. Was he drinking when you saw him last?'

'No, and there was no alcohol in his room. He didn't order any with room service, we've seen his room service order. So, that means . . .'

'I'd suggest, bearing in mind there are no visible signs of injury that I can see so far, and I haven't seen his back yet, that it could be a mode of transmission for something.'

'He was poisoned?' Claudia stared at the pathologist.

'I never said that.' Her tone was rigid. Her face severe. 'You know I can't give you a cause of death in the field. What I'm doing is suggesting areas we can look at when I get him back to the lab.'

Claudia nodded. This killer was unlike most killers she'd ever come across. Whereas most serial killers tended to have the same or similar MO, this guy was all over the place. For the first murder he'd used a dagger and dug it deep into the victim's back. The second victim had been hanged by his hands and suffocated by the force of his own weight, and Zach looked like a possible poisoning.

'What are you thinking?' asked Russ.

'That this guy is unusual in that he doesn't have an MO.'

'You want to get a psychologist in?'

She watched Nadira work on Zach, or the remains of Zach. She couldn't see this person in front of her as Zach any longer and pondered the question. Did they need outside help? Was it admitting defeat or simply requesting another pair of hands? She had so much on her mind she wasn't sure she could think straight. Maybe she should run it by Sharpe and see what her opinion was. Or was that in itself a display of weakness? Not making the decision herself. Damn Tyler and his cellmate for screwing with her head. Damn this killer for taking Zach when they'd had him secured away. Or what they thought of as secured.

She'd failed him. She'd failed his family. She'd failed Ruth and her father.

Russ was looking at her. She had to get a grip. 'Let's wait and see if we get another drawing, shall we?'

He nodded his agreement. It sounded reasonable. There was no reason he would know she had struggled to think in a straight line.

'Can you get him on your table today?' she asked of Nadira.

'It won't be until late this afternoon, but yes, I'll get him on. I had a baby death come in last night, so I have that to do when I get back.'

Claudia shuddered. She hated those cases and was glad in a way they were busy dealing with this, so that her team hadn't picked that case up. So many times they were dreadful accidents. Parents falling asleep in precarious positions out of utter exhaustion. Sofas being the worst one. And little babies, unable to push themselves free when they slipped down the back of the sofa, their mother or father unaware of their predicament. The parents were beyond distraught. Of course, all such cases needed a full investigation, and there were times when an arrest was necessary and harm had been all the baby had experienced in life. These cases hurt her. Claudia hated to think how she would feel when she finally had children of her own.

'Thanks, Nadira. I appreciate it.'

Nadira balanced back on her heels. 'Look, I'm sure there was nothing else you could have done to prevent this, Claudia. Not if I know you.'

Claudia shrugged. The senselessness of the loss of this young man's life was nearly too much for her to bear. 'He was supposed to be in a safe place. We'd removed him from his home to protect him, and yet he still finds himself here and being transferred to your table. What does that say about my ability really, Nadira?'

The vehemence in Claudia's voice silenced the whole tent. The CSI even stopped what he was doing for a moment before realising this was none of his business and continuing his task.

'His body will talk to us. He'll tell us more about what happened. Hopefully it'll help you.'

'Shall we go and talk to the witness?' Russ asked with an obvious plan to get Claudia away from Zach's body.

She allowed herself to be steered away. 'Who found him?'

'A guy on his way to work. He was driving past and saw him sitting in the chair. Thought it looked a bit odd from the road, so stopped to see if the kid needed any help. It was only when he walked over he realised something was wrong and called the ambulance. Didn't know if he was dead or . . . I don't know, not quite dead. Unconscious.'

Claudia pulled the hood of her Tyvek suit down as they strode across the green towards the marked police vehicle that held their witness. Something had to break in this case because she wasn't about to let this killer keep playing his games this way.

CHAPTER 50

The exhibit had been opened to the public before the time he had planned for it to be. The time on the clock he'd drawn on the invitation had said 6 a.m. and yet someone had blundered in just after five.

The Artist rubbed his arms and thought about all the things he'd done wrong for this exhibit to go so disastrously.

First of all, he'd had to locate him and bring him out of hiding. Then, when placing him in the exhibit, it hadn't been as easy as he'd wanted it to be. Not at all like the drawing. The use of the rope destroyed the image he wanted to create, but there was no way to hold the boy up so that his wings sprang up from his back, without tying him to the chair.

It nearly broke him seeing the rope cross the boy's own image of the skull and wings. It was a beautiful mirror image, and having it split in two by the rope had been like having his own mind split in two.

And now the timings had been broken.

He wanted to scream. To shout into the void. How could he be expected to create perfection in art if people — stupid, stupid people — got in the way?

There was one person who was more to blame than any other. One person was messing up all his plans. She had hidden his artwork away from him. She had nearly cost him everything. She'd even got into his subject's brain and nearly made him brave enough to stand up to him, but fear of what might happen to his family had finally made him drink the cocktail of alcohol and drugs he'd given him. And finally, she was here, trampling all over his exhibit before opening time.

As though it were her exhibit.

Well, if that was what she wanted, he could help her out with that.

CHAPTER 51

The man who climbed out the marked police vehicle was overweight, with unruly black hair and hanging jowls, wearing a high-vis jacket that had the word 'Security' on the back.

'You were on your way to work?' asked Claudia.

'Yeah. I work at an industrial site in the city. It's an early start. That's why I was on the road, you see.'

'Can you tell me what happened?'

The guy could easily answer the question with a yes, but Claudia hoped he would use it as an invitation to open up about the morning's events. Most witnesses liked to tell their story, so much so that you got a lot of waffle and extraneous detail you didn't need. But in a murder enquiry there was little that was extraneous. You never knew when the smallest piece of information could break a case.

'I was on my way out to work when I saw him,' the man said. 'It was getting light, and because he's half-naked he glowed in the early sun. He's pretty pale.' The man paused, recognition dawning on his face that it could have been because the lad was dead that his skin was so pasty.

'Go on,' encouraged Claudia.

'I thought he was in trouble. I actually thought he might be a druggy and it might have been an overdose. After all, most sensible people aren't around at this time of day, are they? Never mind half dressed.'

Claudia smiled in response. The aim was not to put words in his mouth, but to be grateful for what he had already said.

'I got a right shock when I approached him. Yeah, I were expecting something, like I said, but he were tied to the chair. You don't do that to yourself, do you?'

Claudia waited for him to continue. People tended to fill the silence.

'I weren't going to touch him and feel for a pulse. If he were dead, I didn't fancy touching that. I've never even seen a dead body before. So I called an ambulance. They were the ones who called you out. Seems you really can't tie yourself to a chair in the middle of the street.'

CHAPTER 52

Dominic was dealing with the house-to-house enquiries. As the sergeant, he was organising the teams, but he was also supporting them by attending a couple of addresses himself. He'd paired a detective from the task force with a uniform cop to visit each address.

It was highly unlikely they would get anything of use due to the hour of the day. Most people were in bed, but it had to be done.

What most rankled him was that Russ was coupled up with Claudia yet again. It was Claudia's duty to split the work fairly, but as far as Dominic could see, she was still leaning on Russ and leaving him out in the cold.

He walked up the narrow pathway to the house he was attending. It directly faced the green that the chairs were built on. Most likely the house that was depicted in the drawing.

He was happy to work alone. He didn't need a uniform presence to aid him with the knock. He was in no mood to make small talk.

Maybe Claudia was making him pay for the fact that Lawton had put Tyler in the spotlight for killing Ruth. Not that she could possibly know he had anything to do with it. Maybe it was just her way of avoiding family while she processed her feelings. Another reason they should never have both been placed on the same team.

He rapped on the closed door, hard enough to wake its sleeping residents. It was possible most were up with all the activity in front of their homes.

It wasn't as though the powers that be knew there was a huge underlying issue when they put him and Claudia together. If they were any 'normal' father and daughter, it wouldn't be a problem. But killing her step-mother and tampering with evidence when she asked difficult questions made the working relationship rather challenging.

As for Russ, in the main he liked the guy. But he wouldn't allow him to put Dominic's own career on hold while he took all the glory. He would have to think about how to deal with that.

It was one problem after another.

The door opened and a mother with a child on her hip peered quizzically at Dominic. 'Hello, can I help you?'

He flashed her his ID. 'DS Dominic Harrison, South Yorkshire Police.' He indicated the green behind him with his head. 'You've probably seen the activity behind me this morning.' He was banking on it as the baby was small and had in all likelihood had her up early. 'I'm wondering if I can ask you a couple of questions?'

The woman looked beyond Dominic to the white tent hiding Zach's body. 'What happened?'

'We can't go into details, but we'd love your help.' Zach's family hadn't been informed yet. There was no way they could leak the murder until they were aware.

She turned to check the house behind her. People, especially people with kids, worried about what strangers thought of their homes. New mothers were not usually on top of the tidying.

'I won't keep you long, and it would be really helpful,' Dominic pushed.

Finally she relented and stepped back, allowing him access. Dominic entered her home just as her husband

— he'd seen a ring on her finger — walked down the stairs, dressing gown wrapped around his slender torso.

'What's happening?' He rubbed his eyes.

'This police officer wants to talk to me about the incident over the road.'

'There's an incident over the road?' He yawned.

Dominic could see the fillings at the back of his mouth.

The baby grumbled.

'Do you mind if I sort his breakfast out while we talk?' the mother asked.

'No problem at all.' Dominic followed her into a bright and airy kitchen-cum-diner and the husband followed behind him.

'I told you something was happening on the green,' she said to her husband as she dumped the baby in a highchair. 'You snored in response, though.'

She huffed at him — disgusted, Dominic imagined, that she was up early with the baby while he managed to sleep through everything. He remembered the fractious times when Claudia was little. The digs about who was doing what. Who had done the last feed or changed the last nappy or had the least amount of sleep, as though it were a competition.

'Have a seat.' She waved at the chairs around the circular table in the room's corner.

The husband clicked the kettle on. 'Can I make you one?'

'A coffee would be good, thanks. It's been an early start.' Not that Dominic needed to remind this couple.

The woman stirred some porridge in a plastic bowl while the baby waited patiently, and Dominic realised he still didn't have the couple's names. He opened his notebook and asked for their details.

'Julia and David Stewart,' the woman answered as she carried the baby's bowl across the room and sat down, pulling the high chair around so it faced her.

Dominic made a note. 'Thank you.'

The baby guzzled his breakfast with barely disguised excitement. The first meal of the day and he was ready for it. His pudgy little hands patted the tray of the high chair and his mouth opened and closed around the spoon as his mother fed him.

Quickly, a steaming mug of coffee was placed in front of Dominic, the smell waking up any still-sleeping brain cells.

He looked up. 'Thank you.'

David smiled and scratched his scalp, still trying to get his head around what he'd woken up to. Dominic sensed it was not normal to wake to a stranger in his house.

Now they were settled, Dominic started on his reason for being here. 'What can you tell me about this morning?'

Again David looked bemused. He rose and walked to the front of the house and peered out of the window. Dominic heard a low 'Oh' as he took in the activity beyond. The ambulance, the police vehicles. The white tent that signified a body beneath it. He returned to the kitchen, looking even paler than when he'd left.

Julia looked up from what she was doing and shook her head. It was clear who had things in order here. No doubt her husband had the excuse that he needed to go to work. And no sooner had the thought gone through Dominic's mind than David took a sip of his coffee before saying, 'I sleep through so much as I'm up for work early. Then I help with the baby when I get home. It's a busy household, as you can see.'

Dominic nodded his agreement, not daring to put a foot in either camp of this family. It was a delicate balancing act, and he couldn't remember how good he'd been when Claudia was small. Of course, he'd still been working and her mother had taken maternity leave, so he might have been guilty of allowing her to take the bulk of the work through the night. Listening to the more modern fathers in the office, though, they appeared to lend more of a helping hand.

'Noah stirred.' Julia brought Dominic back to the question he'd asked of the couple. 'That was what woke me initially. He's eight months, so he's in his own room.' She continued to shovel his food into his greedy little mouth. 'His room is at the front of the house. We use a baby monitor.

There was a car in the background. I thought it unusual for being so late in the night. Or early in the morning. However you want to look at it.'

A thrill ran up Dominic's spine. This woman might have actually seen something. He kept his stance relaxed so that she could continue to tell her story and took a sip of his own coffee. It was good. Just what he needed. 'What did you do?' He pushed for her to proceed.

The baby had finished his porridge and Julia rose and started to make a bottle. Moving easily around the kitchen, placing the dirty bowl and spoon in the dishwasher while waiting for the bottle-filling machine to finish. They never had anything so flash when he was a new dad.

'I saw to Noah first. He was grumbling because he'd lost his dummy. I never wanted him to have one, but it's the only way he settles at night. He can't put it back in himself yet, so when he wakes without it he lets me know, and I have to get out of bed to settle him.'

Dominic allowed her to ramble off topic. Some officers, less experienced officers, would attempt to guide her to the path they wanted her on. But Dominic was aware that as she talked and as she placed herself in her child's room at the right time this morning, she would be right there where he needed her to be, in her mind. She may or may not have witnessed something important, and that was what they were about to find out.

He sipped his coffee again, savouring the warmth. The aroma was waking his body.

Julia sat back down with the baby's bottle and leaned it towards the still-hungry mouth, which was open like a baby bird. The teat was soon enveloped and the baby once again happy.

'It took me a while to settle him,' Julia continued. 'It was still dark, but I had the sense daylight was not far away.'

June brought early mornings. Unless you had blackout blinds or heavy curtains, the day woke you at an unreasonable hour. Dominic understood the feeling of daylight being not far away, sensing it about to break.

'Eventually Noah settled, and I remembered the car engine I heard. I looked out of Noah's window. I worry about cars being broken into or houses being burgled through the night. So I'm alert to sounds I might hear when I'm awake with Noah.'

Dominic leaned forward.

David's mouth was open slightly. He glanced at the time on the microwave. Dominic presumed he would need to get ready for work but wouldn't want to miss what his wife had to say.

'I couldn't see anything. If there had been a car, it had gone.'

Dominic was deflated. David's mouth closed.

'But there was someone sitting in one of the chairs on the green. They had their back to me. The winged seat has its back to the house. The wings are rather large. All I could see was a rough outline of their body and the tip of their head. The size of the chair hid the majority of them. I couldn't even see if it was a male or a female.' She put her free hand up to her mouth as she shook her head. 'I had no idea there was anything wrong. To be honest, tiredness overwhelmed me.'

She turned to David, who looked down at his feet then at the clock on the microwave again before rising.

'I have to get ready for work.' He returned his gaze to Julia. 'Will you be okay? Do you want me to take the day off and stay with you?'

She looked worn out. Like relaying the early morning/late night's events had taken it out of her. And Dominic hadn't finished questioning her yet. 'We're going to need a statement, Julia. I don't know if you'll need someone to look after Noah or not while we do it,' Dominic said in response to David's question.

David looked put out that Dominic had answered instead of Julia, but Dominic just continued to sip at his now-cooling coffee while the couple sorted out their domestic arrangements.

He wished they would hurry, as Julia hadn't finished relaying this morning's events. Dominic wanted every detail from her.

David dropped back into his seat, resigned to the fact that his morning at least was going to be scuppered, and picked up his own coffee mug again.

'What happened next?' Dominic asked of Julia, bringing her attention back to the subject at hand.

She shook her head. 'I closed the curtain and left them there. I presumed they were waiting for someone. Though it was a little early. Oh, first I checked our car in front of the house hadn't been tampered with. That was fine, so I headed back to bed.'

'The car you mentioned hearing, what make or model was it?'

'It wasn't in sight by the time I opened the curtain to have a look outside. You think I missed something important?'

It was clear she'd missed the killer dropping Zach Williams's body off. What Dominic needed was a timeframe. 'Did you check the time when you woke?'

Julia paused. Dominic watched the question running through her head. The neurons searching for the answer. Again, he remembered back long ago to the early days of Claudia being so small and the haze that enveloped you.

'I'm sure I checked the time when I heard Noah but . . .' She pulled the teat out of Noah's mouth to allow milk to flow where his suckling was creating air blocks. His greedy little mouth searching out the bottle his mother had removed from him until she replaced it. She rubbed her forehead. 'I think it was probably around three forty-five.'

'That's really helpful. Thank you.'

'The person on the chair, under the tent, what was it?' Julia asked.

Dominic frowned.

'Was it a man or a woman?'

'He was a man.'

'You think he's anything to do with the guy in the papers?' asked David. 'The one they're calling the Artist?'

'It's not a name we've given him. And at this time we don't know what we're dealing with until we take him back to the mortuary and inform his next of kin.'

Silence fell in the kitchen, leaving just the sound of a greedy suckling baby.

CHAPTER 53

The Artist hadn't been able to get any sleep. He had expected no one to be up and about so early, and it irked him that things hadn't gone to plan. A simple phone call would have sent the police to the right location at the right time, but people, people, they were such an unknown quantity.

Now he had to plan his next installation with detailed precision. Especially with the focus of the exhibit he had planned being the most difficult yet.

But planning was what would get him through it.

He would need to identify a location. Somewhere fantastical. Somewhere that topped everything he had used so far. This was to be his crowning glory.

Could Sheffield produce that for him?

His head was spinning with the thoughts that whirled through his mind.

He could not fail this time.

They would witness his greatness. It would be there for all to see when he displayed the next and final exhibit. After this, there would be no need to show his work any further. This would be his jewel in the crown. And he wanted to move on it sooner rather than later.

His heart raced with excitement at the thought of where he was going next. No need to worry about the failures of the last one. Focus on the next piece of art. Move forward. Always forward. It was an artist's life. To always create. He would show Sheffield what he was made of.

CHAPTER 54

Claudia paced around the incident room like a caged tiger.

She was utterly furious.

Zach had been in their protection and they had failed him. He had succumbed to the wanker the press had named the Artist.

'What a ridiculous name,' she shouted out at no one in particular.

Blank, pale faces stared back at her, afraid of the fury she would rain down on them.

'What is?' Dominic asked. One person who would not be kowtowed by her.

'The Artist,' she hissed. 'A name for someone who creates beauty. What we see from this killer is not beauty. It's ugly and stark and vile.' She turned and paced again, running out of steam a little now.

'We can't help what the press do, Claudia,' Dominic pushed back. The rest of the room sat in continued silence, grateful for his presence this morning. Even Russ Kane, her battle-hardy second, was quiet.

It wasn't about the name at all. It was about the incompetence, and yet she couldn't scream at them for that. Because the incompetence was down to her, not them. But that was indeed what she wanted to do. She wanted to scream the place down and blame someone for the shitshow that she was standing in the middle of, that had allowed Zach Williams to die the way he had.

So instead she turned and railed on Dominic. 'What the fuck? If I want to bitch about the ridiculousness of this killer's media-given name, I damn well will and no one here is going to bloody well stop me. Do you hear me?' She was absolutely raging.

Dominic rose from his chair. His hands curled into fists at his sides.

Russ also rose to standing. 'Claudia?' His voice was calm.

Her head snapped around to look at him, her attention drawn away from Dominic. From the fists at his sides. The pulse hammering in his jaw.

But Dominic wasn't having the interference. 'Russ, I don't need your help here.' His tone was flat with a sharp edge.

'I was talking to Claudia, Dom.'

No one else moved. To Claudia it was as though the room itself was holding its breath, waiting to see who would back down first. The energy was exploding from inside her like a volcano, but Dominic had risen to her display of temper with one of his own. She could see the fear in her team's eyes. No one knew what a clash between these two titans would look like. And in the middle was Russ, calm and quiet but no less fiery. Claudia knew he'd hold his ground. But his stance was different. His reason for being involved was not the same as hers and Dominic's. Whereas they were escalating, Russ was there to dampen the fire.

Both Dominic and Claudia turned on Russ immediately.

'I don't need . . .'

'She doesn't need . . .'

They glared at each other.

Russ took a step closer to Claudia. 'Shall we take this into your office?' he asked quietly.

'She doesn't need mollycoddling, Russ,' Dominic spat.

Claudia straightened her spine. Dominic pushed back his shoulders.

'We don't need to do this in here.' Russ's voice was level and calm, like silk.

'I'd listen to Russ if I were you, DI Nunn.' The voice was like an electric shock through the room. It had appeared from nowhere. Everyone had been so engrossed in the action in the middle of the incident room that no one had seen Sharpe enter. Her heels, which usually gave her entry away, were hidden beneath the animosity being thrown about by the father and daughter.

'Ma'am.' Claudia lowered her stance. Brought the anger down a notch. Recognising where she had nearly allowed things to go, shame flooded her system.

'Like DS Kane said, not in here. Your office, shall we?' And without waiting for an invitation she strode straight into Claudia's office, followed quickly by Claudia.

Russ and Dominic looked at her and she shook her head. She'd deal with this alone. They were to go back to their desks. This was over.

'Close the door,' Sharpe instructed as Claudia moved into her office.

She pushed the door to.

Sharpe narrowed her eyes. 'What the hell did I just walk in on?' She was sitting in Claudia's chair, waiting for answers.

Claudia stayed standing like a naughty schoolgirl in the headmistress's office, rather than a detective inspector in her own space, in control of her own team. Though a minute ago she really hadn't been in control of anyone, least of all herself.

She deserved to feel ashamed of herself.

She deserved the look Sharpe was bearing down on her.

It wasn't as though she had any answers for Sharpe. Anger had been driving her. Pure unadulterated rage that Zach had been murdered when she'd thought he was in her care.

Claudia ran a hand through her hair.

Sharpe softened. 'You thought you had him — the victim,' she clarified as though Claudia needed it.

Claudia gave a short nod, then crossed her arms over her body.

'We can't save everyone.' Sharpe visibly relaxed. The lines on her face that had been like ravines when she'd entered the incident room were mere wisps on her skin now. She stared at Claudia standing in front of her. 'But whatever occurred, Claudia, there's no way I can be walking in on what was happening just then.' The softness was gone from her face. 'Do you understand me?'

'I'm sorry you had to see that.'

'You're sorry I had to see that or you're sorry it happened? I'd much prefer the latter. The first one indicates you wish you hadn't been caught.' She would clearly not take any shit this morning. And certainly not from her detective inspector.

Claudia dipped her head. 'I'm sorry it happened. I don't know what got into me. It should never have got out of hand like that. I should never have allowed it to get to that place.'

'And can you sort it out? It looked like it was about to get physical, and I can't have my sergeants brawling in front of the team and the inspector allowing it — in fact, not only allowing it, but instigating it.' Sharpe was brittle.

Claudia was suitably chastised. Unsure herself what had happened, she did not know how to explain it to her supervisor. 'I can only apologise, ma'am. Emotions are obviously running high. I let it get out of control. I'm sorry. I'll sort it out.'

'You're damn right you will,' Sharpe snapped. Then she looked at Claudia and leaned back in the chair. Claudia's chair. And softened.

'Leaving the disgrace of what I saw aside, I can understand why the team is struggling.'

Claudia should have felt better, but Sharpe's melting only served to remind her of her failing. Of Zach's murder. Of the lively boy he'd been only hours earlier. Of the life he'd had ahead of him where now he had none.

'But you have to focus on where you go from here,' Sharpe continued. 'You can't do anything about what has already happened. You lost the boy. It's a fact. Now you can get justice for him by tracking the bastard down who did this and putting him before a court. Not fighting among yourselves. That does nothing for him. It certainly does nothing in the battle we have to identify and locate his killer. He's a smart man. We need to be even smarter. Remind me we why we put this task force together, Claudia. Find him and bring him in.

'You and Dominic work so differently, that's one of the reasons we put you together. You work by the book, Dominic works more by the seat of his pants. Don't think we don't know that. But he colours just outside the lines enough to get things done. We can cope with his ignoring of the rules because it gets results. You're a by-the-book kind of copper, the kind we need in charge, but you have a good nose. Together you can do this. We need you to do this.'

Claudia hadn't thought about the fact that Sharpe and Connelly had initially put the task force together with just her and Dominic. Since then, she'd focused on creating the team she wanted to have around her. She hadn't considered the reason both of them had been selected. Or that Dominic's unusual policing style had worked in his favour rather than against him in this case.

Because he was her father, she often became irritated by his walking to his own beat. Of course he'd been doing the job a lot longer than she had and he felt he knew better, but she had rank on him.

She scrubbed at her face. It was such a mess.

'Are you listening?' Sharpe pushed.

'Yes. Yes, I'm listening. I was just thinking about Dominic.'

'You two *can* work together, can't you? Do we have to step in and rearrange the task force for you?'

This caught Claudia's attention. 'No. No, you do not. Dominic and I can work perfectly well together.'

'That's not what I was seeing a couple of minutes ago. It looked like Russell Kane was getting in the middle of the two of you.'

'It was my fault,' she admitted. 'I allowed my emotions to get the better of me, and Dominic didn't take it well. Family react to each other a little differently than your usual team members would.'

Sharpe tapped her fingers on the desk. 'I came in here to get an update. This latest development isn't going to play out well in the media. Whatever this is that's going on between you and Dominic, don't let it interfere in the investigation.'

'It's already over, ma'am.'

Sharpe gave a curt nod. 'Tell me what we have. I have to liaise with the press officer so we can release a statement.'

Claudia's stomach sank. She was positive the killer was getting off on the media attention. With the flair he put into the scenes he set and the name the press had given him, it was a given he was lapping it all up.

She would find him and she would make him pay.

CHAPTER 55

Informing a victim's parents or guardians got no easier, and this was the case with Zach's mother and father. They had been a close, supportive family who had enjoyed spending time together, even though Zach had recently moved out of home to live alone. They had been proud of his independence.

Zach's father was tall, and Claudia could see where Zach got his dark and brooding eyes from. There was a real resemblance to the man.

His mother on the other hand was petite but with a midlife expansion around her middle. It made her look comfortable and welcoming.

Following Sharpe's conversation, Claudia had brought Dominic with her to the Williams family home.

The couple were warm and polite until the news was broken and their world was shattered forever.

'We spoke with Zach last night,' Claudia said.

'He said something about the police. What happened?' Through her heartbreak, Zach's mother grasped onto this last sentence. Her son was alive last night. He had been safe with the police. How could this be true?

'We were concerned his life was at risk and we placed him in a secure location . . .' Claudia tailed off at the absurdity of what she'd said. Sharpe had told her to be careful when breaking this piece of information to the family. Sharpe, the one who was worried about legal proceedings more than the grief of loved ones.

Dominic stayed quiet. He would allow her to work her way through this. She had been the one who had been there last night and should be the officer to explain the circumstances.

Zach's father picked up where Claudia had paused. 'Secure?' His voice hitched.

Claudia's stomach jumped.

'Secure? How can you say it was secure when you're here informing us our child is dead?' The sound in the room was loud and violent. 'How secure do you think it was, Detective Inspector Nunn?' Tears were streaming down his face. Fury and grief mingled in a raw emotional telling of his pain.

Claudia's breath caught in her chest as she attempted to bring together the words she needed to calm the room and explain the situation as it had occurred. There was no way to explain it, of course. She had failed Zach. It was her fault Zach was in one of Nadira's refrigerators waiting for her to perform a post-mortem. 'We . . .' She used the plural for the police service rather than laying the well-deserved blame at her own door. 'We don't know what happened, and that will form a part of the investigation. He was secure when we . . .' We again. '. . . left him. We, as much as you, want to know what transpired and how he ended up leaving his accommodation and being . . .' She lost the rest of the sentence. She never normally found it as difficult to issue death messages. Although the emotion of the family inevitably washed over her, she usually steeled herself for what was to come before entering a home. Today was different. With the blame firmly planted at her feet, she was fumbling to deal with the family, their pain and finding her words. '. . . how we find ourselves here today,' she finished.

Zach's father rose from his chair and exploded, spittle flying from his mouth, his eyes popping from his head. 'You dare come here and tell us our son is dead, murdered no less, and you have the nerve to tell us you want to know what happened after you had him supposedly safe last night?'

His wife's face mirrored his own rage, but shock and grief were the strongest emotions breaking through.

Claudia was helpless against his righteous anger. How could she defend herself and her team when she placed the blame squarely on her own shoulders? She would have to bear this torrent of fury. Wait him out and allow him his rage. It wouldn't help him, but it would provide him a release.

She made no excuses. There were none to give.

Claudia left the family broken, but with a promise that she would do her level best to bring their son's killer to justice. A promise that was as vague as it was supportive. She hadn't promised she would bring him justice. She hadn't promised his killer would be brought down within any specific timeframe, and she hadn't promised to never stop hunting him. All she could do was tell them she would try, and she would.

A family liaison officer, or FLO, would be assigned to the Williamses later today. It would have to be a sensitive posting bearing in mind the difficulties the couple had with the police. But it was a necessary one. Zach's parents might have information they didn't realise they were holding on how their son had known his killer. Because, to Claudia, looking at what they had in front of them, he had gone willingly. No one had entered the hotel looking for him. He'd left of his own accord, knowing how dangerous that would be. His family were the people who knew him best. A FLO would work with them to learn as much as they could about Zach and try to paint a picture of the young man and how his actions could have played out last night.

Claudia desperately needed to know how things had gone so wrong.

They climbed into their car outside the Williamses' home, and it was then that Dominic spoke. 'You can't shoulder all the blame, Claudia. You made a decision last night that you thought was the right one. With staffing levels, Zach placed in a safe place, and the killer still outstanding, you decided you needed officers guarding Zach's home address, where you presumed the killer would automatically think he would be. It was a simple decision, really.' He turned the vehicle on and it growled. The sun shone through the windows and Claudia pushed the electric button for the window to lower, allowing air to circulate.

Dominic was talking sense, but it didn't help her subconscious, which was beating her mercilessly.

'We need to make inroads in this investigation,' she said. 'This killer is taking the piss. It's time we turned the tables on him and showed him this isn't his game. We're as capable of playing it as he is.'

CHAPTER 56

A few days passed and once again they were struggling with leads. Claudia had taken to running before work to wake her body and mind up. It meant rising early, but she enjoyed that time of the day. The sound of the birds as they talked to each other in the otherwise empty, quiet streets. Only the odd car drove by on the way to a job that demanded a ridiculously early start.

She enjoyed the peace the time of day gave her and the endless beat the rhythm of her feet provided.

The investigation ran through her mind as her feet trod asphalt, one foot in front of the other. One breath after the other. Everything even and calm.

They had two witnesses to the Zach Williams murder, but they were no help in furthering the case. One had found his body, and the other had heard the vehicle that had brought him to his display place and in turn created a timeline. But neither had given them a lead on the killer.

Claudia's heart vibrated a little harder against her breastbone as her feet pounded the ground and the Artist's name ran through her head. A name that continued to rattle her to her core.

He'd continued to receive near adulation from the press after Zach's murder, and yet the investigation team had been eviscerated. Not that she could blame them for turning on the police. She shouldered that blame and refused to allow any of her team to accept it. They'd discussed it in a briefing, the first day a paper turned on them asking how Zach was killed under their noses. As a team they'd supported her — in their view, she'd done what she could, and if any of them were going down they'd go down together.

It wasn't how it worked, though.

Not in policing. The powers that be liked to throw someone under the bus. They liked a scapegoat.

Claudia heard feet coming up behind her. She didn't flinch. The runner had passed her the last couple of mornings. A fit male who ran with his hood up and his concentration to the floor as he pounded the ground past and away from her until he was out of sight. She never saw him again until he passed her again the following morning.

Like clockwork, head bent, he ran around her, feet moving easily. Claudia continued forward. It wasn't a race. She kept her own pace. It would be very easy when travelling in the same direction as another runner to pick up your speed and try to keep up with them, but she was here to ease her mind before a busy day at work, not smooth her ego in a race.

Sharpe, she mused, had talked to her privately that morning, the morning the press had come down hard on her, knowing she would wonder if she'd be the force scapegoat. She'd told her in no uncertain terms she needed to pull something out of the bag to turn this around. She pulled no punches. Claudia took it in her stride.

Sharpe would always tell her the truth as she saw it.

But how was she to pull it out of the bag? This killer was good. She hated to admit that. She hated that he was clever, intelligent. But that's what they were faced with.

Her heartbeat stayed steady as she followed her regular route. Her feet and her body in tune with the map she had set out.

Her head, however, was another matter. Her mind was a tumultuous mess where the failures of the current case vied for attention with her confused thoughts regarding the statement Lawton had made claiming that Tyler had indeed murdered Ruth.

It didn't ring true.

Tyler had not long ago pleaded with her to listen to him. That he had not killed Ruth because she had not had a child. He was punishing women who left children home alone, to follow their own selfish needs. Putting their children at risk, as he'd once been left at risk. With the scars to prove it.

Claudia had listened to him. She had leaned in to his story and had believed him. She hadn't known what she would do with that belief, but believe him she did. And now his cellmate, this Lawton, was saying Tyler had quietly admitted to him that he had killed the copper Ruth Harrison, as he had killed the others. The lipstick in the grave went to prove that. How stupid could the cops really be to think he hadn't killed her?

But there was one issue with this. One anomaly. There was a lipstick at the place Ruth had been taken from. At her home address blood had been found, signs of a fight. It was Ruth's blood. And with that blood the signature lipstick, like a note telling cops that the Sheffield Strangler had taken her. But this hadn't occurred with any of the other women. So why, then, had he left a lipstick there? Wouldn't it be enough to leave one in the ground, as with the others?

One foot in front of the other. The rhythm beating up through her body. A regular drum as her mind whirled.

It was likely Tyler would be convicted of Ruth's murder with so much evidence against him, plus the latest statement from Lawton. But it didn't feel right to her. She'd have to find time within this current investigation to talk to her father about it.

With this ongoing case they hadn't been able to get together as she wanted. This was important, though. Her own thoughts were a jumbled mess. Heavens knew what her father's were. He was a stoic man and would keep his thoughts to himself. She would have to prod him to find out, and prod him she would. This was too significant to allow to go unchallenged. Ruth deserved justice but someone was playing games. Be it Lawton or Tyler, she wanted the truth, and she was sure her father would quietly be brooding on the issue as well. Together they would talk it through and see what they could resolve.

CHAPTER 57

An email was waiting for Claudia when she sat down at her desk that morning. The results from the tox screen and on Zach's stomach contents had come through, and Nadira had forwarded them straight on to her. She was obviously an early bird as well.

Claudia returned the email with her thanks.

Now she had the attention of the team as the morning briefing commenced. The last few days had been a subdued affair. Not because of a lack of interest, but because no results had been forthcoming. This morning she had something to feed them.

It would buck them up. Revitalise them.

She paced in front of the room, printout in hand. 'It was a challenge to ascertain Zach Williams's cause of death during the post-mortem,' she said. 'It wasn't as obvious as the previous victims and was made all the more difficult by the fact that the killer—' she continued to refuse to call him the Artist if she possibly could — 'changed MO with every kill. Well, this morning we have an answer to that illusive question. Nadira has sent me the results through of his stomach contents and tox screen, and this was where the explanation lay.'

There were mumblings around the room. She waited for them to quiet again.

'Our killer fed Zach a mixture of alcohol, specifically a large quantity of whiskey, along with pain medication — codeine and diazepam, again, both in rather large quantities. He wanted to make sure they did the job.'

'How easy is it to get hold of these drugs?' asked Lisa.

'I don't know. It's a line of enquiry for someone to follow up. They're dangerous drugs. You can't buy diazepam over the counter. You can buy low-level codeine but not in the amounts we're talking about. So he's either being prescribed them and has used his own supply or he's acquired them somehow, and that's another line of enquiry. How do you buy these drugs when you can't get them over the counter? I don't imagine there's any point looking at patients who use them. In a city this size I'm thinking the numbers are quite high.'

Knowing how Zach died was not helping her come to terms with his death. The days between finding him and now had been difficult. The blame had seeped into her subconscious and buried itself deep. There had been no way to dig it out. Not that she had wanted to dig it out. She deserved for it to be there. Now she knew he had been forced to drink whiskey laced with the products of his demise, in all likelihood knowing that was what he was doing — drinking to his death, the fear enveloping him — her own guilt smothered her further. She had been with him, he had thought himself safe. How had this happened?

Halfway through the briefing, an envelope appeared at Claudia's side. She recognised it immediately, and she was torn. Should she open it before the crime scene unit processed it to find out what was inside or do as protocol dictated and wait for them to do their thing?

It wasn't as though they had ever managed to gather anything of evidential value from the envelopes or their contents when they had been delivered.

Dominic rose from his chair. 'It's him.'

She admitted it was.

He dialled for the CSU and requested their immediate attendance. 'Someone is on their way.'

'This is a bloody quick turnaround for him,' Graham noted.

It was, and Claudia didn't like that he was escalating this way. 'It feels like something has upset him.'

'You think because we got to his victim before he did?' Russ asked. 'It made him change what he was doing. Not many people like having their plans changed.'

Claudia's fingers were itching to open the envelope. Instead, she gripped one hand inside the other like she was shaking hands with herself. 'You could have a point there. But if he didn't want us to be ahead of him that way, then why would he send us these drawings? It doesn't make sense.'

'Nothing about him makes sense,' said Rhys.

'Open the envelope,' said Dominic. 'You're not going to destroy evidence by opening it. We've proved that time and again with the last ones he's delivered. Just place a sheet of paper below the envelope as you open it so it can catch any debris that may fall.'

She stared at him, understanding where he was coming from. The instinct to do as he said strong within her. But her training to follow the rulebook was equally as strong, and this time, with a CSI on their way, being a rulebook follower won out. She paced across the front of the room, desperate to open the letter and yet leaving it in place where it lay. 'I opened the previous envelopes and we didn't retrieve any evidence from them. Maybe that was because I opened them. If I do it properly this time around maybe we'll catch a break?'

Dominic huffed at her but kept his own counsel.

Eventually a CSI wandered in. She was wearing a Tyvek suit and a large camera hung around her neck. Claudia breathed a sigh of relief and directed her to the envelope sitting on an empty desk at the front of the room, where she had been perched earlier during the briefing.

She started by photographing it in situ and worked quietly and diligently from there. 'I wouldn't normally open the envelope until we were forensically ready to, but we're aware of the ticking clock involved with this case. So I'm prepared to open the letter for you and work on it afterwards back at the lab. I'll photograph the drawing inside and email it to one of you if you want to give me an email address to send it to.'

Claudia looked at the room. 'Dominic, give her yours. You can put the image on the screen as soon as you get it and then forward it to the rest of the team.'

He nodded and reeled off his email address. The CSI tapped the letters into her camera screen and proceeded to tentatively open the sealed envelope.

The incident room collectively held their breath.

This was another job waiting to be started.

They hadn't resolved or moved forward with any of the other three victims that had been their cases so far, and yet here they were waiting for the image of a fourth victim to drop in their laps.

Claudia could barely stand the tension and paced some more across the front of the room, time slowing to a crawl. Her scalp prickling, she ran a hand through her hair and clawed at her scalp with her nails.

The folded sheet was finally pulled free of the envelope and the room breathed a light sigh.

Dominic's computer screen was on and waiting for the email to come through.

The process the CSI was working through was slow. Claudia wanted to dash up to her and yank the sheet from her hands and open it so she could see what they had to deal with next. But she held herself back. They had a procedure to go through.

The envelope was placed into a plain brown paper bag and sealed. An exhibit label was signed and attached. It was secure and ready for proper forensic examination. Now they could move onto the drawing, presuming it was a drawing inside. It had been a drawing all the previous times. It had to be a drawing this time.

A terrible sickness overwhelmed Claudia as she considered the prospect of the sheet in front of the CSI not being what they were all presuming it to be. Not being a drawing of a victim, but turning out to be something altogether more horrific.

What that was, she had no idea.

But making assumptions was not a good look for the task force. She'd learned that the hard way with her presumption that the killer would be unable to get to his last victim at his 'secure location'. She would talk about it with them after the CSI had gone.

With gentle fingers the CSI opened up the sheet of paper. Claudia couldn't see the contents properly from where she was, but it looked to be a drawing.

She breathed a sigh of relief. But it meant there was another victim, so relief should not be what she was feeling.

The CSI placed the paper on the desk and photographed it, then tapped at the camera screen and practically at the same time Dominic's computer pinged with an incoming email.

She then performed the same process she had with the envelope. Placing it in a plain brown paper bag and sealing it up.

Dominic was staring at his computer screen, unmoving.

'Come on, Dominic. What's taking so long?'

He looked at her, his usual calm demeanour long gone, instead horror paled his skin and enlarged his eyes.

'What is it?' Claudia asked, a niggle of concern at the pit of her stomach.

Dominic forwarded the email to the team and then sent the image to the large screen in the room so that everyone could view it at once.

There was an audible gasp.

Ice ran down Claudia's spine.

For a moment or two she stood on the spot, unable to speak or move.

The niggle that had been curling at the pit of her stomach was threatening to engulf her and come up in a wave of vomit, in front of her whole staff.

As she stared at the image she could see out the corner of her eye that they were all staring at her.

Waiting for a response.

Breaths were held.

The image she was looking at on the screen in the incident room, received from the killer they were hunting, was a drawing of Claudia.

Dead.

CHAPTER 58

Suddenly the silent freeze-frame of a scene around her erupted and everyone spoke at once. The one voice she heard over all others was that of her father. No matter what differences they'd had, he was her father, and his voice boomed out over all the others in the room now.

'He is not getting his hands on you, Claudia.'

She couldn't respond, her tongue heavy as lead.

'Do you understand me? There is no way on this earth that man is getting his hands on you.'

The collective agreement was loud and raucous. The team would do everything in their power to identify him.

They hadn't managed it yet.

The location would be identified.

They hadn't done that yet either.

Luckily they had a head start in recognising Claudia.

She shivered. Zach had had the same head start, and yet he was one of their listed victims.

The room narrowed. Darkness tunnelled in and constricted her vision.

It sounded as though she were underwater.

There was the sense of an arm around her, the word 'tea' was barked out, and she was being shepherded away from the spot she was rooted to. Her feet moved of their own volition, following the gentle guidance. A door closed behind her and she was lowered into a chair.

She was in her office. She looked up at the owner of the arm and was both surprised and unsurprised to find it was her father. Who else would take care of her at a time like this?

Claudia blinked several times. Adjusting to her new reality. A reality where her life may not be as long as she always thought it would be.

'Stop that,' her father said, as though reading her mind.

She blinked some more.

'He will not get his hands on you. Do you understand me, Claudia?'

He was being her father.

There was a soft knock on the door and Lisa entered with a steaming mug. She handed it to Dominic and slipped out as quietly as she had arrived.

Dominic placed the hot tea in her hands. 'Drink this. You've had a shock.'

Was that what was happening to her? Shock? Seeing her own face drawn so clearly in that image. Knowing, just as it had before, that it was supposed to mean her demise. How was she supposed to react?

She leaned back in her chair with the tea in her hand. Of course she knew how she was supposed to react. She was a detective inspector leading a team of driven officers on a hunt for a killer who was now making a threat against one of them. How she was supposed to react was with anger and a steady hand.

She rose.

'What are you doing?' asked Dominic, standing from his crouched position in front of her.

'My job,' she said simply, putting the tea on her desk. Feeling grateful for the support he'd offered when she'd needed it. She looked up at him. 'Thank you, Dad. But I have to face this head on. I have to take my role as DI and run with it, not run away like a scared little girl to her dad. I'm a grown woman and a police officer of rank.'

'But, Claudia . . .' He tried, but Claudia held up a hand to quiet him.

'I know. It unnerved me for a minute or two. But it's time to get back to work.' She moved around the desk towards the door, giving Dominic no choice but to move out of her way. She wasn't going to stop.

'What're you going to do?' he asked, worry etching new lines on his face.

'I'm going to continue working the case. Come on, Dad. Let's go get this bastard, shall we?'

CHAPTER 59

The drawing showed a woman, Claudia, sitting upright, leaning against something, a blade in her chest. The surroundings were woodland, which is why at first glance she thought the item she was leaning against was a felled tree covered in moss. Dark, lush and green. Or they could presume it was green. It was shaded in dark grey, but he had such a sleight of hand it was easy to know what he wanted you to see. But it seemed from the angle of the drawing to be a little too boxy to be a tree.

'This is the worst drawing he's given us for identifying a location,' Graham said. 'It looks to be a wood of some description, and that could be anywhere. How the hell can we decipher this?' His mood was grim.

The overall mood in the room was low and brooding.

This was the first time Claudia had to be honest and say she couldn't see the beauty in the art of it.

But she would say that when it was her face staring back at her.

A little distorted. From the pain, she supposed. The blade dug straight into her chest.

Her heart.

But the intricacies of the flow of the pencil were too much for her to appreciate when she was looking at herself.

The incident room door opened, and to show how unusual this case was, not for the first time, DCI Maddison Sharpe entered.

Claudia flashed a quick look around the office space that asked, *Who the hell told her?* Whoever it was would be in deep shit when she found out.

She wanted to deal with this as any other job that came in and lead the team, as she would any other time. Now Sharpe was involved they were in a different league.

Her face was stern. Her eyes like lasers focused in on Claudia. She stood by the doorway, unmoving. 'Outside.' She turned her back to the room and disappeared back through the door.

The team looked at each other.

Claudia knew where she had gone, where she expected Claudia to follow her to.

But first Claudia had a question.

'Who the hell informed Sharpe?' She didn't care about the reason. Her trust had been severed. She was severely disappointed.

Dominic rose from his chair. 'I did. I sent her an email updating her. I thought she should know.'

Claudia stared daggers at her father. Another reason they shouldn't be working together. If he wasn't her father, he wouldn't have dared to step out of bounds this way. If he'd been a detective on her team unrelated by blood, he'd have been like the rest of them. Worried but following her lead. As it was, he was clearly scared for her and wanted someone of higher rank to know what was happening. To take control and to ultimately protect her.

'How dare you.' Her face flushed as anger surged through her. 'This is my investigation. My face on the image. My decision how we deal with this new turn of events. How dare you undermine me like this.'

She didn't want to do this in public, in front of his colleagues, but the rage was pulsing through her veins. She couldn't control herself. Mixed with the fury that he'd put her in this position was the fear of the killer and his incredible skill for getting around the police and obtaining his target, no matter how much of a heads-up he gave them.

Dominic wasn't perturbed by her cold, hard anger. But instead of looking like they were going to butt heads again, he kept his voice low and level, allowing Claudia to vent her emotions and keeping his in check. 'As your immediate supervisor, she should know. You can't be the next possible victim and also lead the investigation into catching the man responsible.'

Claudia made to jump in, but Dominic stopped her.

'But if you are, then that is a choice that Sharpe or Connelly have to make.'

Jesus. She hadn't even thought of Connelly. How Sharpe would sell this to him. She would have her hands full for the next half an hour talking to Sharpe, trying to keep this in her own incident room. What she didn't want was someone coming in and taking over the lead. She would have to be good when she followed Sharpe downstairs.

Claudia stared at her father, because right now he was treating her as a father would his child, not as a detective on her team. She couldn't scold him. If she thought about it sensibly, how would she react if the shoe were on the other foot? She couldn't possibly answer that.

And with that in mind she shook her head and walked past him and out the door. She would have to argue to keep her own position on this investigation.

CHAPTER 60

The sun was shining down on the smoking shed, and as expected DCI Maddison Sharpe was waiting for her, high pointy shoe tapping impatiently on the grey concrete, a cigarette already between her lips.

'Ma'am.' Claudia approached.

Sharpe stared at the officer in the corner of the shed, shielding from the sun or maybe attempting not to be seen by the DCI. Either way, he took the message that his presence was not required and he quickly stubbed out his cig, discarded it in the bin and stalked away without saying a word.

All the while Claudia waited on Sharpe, knowing she had something to say.

As always, she twiddled her thumbs while she waited. She didn't smoke, but she was becoming used to the smoking shed as a place for Sharpe to have serious conversations with her. A place Sharpe could soothe her nerves while getting on with the business of supervising and policing. And Claudia could imagine Sharpe had some nerves to soothe on hearing one of her staff had been targeted by the latest killer they were investigating.

'How are you?' Sharpe eventually broke the silence.

'I'm fine.' And she was. The initial shock had worn off and she had returned to work mode. The panic had been a mere blip.

Sharpe blew out a smoke ring and seemed to consider this answer.

'I'm going to have to bring in another inspector to lead the investigation.'

Claudia couldn't tell if she was confiding in her or complaining that it inconvenienced her. Either way she wasn't having it. 'I'm not a victim. I haven't been injured. It's a bloody piece of paper with my face on it. I don't see how it compromises what I can do.'

'I don't care what you see or don't see.' Sharpe was cool. 'The fact is you pretty much are a victim—'

'Pah,' Claudia spat at her, for a moment forgetting rank. 'One drawing does not make me a victim.'

'If not a victim, then a target. We have to follow the rules, Claudia.' Sharpe was trying to placate her.

Claudia was not accepting it, no matter the sense of Sharpe's last comment. She fought back. 'Where were the rules when you asked me to investigate and interview my own father?'

Sharpe inhaled and paused before responding. 'They were specific circumstances that required a bending of the rules to save the life of an officer. But —' she stared hard at Claudia — 'the rules were still not broken in that case. As well you know. Otherwise, at this point in time, evidence would be getting thrown out at court, but it's not. Because you did a great job. Within the boundaries we are allowed to colour within. This is different.'

Claudia quieted, no more arguments forthcoming.

Claudia was deeply aware of Sharpe's scrutiny as her supervisor took her in. The quivering outline of her boss clearly indicated her feelings on the matter, and her arms crossing her tense upper body underlined them.

'This is not a statement on your handling of the case,' Sharpe said eventually. 'It's a matter of keeping the lines of the investigation clearly delineated. Where you are being investigated—' she held up a polished finger to shush Claudia's protestations — 'we need another body to oversee that part of the inquiry. But I will allow you to be present, as you have intimate knowledge of the overall case.'

She supposed she couldn't ask for anything better than that and sagged at the compromise. 'Who are you bringing in?'

'Do you know Adam Blackwood from Intelligence? DCI?'

Claudia remembered the brief exchange she'd had with him. In the same place she stood now. 'Yes, I've met Adam. He seems a nice enough guy.'

'I don't care how nice he is.' Sharpe flicked ash onto the warm ground. 'I care about how well he can do his job, and I've heard nothing but good things about him. He's only just moved into his role, but I'm going to ask him to help us out. Or rather, Connelly is. He's speaking to him as we talk.'

Claudia ground her teeth. It was a done deal. Nothing she said down here in the grounds of police headquarters would change the outcome of her position. This rattled her.

'If Adam is up for this, expect to see him in the incident room shortly.'

Claudia rolled her eyes.

Sharpe flicked her cigarette on the ground, ignoring the bin, and with her pointed toe ground it out. 'We'll keep you safe, Claudia.'

She sounded like her father. It really wasn't what she was worrying about. What she wanted was to keep her hands on her own investigation, but that wasn't happening. 'I'm a big girl. I'll be fine.'

'We'll put a close-quarter detail on you until this is over.'

Claudia shook her head. 'No. No. No. I'm not having someone trail around after me like a lost puppy.' She was adamant about this point. It had been difficult enough to be informed a new SIO would be taking the lead on the investigation without the need for close protection screwing up her day. She wouldn't have it. Under any circumstances. She was trained in self-defence. She could handle herself.

'Claudia.' Sharpe warned her with a word. She looked lost as to what to do with her hands and fished out another cigarette from her pocket and lit it.

'No.' Claudia was equally adamant.

'We're still reeling from the loss of Ruth. What do you think it'd do to Dominic if he lost you right now?'

That was a low blow, and it took the air out of Claudia. She gasped at the severity of the comment. It was meant to shock, and it had done its job. 'That was below the belt,' she moaned.

'Yes, but it's had the effect I intended.' She smirked. It wasn't an attractive look on her.

'These are completely different circumstances. For starters Ruth didn't know she was at risk. I'm fully aware and will consciously assess my surroundings at all times.'

'Ruth was an undercover officer. She was working on the Strangler case. Do you not think she was cautious of the situation around her?'

'He attacked her in her own home.'

Sharpe blew smoke out and stared at her pointedly. 'And you don't think it's possible the Artist can attack you in your own home, Claudia? Are you listening to yourself? You're not making much sense.'

The fury was building inside Claudia. At every turn she was being blocked. Whatever she wanted she was being disappointed. How could she gain control of the situation? She hated being treated like this, like a child who needed guiding.

'Look, I've relented on having another SIO in my incident room. Surely you can't expect me to give in about this as well?' She tried for calm.

'It's not about give and take,' said Sharpe. 'It's about doing things the right way and keeping you safe. I have a compromise, though. How about you only have protection while you're at home in the evening?'

'And can we knock it down to a uniform car parked outside?' Claudia asked. 'I really don't need anyone sitting inside the house. And surely a marked police vehicle is going to be enough to put the most hardy killer off.'

Sharpe let out a sigh along with a breath of light-coloured smoke in the bright glare of the sun. 'You fight a hard battle, DI Claudia Nunn.'

Claudia smiled. She was not a child, and neither was she about to be the next victim of the Artist.

CHAPTER 61

The Artist was taking a walk. He was in the location he'd drawn on the invitation he'd sent to DI Claudia Nunn and the location of his final installation.

The birds spoke quietly above him.

It was something you can't place into a drawing. All the external factors of a live exhibit. That's the joy of having a live exhibit, in so much as his exhibits were live. The joy was the surroundings. Like here, where the birdsong would create a soundtrack, though he doubted anyone would notice it once they were here. They'd be stressed and angry rather than being open to what he was achieving.

Prison wasn't an outcome he wanted, but capture would enable the public to finally see him for who he was and what he was creating — the art, rather than the panic the press where whipping up.

He sniffed at the mere thought of the press. They were useful in some ways but they really were a world all of their own. He hoped they would support him in explaining the artistic meaning of the installations, if the police managed to do what they were aiming to do. But whether they did or not, a court case would give him all the opportunity he needed.

He wasn't afraid.

Creating a name that people would recognise for years and even decades to come, that meant more to him than a few years locked up. He was sure he'd still be able to create in prison. After all, they had libraries. They weren't barbarians.

The Artist looked at the small moss-covered wall he'd depicted in his invitation, the place DI Nunn would soon be sitting, and smiled. It was a perfect place. Difficult to decipher — he really didn't want them to stop this one. They had a head start knowing it was Claudia, and in a location that was meaningful to many. If he was creating his last installation, he may as well create it in a meaningful place with a meaningful woman.

A thrill of electricity ran up his spine.

He was ready.

CHAPTER 62

Claudia found DCI Adam Blackwood waiting in her office when she returned from the smoking shed. The CSI had finished and gone.

Blackwood smiled when she walked in.

She noted he hadn't been presumptuous and taken her seat. He was hovering in the middle of the room.

'Ah,' he said when she pushed the door open. 'I do hope Sharpe's had a word with you.' He looked like he'd been caught with his hand in the cookie jar.

Claudia moved around her desk and sat, making it clear whose office this was. 'Yes, I've just come from a meeting with her.' Though she wasn't sure standing in the smoking shed could be classed as a meeting.

Blackwood inclined his head. 'Glad to hear it. I didn't want to have to explain my appearance here myself.' He grinned. 'It could have been awkward. You're doing okay?'

Was he asking about the fact that he'd been tasked with taking over the investigation, or was he asking if she was okay having a killer target her? 'I'm doing okay,' she responded equally opaquely.

Blackwood indicated the chair in front of her desk. 'Mind if I have a seat?'

He was being polite about the situation.

Claudia noticed faces turning towards them through the glass windows. They'd be wondering what was happening in there. There was no one as nosy as cops. 'Help yourself.'

Blackwood, tall as he was, folded himself into the chair and faced her. 'Look, I hope I haven't bent your nose out of shape. This is obviously a last-minute thing. I only just received the email from Connelly. Said it was urgent. Gave me a brief outline of why. Sounds tense.' He leaned forward to put a point on his words. 'I'm here to do anything I can to help, without trampling all over the investigation you've already got up and running. Connelly is worried about you investigating yourself as a potential victim in this scenario, as far as I can make out, and only wants me to cover this part of the case. What comes beforehand is still totally yours.'

He held his hands open wide.

Claudia wasn't sure how to respond to this. He was sincere in his approach. She couldn't fault him in this. He hadn't asked to take over her team. They had pushed it onto him. She was furious, but she was furious with the situation, not with individual people — the killer behind it all excepted. He took all the blame.

'I have to admit to finding the whole thing difficult,' she admitted. 'I can't promise to be the best behaved "victim"—' she placed air quotes around the word — 'but I'll be as courteous as I can while you do your job and I'll instruct my staff to do the same.'

He gave her the same wonky grin again. 'It's all I can ask for, in the circumstances. To be honest, Claudia, I'm not sure how I'd react to this. You appear to be bearing up admirably.'

She laughed out loud. 'I'm glad the act is working. Now shall we go and update the very nosy crowd who are breaking their necks out there as to what's happening?'

The pair walked out of Claudia's office and the necks that had been straining to see what was happening quickly snapped back to forward positions as the team pretended to be getting on with some work.

'Okay, everyone, can we have your attention?' Claudia called to them.

The act of working didn't last for long. They wanted to know who the new guy was, and those who knew him wanted to know what he was doing here in their office space.

Claudia moved to the front of the incident room and Adam followed. 'This is DCI Adam Blackwood. He's from Intelligence. In fact, he's just taken over the department following the retirement of DCI Jennings.'

There were murmurings around the room as staff voiced their thoughts as to why he was standing in their office.

Claudia glared at them, not amused at the rudeness. They soon quelled. 'You saw I had a meeting with Sharpe after the drawing came in. The outcome of that meeting was that we need another supervisor for the area of the investigation that covers this new drawing. A drawing that is of me.' The words *that is of me* nearly caught in her throat. She supposed that was another indicator she wasn't the best person to lead the case. That she struggled with the fact she was being targeted by such a lethally brilliant killer. She was coming to terms with the reality that Adam had been drafted in to deal with this section of the investigation. It was just a matter of relaying this to the team. 'DCI Sharpe advised me that DCI Blackwood here would be taking the lead with this. He's extremely competent, and I want you all to afford him your utmost respect and work as hard as you can for him.' She laughed at them. 'Bearing in mind it's my neck on the line.'

There was an uncomfortable silence where no one else thought this funny, and she coughed and carried on. 'Okay then. I'll still be here to deal with the rest of the case we have running into the previous three victims. It'll benefit Adam as I hold all the information and might be able to help with whatever he needs for current lines of enquiry.' She turned to look up at him. 'I'll hand over to DCI Blackwood to say a few words.'

Blackwood took a step forward and clapped his hands together as though to capture their attention, though he already had it. A smile lit up his features. It was warm. Made him appear welcoming. 'I know I'm a new face to many of you. I do, however, recognise a couple of you from our time around the force over the years, but for those of you who don't know me, I'm DCI Adam Blackwood. As DI Nunn mentioned, I've slid over from Intelligence for a short while, to give you a dig out. That's it. Nothing more sinister than that. I'm not here to take anyone's job. I have a job I'm perfectly happy with and a team I'm already making myself comfortable with. I don't want to have to change that. So let's not get our knickers in a twist about putting anyone's nose out of joint and creating a hostile working environment. We're all here with the same objective, to prevent Claudia from becoming the fourth victim of the Artist.'

Claudia shivered as a cold sensation ran over her body. This was the second time she'd had such a physical reaction while she'd been dealing with this job. She was not usually so reactive. But this case had gotten under her skin.

Particularly now.

There was no other way for her to be. She was the woman in the drawing.

Adam continued. 'Does anyone have any questions? I'd rather clear the air now than have someone brooding, causing friction to grow and problems later on. I want a smooth working team so we can get this bastard and keep DI Nunn safe.'

The room was silent.

'Okay then.' He clapped his hands together again. 'Let's get straight to work. I need someone to run the whole case past me first, then in particular I want the details on DI Nunn's drawing. Who wants to volunteer to be my guide?'

Officers and civilian staff looked at each other. Krish lifted a hand so the new boss would know who was speaking. 'I can do that, boss.'

'And you are?'

'Krish, Krish Dhawan.'

'Great. Thanks, Krish. I'll grab a chair and you can pull me up to speed.' And with that DCI Adam Blackwood found himself an empty chair and pulled it across to Krish's desk and seated himself beside the detective constable. He looked up at Claudia and winked. He was getting stuck straight in. Claudia was grateful for his easy manner, both in working alongside her and not making her feel he was taking over from her and in the way he had handled the team. Now all they had to do was prevent Claudia from being murdered and becoming another statistic.

Claudia walked to the kitchen and made herself a cuppa before taking it back to her office. Once there she opened up her email and the image of herself in the woods.

Sheffield might be a city, but there were so many woods within and surrounding it that it was impossible to determine where this location was.

She sipped on her drink and stared at the drawing, losing track of time. She carried on sipping until the drink was cold and then until the mug was empty, and still the drawing said nothing else to her.

Claudia looked at her watch. She'd been staring at the drawing and trying to decipher it for half an hour, and it was then she realised that there wasn't a clock or a day written in the corner of the paper. There was no timestamp, no clock they were up against.

She didn't know which terrified her the most. Having a ticking clock counting down to your death or having an open-ended image that basically said you were going to die, but when was anyone's guess. You would just have to wait and find out.

CHAPTER 63

The day had been tense. Blackwood had been meticulous about going through the whole case with a fine-toothed comb. Every time Claudia walked out the office, someone jerked from their seat and asked where she was going and demanded she be escorted. It became ridiculous when all she wanted was the ladies' room. An embarrassing standoff had commenced until Blackwood had stepped in and told the team he thought she was safe enough within the confines of the police station.

It had smarted that it hadn't been sufficient that she had been saying this all day, that it had taken the new boy, the man, to give them the instruction before they listened. But eventually she calmed down and understood that they simply cared about her, that their nerves were shot and they were desperately trying to keep her safe.

Now, this evening, her father had decided he was going to spend some time with her. It wasn't enough that there was a marked police vehicle outside her address. No, he had travelled back with her in her car, leaving his in the car park, giving the excuse that she was to cook him dinner. They'd not had their regular Sunday meal due to work commitments for quite some time.

Claudia couldn't shake him from his decision so she went along with it. Now she stood in the kitchen with a pan of water coming to the boil as she chopped pancetta and grated cheese. Tonight they were having spaghetti carbonara. It was far too warm for a full chicken dinner.

Dominic leaned against the kitchen counter as she worked, a can of beer in his hand. Not only was he staying for dinner, but apparently he was staying the night in her spare room.

'What about clothes for work tomorrow?' she asked moving around the kitchen getting the ingredients she needed ready.

'Do you think anyone is going to care if I turn up in the same suit I was in today?' he said. 'Bearing in mind I'm staying here to add to your security. Besides,' he added, 'we could pop by my place on the way in and pick up a change of clothes.' He grinned and took a slug of beer. 'I'm so glad you have some beer in. I'm only having the one, though. No good getting shit-faced, is it? Kind of defeats the reason I'm here.' He laughed and Claudia rolled her eyes, tipping spaghetti into the now boiling water.

Dominic straightened himself. 'How are you feeling?'

Claudia was aware how in turmoil he must be. It wasn't long ago he'd lost his wife. They'd both lost Ruth, but she was his wife. And now his daughter was under threat. Jesus, his emotions must be all over the place. She really did need to take it a little easier on him.

'I'm okay,' she said, actually meaning it. The stress that had plagued her in the office all day had ebbed away once they'd left, which was surprising as there was more opportunity for the killer to access her once she was out of the building. But for some reason, being with a bunch of cops who were all equally wound up about the drawing had strung her out, much as their tension had come from a good place. And leaving them all behind had eased that tension and relaxed her somewhat.

She wasn't scared. There was a marked police vehicle outside and it wasn't just a show of force, it had two cops inside who were bloody good at their jobs. Plus, her dad was here with her. And on top of that, she was a fully trained cop who could handle herself. If this killer wanted her, he had a lot to get through.

'I'm pretty well protected,' she elaborated. 'There's two cops outside and two inside. He's got a fight on his hands if he wants me tonight.'

Her father was serious. 'It's not just tonight, Claudia. This will go on until we catch him.'

Claudia couldn't help herself. She groaned. 'Seriously?'

'You'd rather we give up after a few days and he slips in and grabs you and you die? All because we couldn't be bothered to keep it up or felt it had gone on long enough?' He wasn't messing about.

Again, she had to think about how he was feeling. Plus, she really didn't fancy being dead. 'No, Dad. It's just a lot of effort.'

'And your life isn't worth it?'

She needed to change the subject. Getting a large flat pan out, she fried the pancetta with a crushed garlic clove, turning her back on Dominic. 'How are you feeling about the Tyler thing?' She wasn't aiming to stress him out any further but she couldn't think of anything else to say. Her own stress levels had been rising, and a desperate need to change the subject had resulted in the question popping out of her mouth unbidden.

The only sound in the room was the pan of water and pasta boiling, the crackle of frying pancetta and garlic and the quiet sup and glug of Dominic taking a drink from his beer.

She regretted the question, but the pressure of the last subject was bearing down on her.

Eventually Dominic spoke.

Claudia stirred the pancetta.

'I'm glad it's coming to a conclusion. I need to move on, Claudia. He might not have made the confession to us, which would have been better for me, but a second-hand confession is just as good.' He paused. Took another glug of his beer.

Claudia waited.

'I miss her so much. It's like a physical loss. Like a part of me has been excised.'

Claudia's heart hurt hearing her father talk this way.

'She was my whole life. She's the first thing I think of the moment I wake. The last thing before I sleep. The house, it feels like it's lost its soul. All the memories wrapped up in it haunt me. And if Tyler's cellmate says he admitted to killing her, then it's good enough for me. Though I knew it anyway. Having official closure means I can move on, allow my grief to let go of the obsession it had with Tyler.' Another glug of beer.

Claudia melted some unsalted butter in another pan.

Dominic watched her work. 'You're quiet on the subject.'

She stirred the butter down with a wooden spoon. 'I don't want to upset you.' It was the last thing she wanted to do. He had been through enough.

He smiled at her. 'Look, I think tonight of all nights, while we wait for a crazed killer to make an attempt on your life, you get to say whatever you want, don't you?'

'But it's in opposition to what you've just said.' Tears filled her eyes.

'Tell me, Claudia.' Dominic put his drink down. The can made a quiet clink on the worktop. 'This has affected both of us. It's not just about me. Tell me what you're thinking. Why isn't it a good thing that Lawton said Tyler confessed?'

CHAPTER 64

Dominic watched his daughter carefully. His nerves stretched to their limit as he held himself together. Making it appear like he was calm and caring when all he wanted to do was scream at her to stop over-analysing everything and let things be. But he'd said one thing that was correct this evening. She had a crazed killer on her tail, and no matter how mad he was at her about this, she was still his daughter and there was no way in hell he was going to allow anyone to hurt her. His love for Claudia was real.

She was just a bloody pain in the arse.

'Tell me . . .' He pushed again. He had to know exactly what she was thinking so he could try to change her mindset. He'd hoped his own speech about believing the confession and it helping with closure would ease her in the right direction, but she still seemed to be balancing on the edge. He needed to do something about it.

Claudia tipped the pancetta into the melted butter and threw the empty pan into the sink with a sizzle. 'It just doesn't add up.'

Dominic didn't say a word. He waited for her to elaborate.

She gently stirred the pan of butter and pancetta, picking out the garlic clove and throwing it in the bin. 'You know I spoke with Tyler.'

Dominic's stomach clenched. Of course he was aware of this, but it still made him react bodily.

'You know he said he didn't kill her.'

'And because he said that to you, you can't believe he would say something different to his cellmate?'

Claudia huffed heavily. 'It's not that.'

'What is it then?' He tried to keep his voice on an even keel. He didn't want to aggravate her. Especially not tonight, when her nerves must be shattered as it was. But he needed to know what her thought process was in relation to Samuel Tyler.

'Part of it's because of the conversation he had with me.'

He couldn't help but sigh, and Claudia wiped her brow with the back of her hand.

'I'm sorry,' he said. 'Go on.' He needed to know.

'The reason he gave for his killing spree . . . It made sense.'

This was something Dominic hadn't considered when laying the groundwork for putting the blame for Ruth's murder at Tyler's door. The reason he had murdered the women. There wasn't a lot he could do about that.

'I told you how he said it was because they had children and they were dating. You've seen the scar on his hand?' She was getting animated.

Dominic nodded. He could do little else. He'd heard the story of how Tyler had obtained his scar from the man himself before they knew he was the Strangler, but he'd listen to Claudia if she needed to tell it.

'His mum left him home alone to go on a date. She hadn't fed him, and he was hungry. He tried to feed himself. Bacon sandwiches, of all things. In a frying pan. He'd seen his mum do it before and copied what she did. But he had an accident and spilt the pan of fat all over himself. Now he's physically scarred and blames his mum. He doesn't believe women should go out and date if they have children at home. Ruth didn't have any children.'

Dominic, though aware of this story, was prepared. 'But she was an undercover cop and was trying to put him in prison for the murders he'd already committed. You don't think there's the slightest possibility he killed her to stop her in her tracks? He's vicious and vindictive. And in killing her to take her out of his way, what better way than to cover it up and make it look like one of his usual murders?'

Claudia frowned and tapped the wooden spoon on the side of the pan, resting it on the handle.

Dominic watched his daughter. Maybe she'd already considered this, maybe she hadn't. There was no way to know unless she said more. But it felt like he'd found a hole in her thought processes and he had to keep needling at it. He couldn't allow her to find Tyler not guilty in her own mind. That possibility terrified him. His neck was on the line.

She drained the water from the spaghetti, leaving a little in a bowl at the side, and tipped it into the pan she had been simmering on a low heat and mixed it all together. 'There's also the issue with the lipstick.'

His heart raced. He couldn't take this strain. He was sure he'd done everything right. 'What about the lipstick?'

'There was a lipstick left in the place Ruth was abducted, as well as the location her body was found. Don't you find this unusual? With the other women, there was only a lipstick found at the site of the body dump. Not where they were abducted from.'

'But we don't know where they were all abducted from,' he countered. Desperation getting to him as she pushed him with valid points.

'But some we do. You ran the case, Dad. You know this. Doesn't it look like whoever took Ruth left the lipstick to make it appear like the Strangler had her?'

How could he answer her? It was exactly what had happened. But he couldn't admit to it. He'd be admitting to his own guilt. 'I think you're seeing things you want to see because you're scared of letting go.'

She paused, mixing the cheese and eggs, her hand still in mid-air. 'I don't want to fight you on this,' she said. 'This was your case, and she was your wife, but it really doesn't sit right with me. You're really telling me you see nothing wrong with it at all?' Her face was a mask of confusion.

Dominic didn't know who was more stressed, her or him. He could make her back down, she was so confused. But it would still be bubbling in the back of her mind that it didn't add up. He could see it in her eyes. The place he'd always been able to read her.

As a child, all he'd had to do was look in those beautiful wide eyes of hers and the game would be up. If she was trying to deceive him, she'd give herself away with the anxiety popping in her eyes. If she was sad but not wanting to worry her parents, her eyes would flood with the hidden emotion. And if she was happy, her eyes sparkled with life.

He'd never told her. It had been his secret skill. And he used it now. Her eyes were telling him she wasn't settled. This was going to stay with her. She might turn around and tell him she'd go with whatever he decided in the end, because she cared for him and it was, after all, his wife who had been murdered. She might even go along with it for a while. Do nothing. Let it slide. Listen to her dad. But eventually . . . eventually it would burrow under her skin so deep she would have no choice but to listen to that niggle, that voice that was telling her something wasn't right, and it would all come rushing out. And who the hell knew what kind of mess would come out with it.

There was no way to resolve the issue with her. No amount of talking to her was going to settle her mind and in turn settle his mind.

She finished the eggs and cheese as she waited for him to respond, then very gently mixed them in to the spaghetti mixture, turning the spaghetti over so it was fully coated. It was here she reached for the small bowl she'd put to the side of the pasta water and tipped a little into the pan to create a sauce, and with a fork, lifted the spaghetti through the mixture.

Dominic's mind relayed through his options as she worked, but he was coming up blank.

'I don't know what to say, sweetheart. I don't have all the answers. I just want to move on and I believe Lawton when he says Tyler admitted it to him. What reason does he have to lie?' There was no reason for Claudia to request to check Lawton's visitor's log. Lawton had done nothing wrong. He was not under investigation. When he'd paid him a visit, he'd hoped it would go a lot smoother than this. But now he was on the back foot. He would have to deal with any problems as and when they arose. He was hoping she was going to come through for him. Be the thoughtful daughter and let it go. Even if it was just to give her dad some peace for now, no matter what her opinion.

'I don't suppose he has a reason.' She pulled a couple of plates down from the cupboard. 'It just didn't feel right.' She looked at him. 'But if you're sure you're happy with this?'

He nodded again.

'And you were the investigating officer on the Strangler case and you're Ruth's husband. I can't ask for more than that, can I?'

No, she bloody well couldn't. Thank God for that. He greedily supped from his beer. Not much was left.

'We're taking it at face value then?' He checked.

Using a pair of cooking tongs, Claudia piled steaming carbonara onto the two plates she'd placed on the side and sprinkled the leftover grated cheese on top. 'We're taking it at face value.' She handed him a plate, which he took, and they carried them to the table.

'This looks delicious. Thank you.'

Sitting down with the food together should have been a pleasant evening, but Dominic was tense. His shoulders tight and bunched hard under his neck. A band of pressure around his head and over his eyebrows. He dug into them with the pad of his thumb.

'What is it, Dad?'

How could he say it was nothing? She had a crazed killer after her. But not just that, she also had his future life balanced in her hands. She just didn't realise it. He wondered what she'd do if she knew. Would she save him or would she throw him to the wolves?

CHAPTER 65

Before eating, Claudia paused. 'Do you think I should take some out to the guys in the car outside?'

Dominic looked at his plate. 'No, love. They're here to guard you, not tuck into a full dinner. If it would make you happier, why don't you take them a coffee?'

He was right. A drink was the way to go. 'I have a couple of takeout-type beakers in the cupboard. I'll make them some drinks and take them out.'

'Finish your meal first?'

Her anxiety over the whole night was obviously getting the better of her. She was twitchy, and she needed to wind it down. 'Of course.' She took a deep breath in and tried to steady herself.

'It's gorgeous,' Dominic said, tucking into his spaghetti. 'It really is. Get some down you. You need your strength for the days ahead. If you have some left you can take it to work tomorrow.'

He talked sense. Claudia picked up her fork and dove into the pasta dish. It was indeed delicious. She'd not done a bad job with it, if she said so herself.

As they ate, the conversation was fairly subdued. They'd said all they wanted to say about Lawton and Tyler. She'd backed down to appease her father. Though she was grieving for Ruth this was his loss, and if he thought Lawton was telling the truth and it was what he needed to move on then who was she to upend it all for him?

They ate quietly but companionably. He was here because he loved her and wanted her to be safe. No matter how much she believed she could take care of herself, he was her father and considered it his job to protect her. She accepted that. After all, there was nothing she could do to stop him. It would be easier to stop the killer.

When they had finished eating Dominic stacked the plates and pans in the dishwasher and Claudia made two mugs of coffee with milk, one with sugar and one without. They could fight over which one they preferred between them.

With takeaway mugs in hand, Claudia told her father she was stepping outside to give the drinks to the officers watching the house. He agreed —from safety to safety and back to safety again.

Claudia opened the door and headed out. It surprised her to see it was overcast. The sun had been beating down on them for so long she had forgotten the weather could change. A break in the heat would be nice. Some air to circulate would do everyone good. It was funny, but the British never coped well with long spells of extreme weather of any kind. Changeable weather was what they were used to.

She saw the two cops sitting in their car across the road and made her way over. The air was chill. She shivered, wishing she'd thought to wrap a cardigan around herself. But the days had been so warm it hadn't been a consideration for a while. But it didn't matter, she wouldn't be out here long.

It was still light, the two guys in the car were facing forward, and they hadn't noticed her heading towards them.

So much for watching out for her. What if someone was walking towards her home while she was inside? She was having second thoughts about bringing the drinks out to them if they couldn't do their jobs properly.

The road was quiet. Standing only a couple of feet away she realised something was wrong. The cop nearest to her had his neck at an awkward angle. And he still hadn't moved.

Claudia took a tentative steps towards them. Up close she peered in through the side window.

Everything was wrong.

And she was in mortal danger.

CHAPTER 66

From his vantage point parked a little further down the street, the Artist watched Detective Inspector Claudia Nunn's reaction to the two disabled cops in the car.

He had to admit it thrilled him to see the colour drain from her face before she yanked open the door to assess if they were injured or dead.

That her first thought was to her fellow officers and not getting herself safe was admirable.

It would, however, be her downfall.

He hadn't expected her to come out here like this. He'd had every intention of going into the house and grabbing her from in there when it got dark. Of course, he'd have to deal with the other cop in there first and the fight DI Nunn would undoubtedly put up, but he'd got this far, he would manage.

Putting the two uniform cops down had been easy. Like taking candy from a baby, as they say.

All he'd had to do was put on slippers and a dressing gown and walk down the street with two mugs of tea. He'd prepared for this, bringing the mugs from home along with a drink in a thermos flask, with an added ingredient that would knock the cops out cold in minutes.

He'd approached the car all smiles, telling the officers he was a neighbour and had seen them sitting there for a while and did they want a cuppa. They had looked him up and down in his slippers and dressing gown and greedily taken the hot drink off him.

He'd walked back down the road and left the tea to do its thing.

Now DI Nunn was on the street and he had to make a decision and act fast. If she turned away and went in the house, he would have to handle both her and the other cop. If he moved now, he could potentially just grab her.

He yanked the dressing gown from the back seat and struggled to pull it on, sitting in the front, steering wheel in his way. But he wheedled himself in and fasten the belt around his waist, hiding the clothes he was wearing below. His feet were still in the slippers.

She was opening the door, leaning in, checking the first cop for a pulse. He didn't have long before she'd go rushing into the house to call an ambulance and backup to their location. Unless she had a mobile phone secreted on her person. He couldn't see one, but that didn't mean she didn't have one.

He jumped out the car and practically ran down the street, slowing as he reached her. His nerves, as they always did at this point, at the point of snatching his subjects, were screaming at him. He was jittery and wanted nothing more than to walk away and listen to some music while curled up on the sofa. But that was his nerves talking. He had to ignore them and do this. It was always worth it afterwards. The glow of the installation. The knowledge that everyone was talking about him and his exhibit over their breakfast and dinner was enough to keep him moving forward. It was what he had dreamed of.

'Claudia,' he panted. 'Is everything alright?' She flinched as he approached. Her arms flew up in a defensive stance, ready to fight off an attacker, fear and anger flashing across her face.

He tried to keep his breathing even and calm. If he played this right, it would all go to plan.

'Thomas from down the road.' He stopped moving towards her, pretending he was scared of her sudden moves, and smiled. It was rare people knew everyone on their street. No one knew their neighbours anymore.

She looked at him in his slippers and dressing gown and frowned.

He stepped even closer.

The slippers and dressing gown did their thing, and she turned away, distracted by her two fallen colleagues in the car. It gave him time to make it all the way to her side without her becoming suspicious of him.

Then she turned to him, surprise in her eyes that he was so close, but she started to speak anyway. 'Have you seen anyone—'

He didn't have time to waste. He removed his hand from his pocket and inserted the needle into her arm. Shock skimmed across her face, and a hand came up in an attempt to brush him off, but it soon fell away as her body became soft and malleable.

The Artist wrapped her closest arm around his neck, pushed the door to the police car closed and part walked, part hauled the detective inspector towards his own car. Her feet were now asleep, making it difficult to drag her along the asphalt, her trainers grazing the ground as he moved her forward.

He was taking a big risk in daylight, but if anyone looked outside they would simply see two people walking towards a car. One in a dressing gown and the other seemingly not very well. Maybe they were on the way to the hospital. It wouldn't draw too much attention, anyway.

He picked up his pace. He didn't want the cop inside the house to come and look for her. He had to get her out of here.

Once at his car he pushed her onto the backseat, slammed the door shut and climbed into the front.

Then he slowly drove away with DI Claudia Nunn, his job quietly done.

CHAPTER 67

Dominic made a couple of hot drinks for him and Claudia. She'd been so busy thinking of the cops outside when she made their coffees that she hadn't thought to make four drinks.

What the hell was he going to do with her? She'd backed down on the Lawton and Tyler thing, but for how long? His nerves were strung out. How long could he keep this up? He was in it for the long haul. It had been the choice he'd made the moment he'd laid his hands on his wife and decided to kill her.

He'd not realised how stressful the after-effects would be.

He took a deep breath.

It was only Claudia who was questioning the outcome.

His own daughter.

He couldn't have foreseen this.

But for now she was going to accept things as they presented themselves. He would try to relax and hope it all went away.

What else could he do?

Sitting at the table with his coffee, he realised he'd been there for longer than he should have been. Claudia should already have handed the drinks over and returned. Even accounting for her having a chat with the cops guarding her, she should still have been back by now.

A cold chill gripped his shoulders. His knuckles whitened around his mug handle. Something sinister crept down his spine.

He rose from his chair.

Of course, it was likely she was still chatting. It was possible she knew one of the cops from earlier in her career and was standing there oblivious to the time and how worried he would be.

Dominic was going to check anyway.

Leaving the drinks on the table, he left the house and strode down the small pathway to the road.

The marked police car was where he'd seen it parked when he looked out the window. Two cops in place. But there was no sign of Claudia.

Sickness overwhelmed him in a sudden surge.

He raced to the car and pulled open the door to question the cops, ready to tear their heads off for not keeping Claudia safe.

Then things took a turn for the worse, and Dominic's world turned upside down. The cops were out cold. Their laps were sodden with spilt drinks.

No one was guarding them.

He turned away from the car and looked blindly each way down the street. It was empty. Quiet. She was gone. His daughter was gone. Claudia was nowhere to be seen.

Panic crushed his chest, and Dominic gasped for breath, bending double in the road.

He couldn't lose Claudia. She was his only child. She was everything to him.

If that monster had hold of her, he was going to find him and he was going to kill him. He would slice him apart and make sure he felt every single wound. He would regret putting a hand on his child.

The thought of raining vengeance down on the head of the person who had taken her brought Dominic back up to a standing position.

That was it. He had to act. Do something positive. He couldn't curl up and weep. That wouldn't do Claudia any good at all.

Staring at the two cops, Dominic pulled his mobile out his pocket and dialled Sharpe. She picked up immediately.

'What is it?' Her tone businesslike and blunt.

'He has her.'

'Tell me.' There was no messing around.

'It looks like he's given the cops outside something to drink that's laid them out cold. They're okay,' he quickly reassured her. 'Claudia had come out to give them a drink, actually.' He barked out a dry, bitter laugh. 'I let her come out alone, thinking she was walking across the road to two cops. What harm could she come to?' He pulled himself up short. He needed to stop rambling, to stop feeling sorry for himself. This was about getting the investigation team moving into locating Claudia. They needed all the information, quickly and neatly. He cleared his throat and continued. 'When I realised she'd been longer than I thought she should have been . . .' He paused, thought about it a few seconds, then gave Sharpe a timeframe. 'About ten minutes. I'd been clearing away our dinner plates and making drinks for us. I came outside to make sure she was okay, to call her back in. She was gone and the cops were down.'

'An ambulance is on the way for the uniformed officers, as is a CSI team.'

He thought he'd heard her tapping at her computer as he'd been speaking.

'Stay there, Dominic. Update the CSI team when they get there. Then you can come in and help with the investigation. There's no point in telling you to stay at home. I know that. But you follow direction, do you hear me?'

'I'm going to do whatever it takes to get my daughter back,' he said in response.

Sharpe sighed down the phone. 'I'll see you soon, Dominic. We'll get her back.'

The CSI team arrived a couple of minutes before the ambulance. They'd put their foot down, knowing what was at stake.

Very gently they removed the drinks mugs from the laps of the two officers and bagged them up then stepped aside for the paramedics, who lifted the officers onto stretchers and carried them off to the ambulance and away. No one had any idea what had been administered to them, so it was urgent that they get treatment as quickly as possible.

Dominic thanked the CSIs, grabbed Claudia's car keys and drove into work as fast as he dared. He'd had one beer, but he'd also had a decent meal. He wouldn't usually drive even with one drink, but today he was making an exception. His daughter's life hung in the balance. He would stop at nothing.

CHAPTER 68

The incident room was a hive of activity when Dominic entered.

Sharpe was standing in the middle of the room like a maestro controlling her orchestra. All information coming in to her and commands leaving her with ease. Not a ruffled feather in sight.

She saw Dominic enter and waggled a finger in his direction. He moved towards her. His mind focused on the task at hand.

'What's happening?' he asked.

'We've taken the image we received from the Artist and we've placed it on the front page of the intranet asking if anyone recognises the location she's sitting in. We have a large and varied staff, Dom, and between them they have a variety of interests. It's possible someone will know the place. And as soon as they log on they will be confronted with the drawing asking for help. I'm also doing a press conference in fifteen minutes asking for the same thing, for anyone who knows the spot.'

Dominic looked at the drawing up on the large screen, where it had been since they'd received it. It had no clock. No time of death. 'We don't have a timeframe to work to. No idea of his plans,' he moaned.

'We're working as fast as we can, regardless of what his plans are. We work to our own timeframe, which is flat out.' She let out a small sigh and placed a hand on his arm. 'I'm sorry, Dom, I can't even begin to imagine how you're feeling, going through this again.'

And as if remembering how it had worked out the last time, she apologised again. 'We'll get her back. And she's one tough woman. Don't underestimate her, Dom. We also have teams out doing house-to-house on Claudia's street to see if any of her neighbours saw anything that could be of any help. Anything recovered by Forensics from the marked police vehicle will be submitted and fast-tracked.'

She looked at her watch. 'I have to get ready for the press conference. Your team are on their way in. Some have already arrived. Plus we have extra staff here, as you can see. It's all hands on deck.'

At that point DCI Adam Blackwood pushed his way through the doors.

'I've emailed you a full update, Adam,' she said as he approached. 'Thanks for coming back in.'

His face was serious. 'I'm here for the duration. Whatever it takes.' He looked at Dominic and nodded.

Dominic responded in kind. He felt useless. There was a lot of waiting around. He wanted to do something active. To be out there. Hunting down this killer. Breaking bones. Causing pain. Bringing his baby home.

'I'm sorry this has happened,' Adam said.

Dominic nodded again. His words choked in his chest.

'We'll get her back.'

'We will,' snapped Sharpe. 'And on that note, I'm going to get sorted for this press conference.' She looked to Dominic. 'Do you want to be there, Dom?'

He thought about the excitement of the press pack. The throng of reporters who would be champing at the bit to get this story down. How he would feel in the room with them. It would be gruesome. But if having a grief-stricken parent to stare at got more eyes on the piece when it ran on the TV, then he would put himself through it. 'I'll do it.'

She peered up at him. 'You're sure? I don't want to put you through anything unnecessary.'

She was obviously thinking back to what had happened when Ruth had gone missing. They had arrested him and it had turned out a serial killer had her all along. Or so she thought. And now she was sensitive to how she handled him, now his daughter was missing.

'I'll do anything that might help get Claudia back, and if I have to play a role on TV for more people to pay attention, then I'll do that.'

'Okay then.' She was appeased. This was his decision. Not something they were forcing on him. She looked to Blackwood. 'Keep at it, Adam. And let me know the moment you have anything.'

'Absolutely. You'll be the first I come to.'

Dominic glared at him.

Blackwood coughed. 'The pair of you will be the first to know.'

Sharpe narrowed her eyes at Dominic. 'What did I tell you? You're here so long as you follow directions. This is being run the proper way, not like some cowboy case where you get to run off and do whatever you feel like doing. Adam will relay information to me, and if I'm happy for you to know, then either he or I will inform you. The rank structure applies as always. We won't keep anything pertinent from you, of course, but neither will I have you dictating to a DCI what they will and won't be doing. Am I clear?'

Dominic seethed. His body tensed. He wanted to wrap his hands around her neck. He had no idea how he was being so restrained. But it was the only way he was going to be allowed in the middle of the investigation, and that was important to him. He had to know everything. They wouldn't lock him out. She was simply showing her strength.

He gritted his teeth, quietly took a deep breath, then answered her. 'You're clear. But let me be clear, this is my daughter we're looking for. I won't back away like a good little boy. Not like last time.' That was it, he'd rub it in, remind them how they had screwed up last time. It would help his cause. 'But I'll run with the investigation team as is proper.'

Sharpe looked suitably slapped but shuffled the paperwork in her hands and tried not to show it. Showing weakness was not in her playbook. 'Okay, let's go and do this press conference. Get the drawing out there. See if anyone recognises the location.'

Dominic followed her out of the incident room, leaving the hum of the team working behind him. He knew these people. They would do everything they could to make sure Claudia returned.

It just wasn't enough.

* * *

It was getting late, but the press were crammed into the room. To get them here, they'd been told someone had abducted an officer. There was no other way to bring them out at this time in the evening.

They'd been greedy for the Artist story since the news had broken that he had been sending drawings to the police. A killer playing with the police this way was unique and they were all over it. A cop had been taken, and now they were salivating for the full story.

Dominic could hear them as he waited to go out front and talk. They were like a pack of hounds circling a meal.

Sharpe turned to him. 'You're okay?'

'Let's get this done, shall we?'

She strode out behind the desks and took her seat. Dominic followed and sank into his chair beside her.

Cameras flashed in front of him, the reporters mere outlines behind the bright lights in his eyes.

Sharpe was silent until the room came to order. Then she jumped in, straight to the point. 'Earlier this evening, DI Claudia Nunn was abducted from her home address, we believe by the man the press are calling the Artist.'

Cameras continued to flash.

Dominic clenched his fists in his lap.

'Prior to this abduction DI Nunn received a drawing, as has been the norm during this whole investigation, showing the location where she, as the next victim, will be found. It is this location we are asking the public to help identify. If anyone recognises the site, please contact the helpline at the bottom of the screen.'

The helpline would also be reported by those journalists who were here with print and online outlets, along with the drawing. They had provided the drawing to each journalist as they entered the room. A digital copy had also been emailed to them for ease of use.

'If you have any other information on the abduction, please also use the helpline and let us know. No matter how small or insignificant you feel your tip is, it could help build a bigger picture.' She paused. 'We'll take a few questions.'

She'd used the word *we* rather than *I*. She'd opened it up for Dominic to be involved as well.

Arms shot up. The first question was fired at them. 'How long ago since Claudia was abducted?'

Sharpe checked her watch. 'It's been roughly an hour. Every minute counts.'

All the arms. Another question. 'Why didn't she take preventative action if she had prior warning?'

Dominic sensed Sharpe tense.

'Two uniformed officers were harmed while protecting DI Nunn. Their current status is still being assessed at the hospital.'

There was a buzz in the room as they took this information in.

'Time for one more question,' Sharpe said. 'As you can imagine, we are eager to get back to the incident room and the investigation.'

Arms shot up again. Sharpe pointed to a journalist in the middle of the room.

He looked at Dominic. 'DS Dominic Harrison, yes?'

Dominic straightened in his chair. 'Yes.'

'DI Nunn, is she related to you?'

How did they know this? They really were sharks. But this was why he'd come out, in case he was needed as her father. 'Yes. Yes, I'm her father.'

'And it was your wife who was abducted and murdered earlier in the year?'

Sharpe jumped in. 'Do you have a point? A relevant question?'

'To DS Harrison, do you feel you are to blame as the women in your life are abducted by serial killers? It really is rather sloppy of you to lose another one like this, isn't it?'

There was utter uproar as Dominic bounced over the table and threw himself into the crowd.

Arms were clawing at him. People screaming his name. A red rage clouded his head. The confusion of having killed Ruth and now Claudia being abducted swirled around him and messed with his thought processes.

Then strong arms had him in a hold he couldn't escape from. With no nonsense, he was yanked backwards and out of the room. Two uniformed officers had a tight grip of him. He'd stopped fighting, allowing himself to be manoeuvred into another office space.

Then he was facing Sharpe. She was livid. 'You think that helped?'

He scowled at the officers who were holding him.

'You can let him go. Thank you.'

They frowned but cautiously released him.

Dominic bent his head.

'The story tonight and all day tomorrow will focus on your outburst, not on Claudia's abduction. You do realise that, don't you?' Her voice was low. It was scarier than if she'd been shouting.

The problem was, she was right. 'I'm sorry. I saw red.'

'That journalist was out of order. He won't be at another briefing.' She studied Dominic. 'I should send you home.'

'You can't do that.'

'Give me one good reason.'

He rubbed at his upper arm where one of the cops had held on to him a little too tightly. 'You feel guilty for what happened last time.' It was his only card. He had no choice but to be blunt and play it.

She watched him silently.

He bristled. Had he stepped too far over the line? He was, after all, only a detective sergeant and she was a detective chief inspector. Two ranks higher than him. No matter the truth of the matter.

Eventually she spoke. 'That may well be true, Dominic, but let me tell you this. You've played that card now. From now on, you're under my thumb. Do I make myself clear?'

Dominic nodded. He was under no one's thumb. He was here to learn what information they had, and then he would go and fetch his daughter.

CHAPTER 69

Claudia's eyes were heavy. Her head fuzzy. Her body leaden.

She had no concept of where she was or what was happening. Whatever it was, it wasn't good. She wasn't at home or at work. This wasn't her bed. Something rigid was sticking into her neck, which was at a weird angle.

She clawed through her mind for her last memories. The killer they were investigating had targeted her. Her father had come home with her for protection. She'd made dinner.

Pain sliced through her forehead. She winced. Whatever her location was she was moving. Rolling and bumping. But it was dark. She still couldn't open her eyes. They were heavy, weighted down in the fog of unconsciousness. Her shoulders were killing her.

She remembered the police car. Something was wrong with the cops inside. They were supposed to be protecting her, but they were too still.

Fear gripped her stomach at the memory.

What happened?

Where was she?

Something about slippers?

Things had gone fuzzy then, and all she remembered was fighting the darkness that was grabbing her brain, pulling her down into the inky black. Before it had taken her, she had been pushed into the back of a car.

Shit.

Her eyes flew open.

The darkness barely changed. She blinked to make sure she'd opened her eyes. She was awake.

She was no longer on the back seat of a car as she'd recalled, she was in the boot. Her face pushed towards the carpet and she could smell . . . oil and something else. Something dark and off-sweet. But it was a crude scent. Urine.

This was how he'd transferred the bodies.

But who was he?

The drugs he'd injected her with — she recalled the prick — had left an imprint on her brain. A fog. But she tried to focus in on the face of the man who had approached her when she'd been at the marked police vehicle.

The cops! They'd been down. Injured in some way. Were they okay? Were they still alive, or had he killed them to get to her? She couldn't remember through the haze of her muddled memory, what she'd found when she got to them. Oh, how she hoped with everything inside her that they were still alive. That it wasn't too late for them. No one should be hurt in the task of protecting her.

But the killers face? All she could recall was the fact he was in a dressing gown. No one walked down the street in a dressing gown unless they'd just walked out their house.

That was how he'd gotten so close.

But now she tried to focus in, there was something familiar about his face. She couldn't place it, but that it was familiar should have been a warning shot at the time.

Damn him. Damn her own arrogance.

The car bumped over something and jolted her bones.

Claudia tried to move, to find a more comfortable position, but she couldn't. She had been bent into a shape to fit her surroundings and both her hips and her knees were shouting out in acute pain. Her wrists were tied. She twisted her neck, tried to ease the discomfort, but there was little room for manoeuvre.

She flexed her wrists, tried to see how much give was in the ties, but they were tight.

Behind her was a huge blanket. Rough against her bare arms. She shuddered as she thought about why he'd want a blanket in the boot. To transfer a body?

Fear was eating her up. Slowly, second by second, it crawled onto her skin. Owning her.

She shook her head as much as she could. She wouldn't allow this to happen. No matter how things looked now, she would not be his next victim.

The team would have been alerted. The whole force would be looking for her, in fact. They'd not rest until they found her. Until then, Claudia had to rely on her own wits to keep herself safe. To prevent this man from fulfilling the act he had her in here for. That was her one job. To stay alive until the cavalry came.

And thinking of the cavalry made her think of Sharpe and the close-protection detail she had turned down. How arrogant of her to think she could deal with this alone. But she hadn't been alone. Her father had been with her.

Yet she was still here. Locked in the killer's car, going who the hell knew where.

This guy had proved time and again that he was capable of swerving their investigative lines of enquiry and not only locating his target but doing the job he'd intended all along. She'd still thought she could beat him.

The car turned a corner and she rolled, her shoulder jamming up uncomfortably against the wheel arch. A dull ache ran down her arm. She was desperate to stand up and stretch her limbs.

She should have taken her orders from Sharpe as a subordinate did, instead of arguing her case. Feeling superior to the man in the driving seat.

Who was superior now?

CHAPTER 70

A partial number plate was coming in from the house-to-house enquiries. Claudia's neighbours, it seems, were nosier than Dominic gave them credit for. The reason given for noticing the vehicle was that the man seen getting in and out of it was dressed strangely. He was wearing a dressing gown and slippers, and people tended to notice these things.

One neighbour saw a man in his slippers and dressing gown supporting Claudia, who appeared to be in need of help. She was unsteady on her feet, and he helped her into the back of his car and drove away. Presumably, the neighbour said, to get her help. She was horrified she hadn't done something sooner now the police were at her door suggesting something nefarious had occurred.

Dominic was furious, but he couldn't be too angry with these people. Claudia had been in his care and he himself had allowed her to slip through his fingers and be spirited away right under his nose.

Some neighbours had identified the car as an old Toyota Corolla. Not in the best condition. Not well cared for. Dark grey in colour.

Now with a partial number plate, they had to work through the multiple possible owners it could be.

Dominic was pacing the room while the rest of the team worked.

His mind was scrambled. He could barely focus. What he needed was something targeted he could go and deal with — a solid lead he could chase up, somewhere he could go. Waiting for information to come in and come together was driving him insane.

The helplines were lighting up with callers. More staff had been pulled in to cover them. Suggestions of where the location could be were pouring in, all written up on a board at the front of the room, though nothing jumped out as a serious suggestion. People wanted to be involved in a high-profile case.

'Dom?' The voice behind him made him jump.

He turned.

Adam Blackwood stood watching him intently. 'Do you want to go for a walk?'

Dominic looked around the incident room at everyone doing their best to get his daughter back. No one was messing about. No random conversations happening. The mood was sombre. He trusted them. They loved Claudia. She was one of them. Could he leave them to it? What if something came in while he was outside getting some air?

'I have my phone on me.' It was as if Blackwood was reading his mind. 'If something happens they can contact me immediately. Let's get out of here.'

Dominic gave a curt nod and the two men headed out the incident room and into the now darkening sky of the summer night.

'It's cold,' Dominic said. 'She's going to be cold.' Like she was a little girl who needed wrapping up.

Blackwood did him the courtesy of not mentioning that the cold was the least of Claudia's problems. Dominic understood that, but it had struck him as they had left the building and the chill had seeped into his bones.

They exited by the main doors onto the steep road that was Snig Hill.

'How're you bearing up?' Blackwood asked as they headed up the hill.

Dominic shoved his hands into pockets. 'As you'd expect.'

Blackwood was quiet for a moment. 'I only met Claudia recently, but she struck me as a very competent officer. If anyone's going to keep themselves alive as we get closer, it's her.'

The thought of her not living through this nearly strangled Dominic. He paused where he was. A car drove down the hill past them, its headlights brightening the way in front of them. Traffic was light at this time in the evening.

'Look,' said Dominic, 'I appreciate you bringing me out of the office for a break, but I'd rather be in there in case something comes in. It's making me a little itchy out here. Not knowing, you understand?'

Blackwood inclined his head and turned back the way they had come. 'Let's get you back.'

The two men walked in silence for a few minutes, Dominic lost in thoughts of what Claudia could be facing. His mind racing away with him. He wanted to shut it off. Quiet it. The scenarios that were running through his head were terrifying. The trauma the Artist could be subjecting her to. He was going to cause this man grievous harm.

With his hand on the door, Blackwood turned to Dominic. 'What do you need from me?'

'I need you to bring my daughter home.'

CHAPTER 71

Eventually the car stopped. It parked up.

They were obviously at their destination.

Whatever was happening, they were here.

Claudia remembered the drawing. The woods.

The blade in her chest.

Whatever she did, she had to stop him putting that blade in her chest.

She couldn't save herself once that was in there.

Her feet weren't tied up. She would kick him when he opened the boot. It was a weird angle laying in the boot, but she was in a position where she had to fight for her life.

The engine clicked off and silence blanketed her.

It was like a layer of fear being laid over her.

She shifted her hips so that her bottom was further back, giving her legs room to push outwards when the lid of the boot was lifted above her. Her hands were bound in front, so she could use them as a weapon if need be.

There was no way he was going to put that blade in her chest. She had to fight until she was found by the team, or until she escaped herself.

There was another click as the boot lid unlocked, probably from a mechanism at the front of the car. Thoughts flew through Claudia's head in a flash. To try to climb out and run before he got to her or wait and fight him? If she tried to clamber out with her wrists restrained she could struggle to escape and he could catch her. Her best bet might be to fight when he's not expecting it.

Time was up.

Footsteps down the side of the car told her they were on solid ground. Concrete, asphalt of some description. A road.

He'd be here any second.

She steadied herself, ready to launch. Decision made.

The fear completely overwhelming. Her heart racing. The feeling growing. Like it was going to explode. Her whole body shaking.

She had to push this away, she was about to be in the fight of her life.

Claudia held her breath. She would come face to face with the Artist. But that was just a name. What he did was very real, though. The pain and death he inflicted and the pain he had planned for her, she just wasn't up for feeling it.

The lid of the boot opened. The darkness of night closed in around her and a face peered down.

In the split second her mind caught the image of his face there was recognition. She'd seen him before. But there was no time to think of where. With everything she had she forced her feet up at the body in her way. She felt the contact and *whoomp* as the air was knocked out of him in surprise. He scrambled as his feet clamoured for purchase on the ground. But he was gone.

Claudia pulled her legs back in and twisted so she could get on her knees and climb out of the boot, hands ready to push and fight off anyone who came at her.

As she struggled over the lip of the boot, she saw the man lying on his side. He must have hit his head on his way down because he wasn't moving.

She had to get out of there.

They were on the side of a road in a lay-by next to some woods. She twisted her head for a better look around. Down the road she saw a building.

Safety.

She clambered down, the fear making her sluggish, as well as the remnants of whatever he'd put in her. With gentle steps, afraid to move for waking him up, she manoeuvred around him so she could head towards the building down the road and hopefully get help.

From here she couldn't make out what the building was, but it appeared larger than a house.

She was a couple of steps away, ready to run though her head was still fuzzy, when an arm snapped out and grabbed her by her ankle.

Claudia couldn't help but yelp. Like a frightened schoolgirl.

He was awake.

Then the tip-toeing and stealth stopped. Suddenly it went from quiet and slow to a flurry of movement as Claudia's fear jolted to another level and she tried to bounce out of his grip, pulling and tugging for her freedom. Help was so close.

The man on the other end of her leg scrambled on the ground to keep his grasp and yank himself up. His fingers dug into her ankles. A guttural groan escaped as he struggled to maintain a tight hold. His knees and feet scrabbled as he pulled himself upright to grab her properly.

Claudia was off balance with her hands tied in front of her, her body unsteady and ready to fall. Tears welled in her eyes as she fought to keep her legs free so she could run, but it was a losing battle. With each second that passed, he was climbing to his feet and pulling himself up on her body and gaining better purchase. She would soon be his again, and the frustration was bitter in her throat.

She screamed out, willing someone to hear. But the road was silent, and the moment she had released the sound a hand clamped around her head, encompassing her mouth and shutting her down.

CHAPTER 72

He had to get her into the woods as quickly as possible. The pub down the road was closed now. He'd waited until closing hours, but he couldn't risk the owners coming out to investigate the racket she'd made.

He just hoped they experienced many strange noises out here and would think it was one of the usual. Possibly wild animals fighting. They'd want to stay out of the way. His hope was that they'd be tucked up in bed.

His plan had been for the drugs to keep her out cold so he would wrap her in the blanket and carry her over his shoulder into the woods, quietly with little fuss, but everything was turning to shit.

He obviously hadn't used enough in the syringe, and she'd turned out to be a fighter. She was a cop, after all.

Her legs were free because he hadn't thought he'd needed to tie them.

Stupid mistake.

Now he had a tight hold of her, but she was bucking and fighting him every second.

He really needed to get her off this road.

The Artist drew his right arm back, and with all the force he could muster he punched Claudia on her temple.

Her head swung back as his fist impacted with bone, a *whump* escaping from deep within her before her eyes rolled and she went limp in his arms.

Control returned to him. He allowed himself a small sigh of relief before he dropped her to the floor in a pile. Then he grabbed the blanket from the boot, closed it and threw the blanket over Claudia, scooping her up and over his shoulder.

Things were going to plan again.

She wasn't heavy. She wasn't a large woman. He shifted her into a better position and strode off into the woods with her. His exhibit would now start to go to plan.

CHAPTER 73

They had a breakthrough. Further house-to-house enquiries had completed the registration mark of the vehicle that had been involved in the abduction of Claudia.

Electricity ran through Dominic's veins.

Graham tapped the details into the computer and waited for it to return the registered keeper's details.

They were about to find out who had his daughter.

The screen filled with the answers they needed.

Sean Marlin. Thirty-four years old. Sheffield.

They had a name and address.

They had the name of the man who had taken Claudia.

Sean Marlin.

It cycled through Dominic's brain on a loop.

Blackwood clapped his hands together. The room hushed. 'Okay, that's who we're up against. Rhys, I want you to dig into Mr Sean Marlin. Find out everything there is to know about him.'

'Will do.' Rhys tapped at his keyboard.

'We have his address. It's highly unlikely Claudia will be there, but we need to do a search of his property to see what information we can discover. What information Sean Marlin has left behind for us. We're not going in blind, though. We go in when we know who he is. Get prepared. Graham, can you organise a warrant for the address, please?'

Graham nodded.

'And in the meantime, I'll update Sharpe and Connelly.'

Blackwood moved towards Dominic, took his elbow and steered him to a corner of the room. 'We're one step closer, Dom. We're getting there. You have to hold on. Please don't do anything rash. He's not going to be there. And if you go in without a warrant, you're going to screw up any evidence we might find.'

Dominic gritted his teeth. There was no point getting into a discussion about it. He'd get nowhere and they might physically restrain him. What did he care about evidence? It was nothing to him. What mattered was getting Claudia back safe. He'd nod and keep his cool. 'I know. Hurry it up though, Adam.'

Blackwood patted his arm, appeased by what he'd heard, then turned and strode out of the incident room.

Seconds later Dominic was out of there. The night air had changed. It was damp. A light rain was falling, the kind that was barely visible, but that soaked you through. Dominic pulled his collar up to fend it off and stalked to the car park.

As he drove his mobile rang. It was Blackwood. He ignored it. Then it rang again. He ignored it again. Then Sharpe rang. Dominic shook his head. They would not stop him from doing this. He couldn't turn his phone off in case they had new information he needed to know, but right now he was taking a gamble. He reckoned the only reason they were calling was because he was no longer in the building and they'd taken a reasonable guess at where he was heading.

Traffic was light. It was easy enough to find Marlin's home and get there at speed.

The lights were out when he arrived. The man either lived alone or any other occupant was in bed.

Dominic knocked on the door first and knocked again when there was no response. He checked around the property, looking in windows to see if there were any signs of life. There was nothing. It looked completely empty.

There was an obvious risk the cops were going to be called on him by this guy's neighbours, but they were on their way anyway. He was on a clock. He had to do this. Claudia was running out of time. Marlin didn't have his victims long before they turned up in the way the drawings depicted, and Dominic wouldn't allow Claudia to become a drawing.

On his tour around the property for signs of life, Dominic decided the rear kitchen window was his way in. Screw procedure. Screw waiting for a warrant. It didn't take long to obtain one through the day, but at this time of night they'd have to wake a judge up at home to get it signed. It was so much more time-consuming. Trying to find out which judge was on the rota for these kinds of calls. Locating his address. Getting there and back.

Dominic didn't have the time.

Claudia didn't have the time.

He'd pay for it later. It was something he was willing to do.

The window had been left open a little. Probably because of the weather they'd been having and the fact that it was at the rear of the property. The idiot didn't think burglars came round the rear where it was quieter?

All he had to do was slide his hand in, unhook the latch and open it.

Dominic shook his head.

He'd have thought a killer would have been a little more security conscious. The guy was obviously too arrogant and didn't think he needed to consider these things. Dominic just had to hope there was something inside worth breaking in for.

Once in the premises he lit the torch app on his phone and looked around. It was reasonably neat and tidy. What was he looking for, though? Plans? If he was drawing his murder scenes then maybe he was also writing down the rest of his plans. There had to be some kind of workspace.

A quick look downstairs told him there was nothing down here. Dominic moved swiftly up the stairs and checked behind each of the closed doors, being as gentle as he could in case there was actually someone sleeping who hadn't heard him knocking. How he'd explain himself he didn't know, but he'd deal with that when faced with it.

The first room was a bedroom. There was little in there. A bed, a set of drawers and a narrow wardrobe. It was definitely a male-only room. Bland. No sign of a feminine touch. The colours muted.

Dominic moved into the next room, which was the bathroom.

The next room was what he was searching for.

There was a desk with a laptop in one corner and a large artist's pad in the centre. Different kinds of pencils, for shading, Dominic imagined, laid on top of the pad. A bookcase, and a printer on a small set of drawers. On the walls were two large pinboards, and this was what drew Dominic's eye. Printed off and fixed to the pinboard were maps and locations, stuck with pins for the final detail.

Dominic searched the printouts. He found the one for the warehouse and the lad with the dagger in his back. Then the bridge that they'd struggled to identify.

His fingers walked along the papers, searching out the one piece of paper he was truly searching for. The one he had printed out for Claudia's final resting place, as he would have assumed it to be. But in reality, now Dominic was here, it was going to be his own resting place if Dominic had anything to do with it.

Stress bunched at the base of his head as his eyes and his fingers moved between the printed maps. It had to be here.

Unless, of course, he had taken it with him.

But there were so many. This guy had plans. Dominic had to check them and cross them off when they didn't match the drawing he had seen. When it wasn't woodland.

Slow down, he told himself. The stress was preventing him from seeing what he needed.

He would be able to work faster if he actually slowed down and took a deep breath. The faster he worked, the quicker he would be out of here, before his team came in after him with the warrant. Breaking the door down. Not caring about making a noise or a fuss. They'd slam their way through the house and tear it apart, looking for signs of where Claudia would be.

And if he ever found the location, Dominic would leave it for them. They could follow him there. He wasn't that stupid. It was possible he could need backup, and he wasn't going to risk Claudia's safety by being too proud and taking the evidence.

Then he found it. A map with a pin in a wooded area.

It was the ruins of the Lodge Moor prisoner of war camp. He did know it. On the drawing, what they'd all thought were fallen trees were in fact rectangles of cement. Yes, they were covered in moss, so easily confused for fallen trees. There was not much left of the camp, just the small cement walls and some basements.

Dominic took a couple of photographs of the map with his phone then left the property the way he had arrived.

It was still quiet outside. The rain was falling heavier.

Dominic didn't wait around. He climbed in his car and headed towards the camp, not knowing what would be waiting for him.

CHAPTER 74

Claudia was getting soaked. She was cold. Deep into her bones, cold. Her shoulders ached and her head felt like she'd had a run-in with a lump hammer.

The last thing she remembered was running from the Artist after she'd climbed from the boot of his car. He'd grabbed her, and she'd struggled, but then it all went black.

She was alive still. There was that.

She supposed she should open her eyes and see what predicament she was in. As long as she had breath in her lungs, she would not give up the fight. And he hadn't killed her yet.

Was he waiting for her to wake up? Should she sit here with her eyes closed for a little longer? Figure out what state she was in?

Her arms were fastened behind her now. He'd obviously figured out she had too much control with them in front. She was sitting upright, leaning back against something solid, like a wall. The ground was damp. It was raining heavily. They were in the woods. She could hear the rain as it hit the leaves on the trees. The soft pitter-patter above her in the tree canopy.

She wasn't dressed for this weather, and she was shaking from the cold. It was wrapped around her and seeping up from the damp ground she was sitting on.

Claudia wiggled her fingers to see if there was room to get out of the bonds she found herself in. If he'd been in a hurry when applying them then maybe he hadn't done a good job. But no, they were tight enough.

But as she moved her hand, her wrist caught on something metallic sticking out of the wall she was leaning against. It was narrow. Her fingers probed it. Feeling down the shaft of it, the ridges, the head of it, the lip. It was a screw.

She realised as she was feeling her way around the screw that her body would be moving slightly. He'd know she was awake. She'd have to open her eyes and confront what was happening. But fear kept them clamped shut.

As long as he wasn't shouting at her, she was doing okay. Claudia listened for his activity. He was in front of her somewhere. There was shuffling in the mulch on the woodland floor.

Very gently, Claudia rubbed her ties against the screw. If she released her hands, she was in a better position to help herself.

'I know you're awake,' he said. 'I can see you fidgeting. You can open your eyes.'

Terror gripped Claudia hard. She continued to rub at the screw. Very gently to not cause too much movement with her body. But if she opened her eyes, would it all be over? He wasn't going to stand out here all night with her.

'Open your eyes!' he shouted.

The sound, loud in the quiet of the woods, made Claudia jump and her eyes flew open.

Trees towered above her. She was leaning against a small wall of some description, water pooling in front of her. She was in some kind of rundown enclosure.

In front of her, the man they had been hunting and who had gone by the name the Artist was crouching with his phone, taking photographs of her. Keeping memories of his kills? Her team would be able to catch him and convict him with evidence like that. She was glad of that, at least. Even if the worst happened.

But she wasn't going to be his next victim. The screw was working against her ties, breaking bits off, releasing her binds. Freedom was slowly coming her way. All she had to do was keep him talking. Prevent him sticking a blade in her chest.

He had an ominous smile on his face as he took his photos. He wasn't holding a knife, so that was a good sign. She still had time. All she had to do was engage him in conversation.

All? What did you say to the man who was planning to kill you? While at the same time keeping him distracted from the fact you were sawing at the ties that bound you.

She recognised him. Sean. He was the guy from Brendan and Obasi's photography shop. They'd talked to him. He'd seemed to know very little, when all along he'd used someone close to him as a victim.

'My name's Claudia,' she said, for somewhere to start. Not knowing if he would remember her from their brief meeting.

He looked over his phone at her. 'I know who you are.'

That had gone well.

'Why are we here?' Straight to the crux of the matter.

He took more photographs. 'You're my next exhibit.'

'Exhibit?'

'I'm an artist.'

Had he taken the media name to heart, or was he actually an artist? She had dismissed him simply as the receptionist when she spoke to him, as Obasi had called him. When all along he cried out to be something more. Maybe it was this desire to be more that had driven him to kill Brendan.

The ties behind her were slowly loosening. She had to keep sawing at them on the screw, being careful not to draw his attention to her movements. 'I've seen your drawings. They're very good. How long have you been drawing?'

He paused what he was doing and looked at her. 'Drawing isn't my real love. It's something I can do on the side. My real love is modern art. Installations. Something that people can walk round and talk about. Something I can create that causes people to think.'

Claudia nodded, as if she understood what he'd been doing these past few weeks. Her concentration was on her wrists. There was little holding her in place now. The screw had gradually worn through the ties. A little more sawing and she'd be free.

'I'm sure we can talk about this.' She needed to connect with him and at the same time distract him. 'We met at the photography shop, didn't we?'

He stared at her.

The rain poured down on them. His hair slick on his head. He tilted his face sideways as he contemplated her.

She was free. The binds snapped apart. It took all her strength to keep her arms still and not break them out to the side of her in relief. Her shoulders ached so much. But she needed a plan. She had to decide what she would do next. Because her next steps would determine if she made it out of this or not.

'Why me, Sean? Why am I here?' Her mind whirred. Where was the knife? She had to keep him occupied while she studied her surroundings.

He twitched. As if she had asked him something deeply personal that no one should ever ask. That she should know better than to ask.

'You ruined the last exhibit.'

She'd taken Zach to safety, but ultimately she hadn't saved him. Sean had done what he'd needed to.

Sean's distress with his recollection of the event rubbed up against her own. The loss of Zach. Her inability to prevent his death.

She had to do better this time.

'I might have taken him away, but you still managed to get to him.' She didn't understand his logic. Why was he sending the drawings if not for them to try to save the victims before he killed them?

Claudia scanned the ground around Sean while they talked, looking for the blade from the drawing. She imagined he would keep it close, ready to use.

'You interfered. And from there it all went wrong, they found him too early. The timing was out.'

Claudia thought she saw something to the side of him. Buried in the grass. She needed to get to it before he did. Or get to him before he could use it. Disable him. 'Why send us the drawings if you didn't want us to act on them?'

With the slightest of movements, she readied her body. Tried to prepare it to pounce from this uncomfortable position on the ground. She just needed to choose her moment.

He shook his head violently. 'You've got it all wrong. It wasn't for you to act on. The drawing was an invitation. To the exhibition. My installation. The papers had it right, I'm an artist. It's my calling. I needed to find something that no one else had ever done. And what better than the human form?' Sean was smiling. 'But someone had to see it. It was no good creating it and leaving it alone where no one would find it and experience the wonder of what I'd created. So I had to send invitations. And you were the ideal person. I'd read about you in the paper. I knew your name. You seemed nice. Leaving my exhibits in your hands was the perfect way to go. You were supposed to share the invitations with the world, to tell people about the exhibit.'

The rain was torrential now. The darkness all-encompassing. Sean was a mere outline. His features lit up in the glow from the phone in front of his face. The blade she'd spotted, a faint indentation in the ground. If she was wrong, she was risking her life. If he had it on him, maybe in a back pocket, her life would be over. But if she did nothing, her life was over anyway.

Sean lowered his phone. He was finished with the photography it seemed. This was her moment. She had to act. If Sean put his phone away his next step would probably be to pick up the knife. Claudia had to stop him.

The adrenalin surged through her body. Claudia tensed her muscles. She needed all the power inside herself, and with everything she had she launched herself up and forward.

CHAPTER 75

Dominic pulled up at the lay-by with speed, angling Claudia's car in and screeching to a halt behind the vehicle that the team had identified was registered to Sean Marlin.

He climbed out of the car into the pouring rain and listened for any sound that would tell him which direction his daughter and the man who had her had travelled in. But all he could hear was the water as it hit the ground and fell through the trees at the side of him.

Dominic opened the boot, lifted the bottom shelf and located the wrench. He picked it out and closed the lid.

He was close now and needed the team as backup. There was no time to wait for them to search the house and identify this as the location Claudia was at. He dialled Sharpe. She picked up immediately.

'Where the hell are you?'

He told her.

'What's there?'

'Claudia.'

'We're on our way.'

He thanked her, and before he hung up she spoke again. 'Dominic?'

He didn't have time for this. 'What is it?'

'Don't do anything stupid, but make sure you save our girl.'

With that, he ended the call. Dominic didn't need telling to save Claudia. Nothing was going to stop him.

Dominic didn't have a torch, save for the one that came with his phone, but it would do no good to go into the woods with it lit up. It would alert Sean Marlin to the fact he was on his way. With the night fallen and the added tree cover it was going to be difficult to see his way around in the woods, but his daughter was in there, so he was heading in.

The wrench was cold and heavy in his hand as he stumbled over tree roots and tried to keep his balance. Rain water ran down the neck of his jumper, washing down his face and blurring his vision.

He had no idea of the direction to take, but continued to push himself deeper into the wooded area.

Panic cleaved him in half as he thought of his daughter with the blade in her chest as the darkness surrounded him and he struggled find her. He knew Marlin had taken her to the POW camp, but Dominic had never been himself. He didn't know the directions. It might have been easy to find in the day, but in the night, with the rain pouring in your face, it was an impossible task.

He continued to stumble forward. Then a high-pitched scream pierced the air. Like a wild animal who had been caught in a trap — or stabbed in her chest.

Dominic picked up the direction of the sound, lifted the wrench to shoulder height ready to use and ran through the trees, terror hitching his every breath.

CHAPTER 76

As she'd pushed off from her position on the floor, up towards Sean, something animalistic escaped from Claudia's lungs. A primal rage and power combined. Her wide-open mouth shrieking in his face as she grabbed his shoulders and took him down with the weight of her body.

The shock of her sudden movement sent the phone flying from his hand to the sodden ground, and the pair tumbled after it. Sean released a grunt of air as he landed on his back and Claudia flew on top of him. Her knees pushed into his chest. Her hands clawed into fists and pummelled at his face.

She had to take his capacity to control away from him. Stop him from reaching out for the knife.

It was slippery on the woodland floor and Sean attempted to slide out from under her, using his forearms to push her off. But she was furious and determined. This was her life she was fighting for. She only had one chance to get this right, to defend herself from certain death.

His face turned to the side. His arm started to snake out from under her. Was he reaching for the knife?

She had to stop him.

Her punches were not enough.

Claudia tried to grab his arm, but she couldn't keep hold. His fingers reached forward. Something shifted under his hand. He nearly had it.

They both twisted their bodies in the direction of the knife.

The fight was on.

The rain continued to pour down on them. Thunder clapped and the sky above the tree tops lit up for a moment. The knife was clear to see as the blade glinted for a second.

In the distance Claudia heard what sounded like a shout. But they were both grunting heavily in the battle to retrieve the knife.

Claudia tried to crawl up Sean's body and his right arm, but he was stronger than he looked. She'd had the element of surprise, but now he was fighting to win and he was in this as deep as she was.

She used her knees as weapons as she clawed for the knife. Digging them into his body, sticking her boots in. Then his hand wrapped around the handle.

Time froze. It was as though the pair of them had made a silent pact that this deserved to be savoured. They were in a bubble. The breath stopped in her chest. The rain was no more. Nothing else existed. There was only Sean and Claudia, wrapped in an embrace on the woodland floor.

Then Sean reared and the spell broke.

In a rush, reality came hurtling back to Claudia, rain water soaking her face, the knife flashing through the air, the sneer of victory spreading across Sean's mouth.

Adrenalin coursed through Claudia, her heart thundering. She would not give up. She would not die here. In the wet, on the ground, in the dirt.

CHAPTER 77

Lightening lit up the woods and suddenly Dominic could see around him, and more specifically, in the direction he'd heard the scream come from, the outline of two people, battling.

Claudia and Marlin.

He tried to run, but the ground was uneven. Tree roots tripping him. Fallen trees and logs to jump over. Slipping in the wetness of it all. The rain blurring his vision.

Dominic's brain focused on the few seconds he glimpsed Claudia and Marlin grappling on the wet soil. Claudia fighting for her life.

He closed in on them, and as he did, his eyes cleared.

Claudia was on top, but they were fighting for something. Claudia was attempting to stop Marlin getting it. She was like a wildcat. He was so proud. *Keep going, girl. Keep fighting. Don't give up. I'm coming.*

The ground beneath him slipped again, and he was down. The wrench flew from his grip. He reached out, couldn't find it in the darkness. He swore again at the lost time. Pushed on the wet soil and rose. Looked around, trying to find the wrench in the darkness and his bearings at the same time.

There she is. He was off again.

Marlin had something in his hand. He was rising, pushing Claudia away. She was punching at him, while at the same time trying to cling on to him. Not wanting him to be free of her.

Dominic wanted to let her know he was there but dared not shout again. He didn't want to distract her. He was so close, but the trees were fighting him all the way. Branches flicking into his face. Pushing him backwards.

Through the trees, Dominic could see Marlin freeing himself. He straddled Claudia, and though Dominic still could not see what he was holding, he knew it had to be the knife.

Dominic couldn't help himself. Fear was driving him. He shouted for his daughter.

Marlin started and turned as Dominic ploughed into the clearing.

He locked eyes with Dominic for a fraction of a second and thrust the blade down.

Dominic and Claudia cried out as one. Marlin raised his arm to strike again as Claudia kicked and lashed out beneath him.

Dominic grabbed Marlin around the throat from behind and pulled, squeezing his hands together. Yanking him off Claudia, forcing the very life out of the man who was attempting to take the life out of his daughter.

Marlin roared like a bear and threw himself backwards, flinging his arms out wide. Dominic felt something like a soft punch in his side as Marlin's elbow pulled back, and then a coldness seeping around his waist. He slid to the ground, pain slicing into him. Had he been hurt? Had Marlin caught him?

The darkness began to penetrate.

Claudia screamed. Loud and primitive. A battle cry.

Dominic willed himself to focus. Before him, Marlin and Claudia were standing, each fumbling to take possession of the knife. Blood was soaking through Claudia's top.

But they were both visibly weakened. Then Claudia's knees seemed to buckle and Marlin began to gain dominance.

Dominic rolled onto his side, winced and pushed himself up unsteadily. His legs were shaking, and with one last ditch effort he threw himself at the pair. He had no idea where the knife was. His hands again found Marlin's throat. This time he would not let go. The three of them tumbled to the ground.

Marlin struck a root as his head hit the ground and went limp. At last, Dominic threw the killer off his daughter and dropped to his knees on the sodden ground. He didn't care what state he was in. All he cared about was what state Claudia was in.

He stared down at his only child as she fell back on the soaked woodland floor. Blood blooming around her stomach. Her face pale. Her eyes closed.

CHAPTER 78

Claudia let the rain drip down on her face. She sank into the soil. She never wanted to open her eyes again. The soft woodland floor was enveloping her. Pulling her down.

But the voice was insistent. It was her father. 'Claudia. Claudia. Oh my God, Claudia.' There was pressure on her stomach. Hands pushing down.

Claudia reluctantly opened her eyes. 'What are you doing?'

Relief flooded Dominic's face. 'Thank God. We need an ambulance.' He rummaged around in his pockets awkwardly with one hand while keeping his other hand on her stomach. His face a mask of pure horror.

She raised an arm towards Sean, curled up on the ground next to her father. 'He needs it, Dad. Not me. It's his.' It was an effort to talk. She sucked in air, still disbelieving. She'd survived.

Dominic looked down at his hand on Claudia's stomach, soaked in blood, and shifted the hem of her top. Comprehension dawned on Dominic's face as he looked at the man he'd pushed aside to get to his daughter.

Sean lay quiet. The blood pooling around him. A hand protectively holding the knife that was still lodged in place.

Dominic removed his hand from Claudia's abdomen. 'Oh, thank God.' He bent his head and closed his eyes. 'But you're still injured.' Blood streamed down from her shoulder. Her arm hung at her side awkwardly. She was in pain.

'Dad, the ambulance?'

He opened his eyes and looked at her. Something silent passing between them.

'The ambulance,' she said again.

'Yes, the ambulance.' He slumped down beside her and it was then that she saw his own blood. Her heart swelled. He'd kept himself awake long enough to save her and now they were safe he was rapidly losing consciousness.

'Dad!'

The ground around them was slick. The air was heavy with the tang of copper. Flies hummed over them, landing to inspect the glistening mulch. Then voices and the thud of footsteps could be heard running towards them through the thick undergrowth.

The cavalry were here.

CHAPTER 79

Claudia took three weeks off work after her ordeal in the woods with Sean Marlin.

She'd told Sharpe and Connelly she didn't need her sick leave extending. It was hardly the longest abduction in history and the wound in her shoulder was healing.

Sharpe had argued that, what with Marlin dying from his wounds, she might want to take some time to process things, but Claudia had fought back, arguing that if the CPS agreed it was self-defence then she was not going to allow it to play on her mind.

And she wasn't. He'd tried to kill her. He hadn't been messing around. He'd genuinely wanted to push that knife into her chest and for her to die and complete his masterpiece. The fact that the blade had ended up inside of him instead of her had been a complete accident, but all the same, it was his doing. She was not going to worry about it.

The lift took her up to her floor as she thought about her return. The team would have completed the paperwork for the file. The murders that Marlin had committed would be classed as detected, no further action, due to his death and the fact they'd managed to gather all the evidence they needed at his home. He'd taken photographs of all his victims in the same poses he'd drawn them in, as well as making multiple drawings of the crime scenes. It seems he'd sought to perfect them before sending them on to Claudia. He had Brendan's gym bag stuffed under his bed. Dirty, stale, sweaty gym gear festered in the bag along with a water bottle, a towel and a pair of trainers. These items were tested and proved to be covered in Brendan's DNA. Marlin had wrapped Zach's phone in Brendan's towel in the bag. Still turned off. Marlin's home also contained the maps of the locations used. The DNA and urine from his victims, found in the boot of his car, had been the final bow on the file.

Luckily, the two cops who had been guarding her had not succumbed to the poison and were not on the victim list. They had, Claudia had been informed, returned to work, long before her. She'd sent them both get-well cards, thanking them for what they had done in their attempt to protect her. But now she was back she would make time to check on them in person.

During her weeks of leave she'd spent time relaxing. Yes, logic told her she was not responsible for what had happened, but she *had* killed a man.

Not on purpose. But still, she had been involved in the man's death. And deep down, she knew that she would be dealing with it for some time to come.

In the meantime, she was on the fast-track promotion scheme. Being traumatically affected by events would not help her career plans.

The lift doors slid apart and the corridor yawned, exposed in front of her. Empty of foot traffic at this time in the morning. She'd wanted an early start so as to not be greeted by a huge array of faces. That was not what she wanted.

Claudia strode quickly to her office, keeping her head down.

Her father had visited her a couple of times during her leave. It had been some of the most difficult periods she had ever spent with him. He had wanted to make sure she was coping with everything, but Claudia wasn't ready to analyse it more than she needed to.

Dominic had stumbled awkwardly around the subject and eventually allowed her peace. He had healed pretty quickly from his own stab wounds. Nothing major had been hit, thankfully.

Her office was as she'd left it. Some files had been removed from her desk pertaining to the Marlin case, but other than that it all looked normal.

Last night Sharpe had called her and organised a meeting for first thing in the morning with both her and Dominic.

This had been their first case as the newly formed task force. Had they failed because Claudia had been taken and the offender had been killed? What would happen to them? Would they all go back to their previous assignments?

The questions swirled through her mind as she switched her laptop on and checked her emails. They would keep her busy until it was time to deal with Sharpe.

Gradually the incident room started to fill. Staff entered, and at first they didn't notice her. After all, she hadn't been in her office for the last three weeks. But then out the corner of their eyes they saw movement and spotted her. Their faces brightened and they raised an arm in welcome recognition. Claudia waved in return and sighed with relief that none of them had run in to talk to her. They were giving her space.

The clock ran round and eventually it was time to see Sharpe. She and Dominic walked together in grim silence, until he broke it before they reached Sharpe's office.

'How does it feel to be back?'

She had to accept this was going to be how it was for a couple of days. 'I think it's what I need.' She'd had a session with a force-mandated counsellor before being allowed to return. She'd said the same thing to him. He'd agreed to allow her to find her feet within the parameters of work guidelines, so long as she promised to call him if she had any major problems. She'd agreed. She believed she could cope with work. It was the people talking about it that she would struggle with. They were trying to be kind, of course, but Claudia needed to be left to deal with events in her own way.

Dominic gave a curt nod. He'd pushed against this wall enough to know he'd get no further.

Maxine greeted them with a smile. 'She's waiting for you, go right in.'

The normalcy from Maxine was like a breath of fresh air. Claudia could have hugged her right then and there.

Sharpe was indeed waiting for them. Standing at the window, staring down at the world below her. The great heat they'd been dealing with had broken. The sun was still shining, but there was more breeze in the air. It was easier to breathe.

Sharpe turned as they entered, her gaze landing on Claudia, arms crossed over her chest. Stance pensive. 'Why is it your family that's always in the middle of something difficult?' she asked with a sigh.

There was no answer forthcoming, so she waved a hand in front of her at the chairs and told them to take a seat. They did as directed.

Claudia's nerves got the better of her. 'What is it, ma'am?'

Sharpe sighed again and sank into her own chair. Giving nothing away until she was ready. 'It's good to see you,' she said. 'How are you feeling? Ready to be back?'

'I'm healed from the stab wound. Whatever drugs he used on me were out of my system pretty quickly. I'm good to go,' Claudia said.

Sharpe nodded. She wouldn't know the ins and outs of Claudia's counselling sessions but she would have an overview. She'd know that she was mentally fit to return.

Dominic grunted a response that was practically inaudible. Sharpe smiled at him, but Claudia knew she had his page marked. She would have made sure he was properly fit before returning.

'Do let me know if I can do anything to help,' Sharpe said.

'Of course.' What was the real reason they were sitting here? Her chest tightened as she waited for Sharpe to go on.

Eventually she spoke. 'I have some bad news for the pair of you.'

Claudia straightened in her chair. Preparing herself for whatever was to come.

'There's been an incident in Doncaster prison.'

A chill ran down Claudia's spine.

'Craig Lawton has been killed.'

Craig Lawton. The cellmate who had given a statement that Tyler told him he had killed Ruth.

Dominic was silent beside her. Claudia's mind whirled.

'What happened?'

Sharpe paused before she spoke, gathering her words. 'He was being transferred out to another prison because of the statement he'd made. While the paperwork was processed, he'd been moved out of Tyler's cell and into another wing for his own protection. They thought he was safe, but he was found shanked in the shower block. It was too late. Nothing anyone could do.'

Claudia's scalp crawled. 'Tyler?'

'It can't be proved, but it's more than likely.'

She had planned to talk to him, but time had slipped away from her. The investigation into the Artist had taken her every waking moment even before the injury. Now that chance was gone and she would never know the truth behind the statement. If the conversation had really happened. If there was anything else behind it. If there was anything more he could tell her. All she wanted was the truth.

'I take it his statement stands,' said Dominic.

Sharpe nodded. 'Of course. It'll be read out in court under hearsay provisions, section 114 of the Criminal Justice Act.'

'With no chance of a cross-examination,' said Claudia.

Dominic looked across at her. 'I for one am glad it's over. I'm tired of having this hanging over me. The sooner he goes to trial and is sentenced the better, as far as I'm concerned.'

Claudia looked back at him. There was nothing else for her to say. Not now. But it wasn't over.

It was far from over.

THE END

ACKNOWLEDGEMENTS

A book comes together because people come together, and it is these people I wish to thank for bringing *Seconds to Die* together.

Huge thanks go to my editor, Emma Grundy Haigh, for her insight and belief in the story. For pulling it all together and cheering me on as I worked. Thanks to Laurel Sills for editorial input, Anna Harrisson for the copy-edit and Matthew Grundy Haigh for proofreading. Police systems really aren't that sophisticated! Thanks to Nina Kicul for her help and support this year.

Thank you to my wonderful agent, Hannah Weatherill, who responds to emails at such speed I feel like I'm the only client she has. That's super agenting right there. And to all at Northbank Talent Management who work to keep everything ticking over.

Thanks to Graham Bartlett for policing advice on issues I might be a little rusty on. I'd rather check than get it all wrong. Of course, this is fiction, so a little leeway is allowed, but if you spot any faults, they're not because of Graham.

To the crime writing community who keep me buoyed and the readers who take a chance on a new book and then maybe come back for more. Without readers this would be a lonely journey, so thank you.

And finally, to my family, who give me the space to write without distraction. I love you all.

ALSO BY REBECCA BRADLEY

DETECTIVE CLAUDIA NUNN
Book 1: BLOOD STAINED
Book 2: SECONDS TO DIE

Thank you for reading this book.

If you enjoyed it please leave feedback on Amazon or Goodreads, and if there is anything we missed or you have a question about, then please get in touch. We appreciate you choosing our book.

Founded in 2014 in Shoreditch, London, we at Joffe Books pride ourselves on our history of innovative publishing. We were thrilled to be shortlisted for Independent Publisher of the Year at the British Book Awards.

www.joffebooks.com

We're very grateful to eagle-eyed readers who take the time to contact us. Please send any errors you find to corrections@joffebooks.com. We'll get them fixed ASAP.

Printed in Great Britain
by Amazon

68037673R00201